Wildfire

The Rise of a Hero

Books by Jordan S. Keller

Ashes Over Avalon Trilogy
Wildfire

Coming Soon!
Ashes Over Avalon Trilogy
Burnout
Combustion

Wildfire

The Rise of a Hero

Jordan S. Keller

SPEAKING VOLUMES, LLC
NAPLES, FLORIDA
2022

Wildfire

ISBN 978-1-64540-762-1

For Paul.
For filling my life with stories and
telling me I'd always find my niche.

Chapter One

The building burned like a tinderbox.

The flames were relentless, the heat stole Abigail's breath. The fire blazed into an all-consuming monster, turning the apartments into pyres. Its ravenous hunger burned through the floors, broke through locked doors, gnawed its way deeper inside the complex. The blazing monster didn't notice the feeble counter attack from outside. It was too preoccupied with consuming everything in its way. Furniture. Photos. Appliances. Clothes. Nothing satisfied it.

Abigail ran toward it. She followed the flames deep inside the building to the central units where fire crews had been unable to access safely. Curious flames licked against her skin, but Abigail paid them no mind. Adrenalin pulsed through her veins, allowing no room for fear to distract her.

A hero saves people, and that was Abigail's only goal.

Following the monster into a windowless bedroom, Abigail found a small boy huddled in a corner. She crossed the room and picked up the boy before the fire decided he would be a better meal than the toys it consumed on the floor. Abigail tore her golden cape from her shoulders and draped it over the boy.

"I'm getting you out of here!" she shouted over the flame's roar. "Whatever happens, do not let go."

The boy nodded under her cape and tightened his arms around her neck. Abigail carried him through the flames, down three stories, and out the front door. The fire burned around them but couldn't touch the boy under the cape's fire-retardant material. The flames tried to grab Abigail but couldn't grip her skin or costume. Once outside, the snapping sound of fire was replaced by the hissing of water striking baking brick. The roar of the flames was replaced by the roar of a crowd.

Abigail uncovered the boy, watching him take his first gulp of clean air. His mouth and nose were coated in black ash, and she used a gloved finger to wipe it off. A gurney rolled beside her, and Abigail set the boy down and reattached her cape to the clasps on her shoulders.

"You're safe now." She smiled at him while a paramedic covered his mouth with an oxygen mask. "You're going to be A-okay."

Tears fell from the boy's eyes, leaving rivers of clean skin under the ash and soot still clinging to his face. The oxygen mask fogged as he tried to speak, but his words were lost in the noise around them. Abigail squeezed his shoulder and returned to her battle.

With the apartments empty of civilians, the firefighters were able to fully unleash their water cannons. Smoke poured from the building, the blaze refusing to give up so easily. Glass shattered from the higher floors as a heatwave forced its way out. Black, putrid smoke oozed from the highest floor.

"Inferna!" a gruff voice shouted at her from the front line. The man was also dressed in costume instead of the firefighter's dark gray turn-out gear. "Take this line inside. I'm going to vent the roof."

"Yes, sir!" Abigail grabbed the water hose and ran back into the building.

Abigail worked her way to the back of the apartment complex, kill-ing the blaze in corners the firefighters couldn't reach from the outside. Although terrifying at first, this tactic had become second nature to the young sidekick. With her fireproof body, she could help douse the fire from within while the firefighters remained outside and away from the danger. The building heaved around her as her crime-fighting partner, Volcanic, vented the roof. The flames were pulled up violently, like dust bunnies into a vacuum. Abigail doused the remaining fire spouts and the stubborn embers clinging to baseboards and hiding behind doors.

Fighting fires wasn't their only job description, but it was the reason the heroes had been dubbed The Fire Killers.

Abigail emerged from the building after snuffing out the remaining flames. The complex was now a soggy mess, but the monster had taken no lives. That was a victory for all of the heroes. Super and ordinary. Volcanic leapt down from the roof, landing next to his sidekick. The pair were dressed similarly, like many heroes and sidekicks. Volcanic's navy and orange bodysuit was made of the same fire-repellent material as Abigail's costume and cape. He wore dark grey gloves, boots, and a half-face mask that covered his eyes. Really, though, he should have covered his permanent scowl.

Rated the number one solo hero in San Arbor for the last five years, Volcanic was powerful, fast, and possessed unrivaled flame abilities. Crime in the city had dropped eight percent in his first year, and the decrease had been steady ever since.

Volcanic was a perfect crime-stopper, but he was not a perfect hero. At least not in the eyes of media reports and tabloids.

When reporters entered the scene, their cameras focused on Abigail, her red and blue costume easy to find in the quieting chaos. The sidekick's costume resembled the style of 80's comic book heroes. The red skirt swirled around her knees with each step, and the blue top matched her blue ankle boots. She waved to the civilian crowd, who were obeying the first responders' barricade, before turning to the reporters.

"What can you tell us about this tragedy?" one reporter asked, his puffy microphone pressed against Abigail's nose.

"How did the fire start?"

"Could it have been put out sooner?"

The reporters fired off questions as quickly as a boxer's fist, geared to leave the interviewee winded and weakened enough to make a mistake in front of the cameras. If a hero couldn't handle the pressure of story hungry reporters, they would be knocked down like the villains they fought. Thankfully, this was a skill that Abigail listed on her resume.

"Today isn't a sad day," Abigail declared with a wide smile. Volcanic loomed two steps behind her with his arms crossed. "We were honored to be called by the fire chief to help with this incident. Together we saved everyone inside. This building will be rebuilt, and these homes will be restored. As for the cause of the fire, that is under investigation."

"Do you think it was the work of a villain?"

Abigail shook her head at the reporter, her blonde curls bouncing like she had stepped out of the salon instead of a burning building. "It's too soon to tell, but we do not believe so. I'm sure it's something as explainable as a—"

"What if it's the Flame Villain from before?"

"Do you have comments on his possible residency in San Arbor?"

"Will the Fire Killers be able to stop him if he is here?"

Abigail reached for her neck out of habit but stopped herself. A dark purple burn scar in the shape of a hand disfigured her flesh. Its four fingers wrapped possessively around her throat. That Flame Villain had been the only thing to ever penetrate her fireproofing. She refused to have the scar removed until he had been defeated.

"If that villain is here then he will be stopped," Abigail growled. She regained her composure as the boy she had saved ran over to her. Scooping him up, Abigail wiped a piece of ash off his cheek.

"Thank you for saving me." The boy's voice came out scratchy.

Abigail tightened her arms around him. Cameras clicked within the crowd. "You were super brave in there! Maybe you could be a hero one day too."

"Like you?"

"Like us." Abigail caught Volcanic's gaze and motioned him toward her.

The hero, clearly annoyed, knelt to be eye level with the boy. Abigail smiled. The boy smiled. Volcanic didn't frown.

"We're burning up!" the three of them chanted the Fire Killers' motto, the ending punctuated with giggles from the boy.

The camera lights clicked off, and the reporters vanished into their news trucks to finish their stories before the five o'clock newscast. There was no doubt this event would be the top story. The crowd thinned out once the danger and media storm were over, and the firefighters ventured into the building's remains to start their investigation. Abigail lowered the boy to the ground and waved to him as he returned to his family's side.

The popularity was a bonus of being a hero. The true joy was saving people.

"That was incredible!" A lanky man approached Abigail with a clipboard. He was younger than her by a few years, and she wondered if there was still time for his body to catch up to his long limbs. His costume mask, made to look like diving gear, hung around his neck. "I have your times recorded, but I couldn't keep up with the body count—"

"That's what you call dead people, Flipps," Abigail corrected the intern. She tugged his mask back over his eyes. It was lopsided. "Call them 'saved,' and we rescued six. The other seven residents were able to evacuate, and the remaining ten weren't home."

Flipps scribbled on the paper attached to his clipboard before adjusting his mask. "This thing is so itchy."

"Take it to Diane in costumes. She can fix it for you."

"Do you think it's true?" Flipps whispered. "Do you think the Flame Villain is here?"

Abigail sighed. "Has anyone seen him? Besides this—" she pointed at the charred building behind her "—has there been any arson-related attacks?"

"No, but—"

"No one has seen that villain in two years. It's a shame that he wasn't caught then, but that doesn't mean he's stalking San Arbor again."

Abigail wanted to curse his name but saying it aloud would give him credit. He would remain nameless to her. He would remain obsolete, a pest she would exterminate.

Flipps abruptly straightened, and Abigail heard his breath hitch.

"Get the car," Volcanic ordered.

"Y-yes, sir!" Flipps tried to salute his boss, but the movement resulted in the kid slapping his head with the clipboard. He ran off.

"You could be a little nicer," Abigail criticized.

Volcanic glared down at her from his mountainous height. "If he's scared of me he'll never make a good hero."

"He's just here for the summer intern program. He wants to be a swim coach, not a hero."

"Then he should have interned at a pool."

It was Abigail's turn to glare. Volcanic really didn't have much of a high horse to sit on. In his first five years as a hero in a neighboring city, he had destroyed most of the underground gang activities, but, using such violent methods, some people had confused him for a villain. Tabloid reporters claimed he was the true leader of the gangs and drug trades. True to his name, Volcanic burnt down an interview set with an agitated blast when he was supposed to address the rumors.

The rumors quit, mostly out of fear, and he started working in San Arbor a year later.

"You could have moved a little faster rescuing the kid," he grumbled.

"He's safe," she reminded. "They're all safe. Hopefully, that will increase your ratings."

"That's not why we do this." Volcanic crossed his arms.

"No, but that's why your company hired me." Abigail adjusted her cape, trying to keep as much of her scar hidden as she could. "Every hero's a celebrity now, and people eat that up. The line between hero and villain can be swayed by just one badly edited viral video."

"I told you never to bring that up," he growled.

"Sorry," she muttered half-heartedly. "Should we get back to HQ?"

"For more training," Volcanic decided. "You were sloppy today."

Abigail rolled her eyes but didn't protest. They waited in silence for Flipps to bring their car around. She chewed the inside of her cheek. "What if he *is* back?"

"You stick to our plan."

Chapter Two

A caravan of vehicles paraded around the apartment parking lot as firetrucks, ambulances, media vans, and Saves the Day personnel left the charred remains of the building. The excitement of the heroes, both super and everyday, also left with the cars. Those affected by the fire could no longer distract themselves from their homes pillaged by flames. Abigail frowned at the complex wishing she could do something more. Unfortunately, her abilities were only good for destroying things; she could never rebuild what was already gone.

Matter manipulation remained elusive even in a world of superheroes.

Returning farewell waves to a few unknown citizens, Abigail turned her sights toward the tall buildings emerging out of downtown. Normally, she would have ridden home with her team, but after this fire she knew a walk would be better for her mind. Although not hiding in her city, the Flame Villain hid in the dark and quiet places of her mind.

She was just an intern when the Flame Villain attacked; unlike Flipps, she had wanted to be a hero. Abigail was twenty-two and felt invincible due to her flames. At the time, she worked for a startup hero company that wouldn't make it past their third year. Each night, Abigail patrolled a local hangout area for the younger, college crowd. It was good marketing. She popped up on social media almost every night wearing a sequined mask and company logo t-shirt.

One of the bars even let her guest bartend when they were slow. She always melted the ice while handing drinks across the bar top. If the buyer had any ice left when they received the drink, they got it for free. That was good marketing, too.

The day after the villain's attack on the bar, she appeared on the front page of the newspaper. As a victim, not a hero. That was not good marketing.

The Flame Villain had attacked without warning. He moved through the crowd like he had summoned it, blending in with the people. Some bought him a drink, some even asked him to dance. Abigail paid him no attention. He looked like an ordinary person, and she was there to stop criminals. She kept serving drinks.

When the bar was smothered in blue fire, he no longer looked ordinary. The burn scars across his face made him look as deadly as the blaze. Both he and the indigo flames danced sinisterly atop the hardwood floors. Bottles on the bar back shattered from the heat. Irish themed posters turned to ash against the walls. Abigail saw the attack as if she watched it on a movie screen, it was burned into her memory, just like his hand had burned into her neck. She ignited her flames, cherry-red light swarming around her wrists, and faced down the villain.

His assault on the bar paused; Abigail assumed he hadn't expected a hero to arrive so quickly. They stared each other down, his blue flames waiting for a command, Abigail buying time for the patrons to escape. That was the only victory of the night.

The bar caught fire like it was made of tissue paper. The walls engulfed, the floor, the ceiling, everything came alive with blue fire. Abigail was losing her breath, her flames growing smaller with the lack of oxygen. He walked the space between them, easily dodging her punches and heel kicks, and knocked her down with one ground sweep.

Abigail was twenty-two and felt like she was dying on a bar floor.

When his hand gripped around her throat, Abigail was certain her life was over. Her dreams of being a hero, her dreams of seeing the next day, ended by flames hotter than her own. Her vision spotted, her eyes watered from the smoke, she smelled burning skin—

"Inferna!" shouted a voice outside her memory.

She looked around. White umbrellas from an outdoor dining patio replaced the imagined burning walls of the bar from her memories. She hadn't realized how far she'd walked. Almost into downtown, this street was lined with locally owned eateries and boutiques. Two small children stood behind the wooden partition and waved to her, calling out her hero name. Eager for the distraction, Abigail jogged to them and delivered both kids a high five over the fence.

"Hey kiddos." Abigail squatted to be at eye level. "Whatcha' guys up to?"

"I love your cape!" the girl announced.

"Can I wear your mask?" the boy asked, his fingers already stretching toward the fabric.

Abigail straightened, avoiding the fingers slick with a brown sauce left over from his lunch. "Don't you know it's dangerous to take off your mask in public?"

"But, you're so strong." The boy's determination didn't waver. "You don't need to wear it."

"But you do?"

The boy nodded.

Abigail gently squished the boy's bicep and pretended she felt steel beneath his flesh rather than just bones and toddler fat. "Wow! I think you're the super strong one here. Are you sure you're not a hero in hiding?"

Both the boy and girl giggled, and their mother emerged from under an umbrella to aid Abigail.

"Does your mom know you're a hero?" Abigail whispered to the boy which caused him to giggle more.

"Guys, come on, leave Inferna alone." The mother gave both the children a shove away from the fence. "I'm sure she has more important things to do than listen to you two harass her."

Besides a training session with Volcanic, the only important thing Abigail had was waiting for the next call. "I don't mind."

"Momma." The girl tugged on her mother's shirt hem. "Momma take our picture!"

The woman sighed and looked at Abigail. It was then the sidekick noticed the half dozen other camera phones out and trained on her. Some of the tiny lenses snuck around umbrella polls and plastic menus, others were held out an arm's length away and several inside diners entered the patio bumping into tables and chairs. Sometimes it was easy to ignore the ever-present cameras pointed at her, other times it was difficult.

Especially when one was a foot from her.

"Do you mind?"

Smiling for photos was not the reason Abigail donned her cape, but it was one of the many items in her contract. She was legally obligated not to say no. "Of course not. Come here."

Pulling the children close to her, all three smiled for the camera. Several other clicks rang out as onlookers also snapped a photo. Abigail released the kids, and they finally listened to their mother, stepping away from the fence.

"Bye-bye!" Abigail snapped her fingers and a spark of flame danced atop her hand as she blew a kiss at the kids. They smacked their own kisses back at her.

Despite the nosey camera phones, giggling children, and scraping of metal chairs against concrete, Abigail heard it. The frantic coughing. The desperate beating of a fist against breastbone. The frightful wheeze of strained lungs. The sounds of someone choking.

Abigail leaped over the fence. An older man's red face was turning blue on the other side of the patio. He gripped the table and unsuccessfully took a breath. Abigail shoved the giggling children aside. She leapt onto a table, knocking drinks and menus onto the floor, and ran to the old man's side.

With training she took a year ago, Abigail knew to check a choking victims throat for blockage before applying any physical touch; if the victim was able to speak, she was to ask them for permission to treat them first. The training had been to protect Saves the Day from lawsuits and not the victim from choking.

Abigail ignored that training and wrapped her arms around the man, pulling him from his chair and performing the Heimlich maneuver.

A half-chewed ball of meat spewed from the man's throat and landed on a different table between Abigail and a recording cellphone. She turned herself and the man away from the device so they both had a moment of privacy.

"Are you okay?"

The man rubbed his abdomen where Abigail had applied the most pressure. "I will be thanks to you."

"I am not a medical professional," she quickly recited a line from the handbook Saves the Day supplied each year with updated scenarios and guidelines. "Even if you feel okay, you should still see a medical professional. I can call an ambulance if you request it."

The man patted her forearm, still wrapped protectively around his shoulders. "It was just a bit of steak. I'll take smaller bites from now on. I don't need an ambulance ride. You got the job done."

Even though she broke several codes, Abigail felt good. A hero saves people and waiting for a first responder would have signed the old man's death certificate. It was only because she wore a mask that so much red tape kept her from helping someone. She helped the man back into his seat, said a final farewell and continued on her way.

Taking several back alleys and one shortcut through the park, Abigail arrived at Saves the Day Hero Company Headquarters without any more distractions. From fans or haunted memories. The nineteen-story office building was the tallest on the block, and its mirrored windows reflected every movement on the surrounding grounds. Well-trimmed hedges and colorful displays of flowers along the walkway tried to give the building charm, but Abigail always thought the corporate building looked cold and unwelcoming.

Not everyone in San Arbor shared that thought, however. A hodgepodge group made up of parents, children, an elderly couple and one fanboy Abigail knew she'd seen here before followed a sharply dressed tour guide through the civilian exit. They carried plastic shopping bags stamped with the gift shop logo and pamphlets containing either a map of the building and its various levels to support the hero company, or a list of where to see the heroes at their next arranged marketing stop.

Last month it had been at Pike's Best Donuts and Bagels and the bakery had ran out of stock before noon as people lined up to "buy a treat and meet Volcanic and Inferna, while supplies last." Abigail always wondered why all crime seemed to conveniently stop during those events.

As she waited for the tour group to turn away from the building, Abigail watched the massive billboard above the door replay the current ad for the Fire Killers. In front of a green screen coded to look like lava, Volcanic blasted two jets of fire twenty feet on either side of him before Inferna rolled into frame completing a series of martial arts moves that took more time to film than to master. The digitized versions ended the ad leaning their backs together and chanting the motto again. They looked good together as a pair. Inferna's wide smile and soft features kept the viewer from focusing on Volcanic's intimidating grimace. Abigail knew the only reason Saves the Day hired her was to make Volcanic look better on screen, but she knew the only reason she accepted being his sidekick was the promise to become stronger. Strong enough to defeat the Flame Villain.

With the tour out of sight, Abigail tapped her ID badge against the first scanner at the employee door, used her eight-digit passcode at the second door, and opened her teal eyes wide for the retinal scanner at the elevator. Finally, she was released onto the fourth floor, the start of the private levels, and could return to her office and wait for their next call.

Before she got there, The Saves the Day Media Loss Prevention Team swarmed her like a volt of vultures at a fresh kill. The three employees looked exhausted with dark rimmed eyes and hands that jittered with either too much or too little caffeine. Abigail doubted they were there to congratulate her on the fire call from earlier.

"Hey Greg." She mustered enough cheer in her greeting to pass as a professional party clown. "What's up?"

"Don't start." The leader of the trio handed Abigail a data tablet paused on a video. He clicked the play icon and Abigail watched a recording of her saving the choking man. "You know the protocol. Why didn't you stick to it?"

"If I did, the man would have died."

"If you hurt him this whole company could have died."

Abigail tapped the data pad and paused the video. "Doubtful."

"You have to follow protocol," Greg reiterated, taking the tablet back.

"My job is to save people. That man needed saving and I was there to do it."

"And, by the looks of the crowd there, someone else could have done it. Without the threat of burning him."

Abigail gritted her teeth. "I couldn't take the chance of someone *not* acting. How bad would it look for the company if I let that guy choke?"

One of the other MLP members typed into their data pad and showed the results to the third.

"Not well," they declared to Greg.

"I'm a hero first," Abigail said before Greg could interject. "I will do that job before anything else."

In a whisper too loud for the otherwise quiet hallway, the third MLP member said to the second, "Kenneth has been rubbing off on her."

Abigail rolled her eyes. "What are the company numbers? After my 'break in protocol'?"

The two MLP members examined the data pad together. "Still on the rise after this morning's fire."

"See?" Abigail smiled at Greg. "No harm and no foul."

"Watch yourself," Greg warned. "We cannot have two Volcanic explosions in our careers."

"I'll keep that in mind. Where's the big man, anyway?"

Abigail playfully looked around them. Not even the fake plants collecting dust in the corner could hide their number one hero.

"Training Room Alpha," MLP number three answered.

"Waiting for his—" —Greg checked his watch— "—42 minute late sidekick."

Abigail ran to the topmost training room, stripping away parts of her costume as she shouted at the elevator to move faster. She was indecent when she tumbled into the small locker room attached to the training room. She covered herself with a tracksuit, dumped her belongings into a locker and entered Training Room Alpha out of breath, blonde locks spilling from her bun.

Volcanic eyed her from across the room. His usual scowl was deeper than normal. They both wore the same dark track suit with padded gloves and shin guards, but he somehow made it a threatening fashion statement, while the loose jacket sleeves draped over Abigail's hands. She rolled the sleeves over her elbows and strolled deeper into the room, taking steadying breaths through her nose. As her oxygen levels increased so did the heat inside her veins.

"About time you showed." Volcanic summoned a fireball in his hands.

The hero put professional baseball pitchers to shame. The force from the fireball was enough to cause serious damage, let alone the actual heat known to melt cars and steel doors. It embedded itself into the floor three inches from where Abigail stood. She did her best to ignore it.

"I ran into some trouble on the way back."

"You should have ridden back with us."

"Are we really here to discuss carpooling, or are you going to train me?"

His answer came in a series of fireballs. Abigail ducked, dived and dodged the ones she could and encased her arms in fire to knock back the ones that came too quickly. The ceiling fans turned on automatically once the room filled with enough smoke to cover the sensors. The devices didn't remove the smoke fast enough, and Abigail lost Volcanic behind a wall of smoke. The flash of yellow before he pitched another fastball was her only hint at where the attack would come from.

Heat from one scorched the side of her cheek before it exploded against the wall. She leapt back as a second exploded on the ground in front of her and backed straight into the wall. She dove to the ground to avoid the next three. They left char marks along the wall where she had just been standing.

She blew fallen hair away from her face and spotted Volcanic's boots across from her under the smoke cloud. With a pause in the attack, the fans were able to clear the room of the obstruction. Annoyance snapped sparks from her fingers when she saw his face. He looked bored. He readied another fireball.

She was a sitting duck where she lay on the floor.

Abigail gritted her teeth and flipped back onto her feet. She jumped to the left to dodge another searing shot. Volcanic flicked the blaze at her without a care. He fired again and aimed a second blast at Abigail's landing spot as she dodged the first. She raised her arms just in time to block her face. The fire rolled off her arms, and she shook the embers off her hands and out of her hair.

"Is that all?" She wiped the sweat off her forehead with the hem of her shirt.

"Are you getting tired?"

"Just bored. I've been doing your practice drills for months now. When are you going to teach me something new?"

"When you're ready."

Fire licked around Abigail's wrists, turning into flaming gauntlets. "I am ready."

"You're still just a child," he said. "I was ten years older than you before I could even summon it."

"You didn't have a teacher," Abigail pleaded. "Just show me one more time."

"One time and you drop it."

"That's all I'm asking."

Volcanic pointed one finger at her. At the tip, a small blue flame ignited around his nail like the start of a zippo lighter. The legendary blue flame. The hottest known flame that a human could produce. The power Abigail had sought after the villain attack. If she could wield it, then she could defend against it. She mimicked Volcanic's stance and raised one finger at him. A cherry-red flame appeared at the end of her finger.

"Concentrate," he commanded. His normal voice was just as un-welcoming as his hero voice. "Push past your limits. Burn hotter than you can stand."

Abigail's flame only grew in size. It refused to rise in temperature. The cherry-red orb turned into a baseball, a basketball, a beachball. She threw it to the ground where it extinguished into smoke. She tried again. Again. Again. And again. But the flame remained red. Like always.

Volcanic put out his blue flame. "You're not ready."

His words were just as disappointing as her lack of power.

Abigail slammed her fists together creating a shower of sparks from her knuckles. "When will I?"

"You may never be," he answered. "Your abilities may never rise to this."

Abigail exhaled a breath to keep her hands from igniting again, but her eyes still burned. They might have well been the only blue flame she'd ever master. "How am I going to defeat him, then?"

"That was always on you to figure out. I only said I'd help you where I could."

A lot of help you've been. Abigail thought.

"I grabbed something out of tech for you," Volcanic confessed.

He was a man of few smiles and even fewer gifts. Abigail watched suspiciously while he retrieved a gadget from his pocket. It was a small pistol, about the size of a dollar store squirt gun, except it looked far more fragile. There was only room for one bullet. He tossed it to her, and Abigail turned it over in her hands. She had been mistaken, there was only room for one *dart*.

"What is this?"

"A tracker. The dart is laced with nanotechnology that activates once inside a target's bloodstream. With this prototype, the signal will only last a few hours. You can pair it to your phone."

Abigail was impressed with the technology but still uncertain of the gift. She aimed at Volcanic through the tiny plastic sight attached to the top. "Why'd you sneak this out to me?"

"If he *is* back, you should be prepared. You can defeat someone in more civil ways than beating them up. Arresting him will be as good as any victory."

Abigail didn't believe that, but she slipped the gun into her pocket.

When a rescue squad did arrive at the scene after the bar attack, they had found only the unconscious intern. The Flame Villain had escaped. He had been evading the police ever since.

"Thanks."

The door to the training room burst open without a knock, and Flipps panted in the doorway. He looked as if he had run up several flights of stairs. Sweat beaded down his bright red face.

"Sir," he gasped, "you're being requested! The whole company is."

"What's happening?"

"Downtown, at the square, there's an attack."

Volcanic and Abigail were already through the doorway, shoving Flipps onto a bench beside the lockers.

"Do we know who it is?" Abigail stripped down while she talked, getting her costume on as quickly as she could.

Flipps shook his head. "There's too many of them. No one's pinged our database yet."

"What are they attacking?" Volcanic pulled his mask on.

"Everything! The department store, the bank, and the Luxury Hotel."

"Where that car show is?" Abigail asked, and Flipps nodded.

Volcanic sighed. "I knew building those three on the same square was trouble. Three high profile targets in spitting distance from each other. Flipps, get the car."

"It's already around front, sir."

"Get in it," he ordered. "If this thing is as wide scale as I think, we're going to need all boots on the ground."

Flipps paled. "But, sir, I—"

"You intern with heroes; you have to do hero work at some point."

Abigail slapped Flipps on the shoulder. "It's just as easy as swimming. Promise."

Volcanic spoke into the communicator device on his wrist. His voice echoed from the speakers throughout the entire building. "All sidekicks, work with the first responders to evacuate the area. All heroes focus on apprehending the criminals and villains."

Abigail accepted the notification on her phone that it had finished pairing with the nano tracker. She slipped it into the bag on her hip containing the other tools she was permitted to have. The prototype tracker didn't fit with the zip ties or radio.

Chapter Three

The car wasn't anything special. The only thing linking the Land Rover to the Fire Killers was the paint job. Saves the Day Hero Company had issued the solid black vehicle to have flames painted on both sides and up the hood. It was gaudy. Abigail loved it. Volcanic hated it. The citizens of San Arbor usually shouted "wee-woo" when they saw it drive by; cheering on the car as much as the heroes who sat inside.

The citizens didn't have time to cheer as they fled the downtown central square. They ran down the sidewalks, they spilled into the streets, they abandoned their cars at intersections. Abigail ditched the car several blocks away from the square when the street became impossible to traverse. She forgot how populated San Arbor was until the streets were flooded with panicked citizens. They moved in faceless waves.

The Fire Killers and Flipps exited the car and ran straight for the square. The crowd parted around them as first responders and sidekicks directed people away from the scene. The closer they got the worse the terrain became. Cars had crashed, storefront windows were shattered, and several busted fire hydrants created geysers over the asphalt.

Abigail slowed to better assess the situation. A group of criminals was breaking into the department store. The red flashing lights from the alarm system unsuccessfully stopped them from filling their bags with jewelry and money from the registers. One of the criminals was rounding up the staff at gunpoint.

The bank across the square had successfully started its safety protocol. Thick iron bars were over every window, and the revolving door was locked in place. Just under the noise of the stampede, Abigail could hear screaming from the direction of the bank. The safety protocol had been activated too late. The civilians were locked inside with the criminals. The square was so chaotic Abigail couldn't tell what the main objective was. Perhaps that was the point, or the only objective was to cause panic. To cause fear.

"Take care of the looters." Volcanic instructed her, his heavy voice was calm in the buzzing around them. "Meet me in the bank when you're done. Flipps, stay with me, we'll need someone to escort the hostages to safety."

Abigail didn't need to give him an answer. Volcanic wouldn't have heard it anyway. He was halfway across the street before he finished giving his order. Flipps struggled to keep up with him. Abigail ignited her arms and jumped through the already broken window of the department store's main entrance. She burned herself a path through fashionable mannequins and saw her first target. A masked man was shoveling money inside a backpack behind the makeup counter. He jerked his head to her, and his eyes widened at the sight of her fire. Abigail leapt over the counter and punched the man in the jaw. He crumpled to the ground and tiny embers ate away at his mask. He shrieked terribly as the embers found flesh. Abigail yanked the masked over his head, tossing it away from him. The embers eating the fabric returned to the fire burning around her wrists. She hauled him to his feet, zip tied his hands and ankles together and tossed him out the window. He flopped onto the sidewalk like an oversized fish.

Once the initial threat was gone, Abigail took inventory of the situation. This front section of the department store was empty. A trail of knocked over clothing racks marked the other criminal's heading. The new summer trends lay trampled on the tile; their triple-digit price tags forgotten in the heist. Abigail turned her flames down and advanced through the store. She would find the remaining crooks and take them down. That was a hero's job.

Something to her left moved and Abigail whipped around with a blazing fist. The frightened face paled under the light, and the fire reflected painfully in the man's eyes. The man shook inside his suit jacket. He wore a lanyard with the store's name stitched into the fabric. Abigail extinguished her fire.

"Are you okay?" she asked, taking notice of the blood dripping from the side of his face.

"We need help."

"Show me."

The man led Abigail to a circular check-out desk. Behind the counter were three other employees. Their hands and feet were tied together, and their mouths gagged with designer ties. It was the oddest fashion installment Abigail had ever seen.

"I don't have anything sharp enough to cut them loose," the man explained. He repeatedly looked over his shoulder. "Do you know where the criminals are?"

"Not yet." Abigail ducked under the counter and used a small flame to burn through the coarse rope. The skin beneath was already turning a bright red. "Further in, I think." She worked quickly, slicing through the binds, and gently removing the gags. "Outside is a madhouse right now. Did any of you see how this started?"

"It happened so fast," one woman answered, rubbing her wrists. "It was like a city bus unloaded all those people and they just started attacking everything."

Abigail pulled the woman to her feet. "Get outside and head south on Main Street. You'll find people to help you get to safety. Stay together and watch out for each other. Okay?"

"Be careful, Inferna."

She gave them a courageous and comforting smile before running deeper into the store. Without Volcanic, or a blinking media light, Abigail didn't need to worry about being "too sloppy." She advanced through the store with one simple goal: stop the bad guys. As she neared the brightly lit jewelry counters, Abigail heard excited chatter and what sounded like coins bouncing against the floor. She stalked the jewelry counters using the formal dress section as cover. At the diamond counter, two other criminals dumped jewelry into a duffle bag. They hadn't noticed her.

"Think we'll be able to keep any of this?" one asked.

"I'm not taking the chance if we can't." The other stuffed a shiny diamond pendant into his pocket.

Abigail darted out of a collection of prom dresses, lit her shins on fire, and round housed one of the men. Her mind slowed, and she imagined her enemies with targets on their bodies. Her attacks hit hard and accurately. This was far better than dodging fireballs in a training room. Abigail didn't watch as the criminal flipped over the counter and fell into a rack of coats where the draping fabric pulled him under. Letting her momentum spin her around, she used the remaining force to leap on top of the last criminal. They crashed onto the floor amongst fallen and forgotten loose jewels. She grabbed the sides of his head and knocked his head against the ground until he passed out.

Reaching for more zip ties, Abigail's fingers brushed the tracker gun inside her utility belt. She tied the unconscious man's wrists and ankles together before returning to the criminal who was trying to escape the coat rack. He slipped on a sleeve the moment they locked eyes. She lit one hand, the blaze making shadows dance on her face that twisted her smile to a smirk.

"How badly do you want to get burned?" she threatened.

The criminal compared the short space between them to the larger distance between himself and the nearest exit. The fire crackled and Abigail stepped forward. The criminal lowered his head and offered her his hands. Abigail tied them together and led him through the department store. Two officers were on the sidewalk properly cuffing the man she had thrown out the window. She handed over the other criminal.

"One more is inside by the diamonds," she explained. "All three are ready for transport."

"We've got it from here, Inferna," one of the officers said. "Thanks."

Abigail nodded before dashing to the bank. Volcanic had probably found a way inside by now, either through a hidden door or one he made from flames. She moved through the panic as more civilians ran away from the towering buildings. A large police force was working the Luxury Hotel where a foreign car from the show hung halfway through a second story window. Abigail still couldn't find a target. This display was too big for just a robbery. It was too ill-thought-out for one, too. She pushed her way closer to the bank, moving around the empty food carts and through people running the opposite way. She felt like a fish swimming upstream in the faceless waves.

None of the moving people saw the man watching from the center. None of the other heroes saw him sitting at a red metal table. None of the first responders saw his takeout lunch half-eaten in front of him. But Abigail saw him. She would always see him. She saw his black duster coat in her nightmares. She saw his hand every time she looked in a mirror. She saw his shadow at every call.

The Flame Villain.

The Flame Villain was in San Arbor.

Abigail forgot about the bank. She forgot about her orders from Volcanic. She forgot about the people running away. All she saw was him. All she saw was how he watched her across the four metal tables stationed between them. All she saw was his grin split in half by the scar that ran from his jaw, across his nose, over his right eye and disappearing under his hairline.

"Hello hero," he said casually. Abigail watched his gaze dangle over his handprint on her neck before returning to hers. "Here for the show?"

Red flames caressed her forearms and legs as she readied an attack. "Hope you enjoyed that lunch, because it's the last meal you'll have as a free man."

"A bold assumption." The Flame Villain stood and kicked the table toward her, a brilliant flash of blue fire following it.

Abigail focused all of her flames to the soles of her feet and created a rocket boost to jump over the improvised torpedo. She landed but staggered into another table. The Flame Villain ran down a darkened alley to the next street over. Abigail chased him. The blue flames oozed off his body with each step and ignited everything on the ground. Lost papers, trash bags, road signs, cars. He left a wake of melted destruction which Abigail followed, her own blazing footfalls burning into the asphalt.

The Flame Villain turned and fired a blast at Abigail. She rolled under it letting the blast destroy a laundromat. The villain tried again, and this time the blast hit a deli. He laughed, and turned down another street as cinders, glass, and chunks of sausage rained down.

"Careful hero," he taunted over his shoulder. "We'll burn the whole city down."

"I won't let you!" Abigail roared. She rocket-boosted herself into him and knocked them both to the ground. She grabbed the collar of his duster to keep him still.

The Flame Villain sighed and rolled with enough force to knock Abigail off him and onto the street. He pinned her hands beneath his knees. Abigail squirmed under his weight and tried to buck him off. She froze as his right hand circled around her throat, his fingers lining up with the scar he had caused before. His other hand sparked to life, the deadly blue flame filling Abigail's vision as he lowered his hand toward her face.

"Skin is so easy to burn," he mused to himself, and lowered the flame closer to Abigail. The heat was so intense it rendered her fire-proofing useless. A cloth napkin had a better defense.

Abigail panicked. The number one thing for a hero not to do. When someone panicked, they didn't think. Abigail didn't think. She only re-acted. She only fought. She only screamed.

Her cherry red fire spread from her wrists and ankles and covered her whole body. The air around her couldn't cope with the rapid expan-sion of heat and exploded. White light filled the street with a bang, and then vanished. Abigail was free. The weight of the Flame Villain was gone. The blue fire was gone. She scrambled to her feet. Her ears rang from the blast and her head spun from the shockwave. The street around her was now a seven foot crater, and the buildings around it were cav-ernous as all their windows were blasted in. The villain stood on the other side of the ridge line, shaking the debris from his jacket. Gray ash peppered his black hair.

"Unexpected," he commented. "Almost got me. Almost."

He had the high ground. From this angle, he could run and be too far away when Abigail was able to crawl out of the hole. Or he could fill the crater with fire and kill Abigail. She knew she wasn't fireproof to him. He knew it too. She watched him like a rabbit staring down a coyote.

The Flame Villain turned and ran.

A selfish wave of relief washed over Abigail before feeling the wave of anguished defeat. She wouldn't lose to him. Not a second time. Not when she was so close. She clawed up the crater, leaving melted foot and handholds, but by the time she was out he was too far. Just a speck of black running through the empty street.

"Almost got me. Almost."

It was a long shot, but she was desperate. Abigail pulled the tracker from her pocket. One graze of the dart would be enough to implant the tracking nanotech. Abigail didn't know the range of the dart. Abigail had never shot a gun outside of a shooting range before. But she had to try. She lined the sight against the Flame Villain's back and squeezed the trigger.

The dart left the chamber and whizzed away from her with a high-pitched whistle. She wouldn't know if the dart worked until the nanotech activated. If she had even hit him. If the prototype even worked. The villain disappeared further down the street.

Abigail turned around; having to watch the Flame Villain vanish again soured her stomach. Volcanic stood on the other side of the crater watching her, absorbing the scene. She lowered the tracking gun, then dropped it to the ground. Volcanic leaped over the crater as if it had been a pothole and grabbed Abigail's shoulders.

"Are you okay?" The concern in his voice surprised her. The anger that followed did not. "What were you thinking? You had your assignment!"

"He was here!" Abigail shouted back. "He was here and I almost had him."

Volcanic shook his fist at the street, at what it had become: a disaster. The roadways through which Abigail had chased the Flame Villain would look similar. The street around her was sticky from the molten asphalt. The first-floor windows of the buildings were gone. She had caused as much, if not more, damage than the Flame Villain had. The only thing worse than a hero losing a fight was losing a battle to corporate. These repairs would come out of her paycheck.

If she continued to get one after today.

Beating the first responders to the scene, the media rolled in like a tidal wave. Their cameras capturing everything, their reporters shouting at the duo, the lights shining brightly at Abigail.

Volcanic stepped away from his sidekick, crossing his arms. "Go back to HQ. Don't talk to anyone. I'll clean up this mess."

This was worse than losing to the Flame Villain. At least there was a sliver of hope that the tracker would go off. Abigail knew what waited for her at HQ. The deal she made with Volcanic a year ago was clear, and she had just burned it to ashes.

Chapter Four

The walk back to Saves the Day Hero Company felt much longer than it should have. Abigail kept to the back streets. She didn't see how the rest of the attack unfolded. She didn't see how many criminals were arrested or if their main target was ever revealed. The back streets were cold and empty and didn't help her mood. She felt like the last person in San Arbor. She stopped at an open dumpster and dropped her melted shoes inside. Her body was numb to the uneven pavement cracks.

Abigail had faced down numerous villains. She had defeated enough criminals to fill a county jail. She had served San Arbor whole-heartedly since she first donned her mask. She had never been this nervous as she walked back to Saves the Day, the one place she should have felt most at home. It was more like walking into a snake pit.

She used the back entrance when she finally did arrive. She rode the service elevator to her and Volcanic's office. It was modern and impersonal. Volcanic's large oak desk was as clean as an operating table. Hers was messy by comparison; a framed photo of her family, a cup of colored pens, and a calendar of baby animals. They had brainstormed new attack patterns in this room, broke cases that had been abandoned by others, evaded the company Christmas party, and become friends in this office.

It now mocked her. The empty desk and lack of personal items on Volcanic's side should have been a warning. The ignored photo of Volcanic and an unknown boy should have been a warning. Abigail squinted at the boy, but still couldn't place him. She always assumed he was Volcanic's son, or a nephew, since they looked nothing alike, but he never mentioned him. Abigail had asked about the boy once, and Volcanic slammed the photo down so hard it cracked the frame. She realized now he never replaced it. The glass was cracked right between them.

Abigail found a change of clothes in her desk and retreated to a private bathroom.

She knew this wasn't going to fix anything. She could scrub all the soot and road debris from her skin, but it wouldn't wash away her actions. Or how the company would think of her now. She needed to wait until corporate summoned her.

Abigail was not good at waiting.

She scrubbed her feet until she almost slipped in the shower. She scrubbed her hair until she started to pull strands from her scalp. She scrubbed her arms until they turned red. She stayed hidden in the shower until the water ran cold.

After dressing in day clothes, jeans and a long sleeve shirt depicting Inferna and Volcanic, her waiting was over. The intercom summoned her to the top floor. She prayed the elevator broke down, but nine floors later Abigail stood in front of the long desk inside the company's boardroom. The seven sets of eyes that stared her down felt like a firing squad lining their sights against her heart. She swallowed hard. Volcanic sat at the center of the table, directly across from her. The seat on his left was empty. It had been her seat. How long would it be until they filled it with a new sidekick?

The other chairs were occupied with the department heads of Saves the Day Hero Company. Mariann Kline, the head of marketing, had broken three pencils since Abigail walked in. Tucker Shaw, the lead support item designer, had the prototype gun she fired on the table in front of him. The gun looked much bigger as it also stared Abigail down. The head of finance, public relations, and recruitment were also seated around the table.

On Volcanic's right side was a tall, grey-haired man dressed in a dark navy suit. Abigail had only seen the brand of suit in storefront windows in the boutique shops downtown. They were worth more than one month of her sidekick paycheck. The man's face was plastered around the building almost as much as their star hero. Devon Kreech. The founder and president of Saves the Day. His large hands were laced together on the tabletop.

"Play the reel." Devon Kreech was not super, but he commanded the room like he was. His voice was a glacier: cold and still. His mind already decided. Cemented in a decision that wouldn't change unless the world did. But, even if it did, a man like him would have a backup plan in place.

Devon Kreech was a visionary. Devon Kreech was a tyrant.

Thick shades fell over the windows, the overhead lights dimmed, and a TV screen flashed to life on the side of the room. A news package played several different pieces of camera phone footage that tracked the chase and battle between Inferna and the Flame Villain. Abigail watched as it captured the damage to the buildings, the destruction of the street, the fires set, but worse, it captured her ignorance. Hiding in alleyways and behind cars were civilians. Several times either red or blue flames licked close enough to sear clothing. Close enough to burn hair. Close enough to scar.

Dark red letters captioned the footage as *Inferna's Eruption?*

"The whole city thinks you've gone postal." Devon Kreech said after the video. The lights remained dim and the TV screen covered half his face in light and the other half in shadow. "I can't say I blame them. That blast?" —from a thin remote hidden in his clasped hands he rewound the video to when she caused the crater. "You were specifically told to never use that kind of force inside the city limits."

"I didn't know what else to—"

"Why?" Devon stopped her. "Why did you chase after this villain when you were given direct orders to stay?"

Abigail lowered her gaze; she knew it was useless to lie and she didn't want to see their reactions. "Revenge."

Devon laughed. It was dry ice; cold enough to burn. "That's not what a hero does. Kenneth, please explain to your sidekick what happened in the bank after she ran off?"

"We were ambushed," Volcanic obediently answered. "More villains were digging in under the vault. It was a trap."

Devon's voice darkened. "Thank goodness you were there. You saved everyone in there, right?"

"Wrong."

Devon turned back to Abigail and raised three fingers. "Two bank employees were shot, both are in surgery now. It's not looking good for the vault guard who was hit in the chest." Devon lowered two of his fingers. "Since you were supposed to be there, our staff didn't know to send more heroes. Flipps? The young intern, you know him. Today was his first mission and he was only supposed to help with evac. After this, I have to tell a mother that her twenty-year-old son is dead."

The room fell silent. Acid burned in the back of Abigail's mouth. It was the first trigger pulled by the firing squad aimed at her. *A part-time lifeguard never should have been sent inside an active crime scene.* Abigail would not let Kreech blame her for Flipps's death, but that didn't make the news any easier. She didn't think she was brave enough to have that conversation with a parent.

"Moving on," Devon Kreech continued. "This device was checked out of Shaw's office without any paperwork explaining which of our *heroes* had it. Will you tell me how you ended up with it?"

Volcanic stole it for me this morning. "I took it."

"Not looking very heroic again." Devon Kreech pressed a button on the remote and the video screen changed to a graph. Abigail knew the graph: it was ratings. Saves the Day ratings. She could pinpoint when she was hired based on the graph. When Volcanic was twenty-seven points lower than the other heroes in neighboring cities and rival companies. It brought the entire company down by eight points. Once Volcanic had a friendly sidekick who knew how to interview, and could coach the hero to do it himself, the ratings improved.

Today, just hours after the attack, the graph was sinking. Inferna's solo numbers plummeted. The decreasing line was as sharp as a knife.

"Your contract with us is based on one thing, what is it?"

"To improve Volcanic's ratings."

"And?"

"And, the company's ratings."

Devon *tisked* his tongue against his teeth and shook his head. "Kenneth, do you have anything to say for your sidekick?"

Volcanic shook his head before looking Abigail in the eyes. "No."

"Then it's decided." Devon clicked off the screen, and the overhead lights powered on. "Abigail Turner, you are fired."

It was the second trigger pulled by the firing squad.

"Yes, sir." Abigail swallowed her pride. Her anger. Her betrayal.

Everything that she had worked toward had been taken from her in minutes. Years of martial arts training, a childhood lost to flame control, a degree in criminal justice, all stripped to useless skills without the permission to do hero work. The only thing Abigail knew how to do was save lives and breathe, and right now she was forgetting to do both. Tears burned in the back of her throat, but she refused to shed them.

The only person who could have stopped her execution had declined to help her. But that had been their deal. Except she had been the only one to keep her side of it. Volcanic had done nothing but use her. The ratings graph proved that. His feigned ignorance was the only thing that saved him in the boardroom.

She turned to leave the room, the seven sets of glaring eyes, and the treachery that painted the walls. Kreech's voice hauled her back and she shut her eyes tightly as he spoke.

"Get dressed and go to level six. Your apology and resignation statement will be waiting for you."

Abigail lifted her chin and forced the tears lining her eyes to stay inside. "Yes, sir."

Abigail removed the few items she wanted to keep from her desk and slammed the drawer shut. She left the news article clippings of her and Volcanic's debut, a stupid photo of Inferna and Volcanic at a company lunch, Saves the Day labeled water bottle, and anything else that connected her to this place. She'd set the whole room to flames if she wasn't being watched.

Volcanic stood on the other side of the office. He looked like a statue; his face hard as stone. Probably his heart too. In his bear sized hands, he held a clear plastic bag with her Inferna mask inside. She eyed it suspiciously. Someone from costumes had taken it, and the rest of Inferna's costume, after she filmed her contractual resignation.

"It's the least I could do," Volcanic whispered.

He took a big chance to take it without permission. Abigail knew that. She didn't care. She'd rather him rip it in half. That way the costume would match the torn apart sidekick.

"No shit." Abigail spat. "There's nothing the great hero Volcanic can't do!"

"You knew the rules."

"You know me! You didn't even defend me in there."

"I couldn't. You know that." He sighed. "You knew you weren't ready yet. Why didn't you wait?"

"I had the opportunity," Abigail muttered. "You got me the tracker so you must have thought I was ready too."

"Ready to investigate, not start a fight!" he yelled.

The commotion attracted the security guard standing outside the office door.

"You did this," Volcanic said softly. "You made this bed."

"And you made yours," she snarled, shoving him with her half full banker box. "Goodbye."

Volcanic dropped the bagged mask inside the box. It was the final trigger pulled. Abigail's tears fell when she descended the elevator her final time. Her mask fell to the bottom of the box with the rest of the trash. She fought the desperate urge to fish it out.

Chapter Five

The television mounted over the bar was muted, but Abigail knew what the newscasters were saying. It was the only story the media was talking about that evening. It wasn't the bank robbery, the attack on downtown, or the murder of a young man who wanted to be a swim coach. It was that Volcanic fired his sidekick. It was Saves the Day stock value dropping nine points. Two opposing opinionated people yelled about the day's events which did more to confuse than inform the audience. The news revolved around everything that wasn't important.

Abigail sipped on her whiskey. The bar crowd was a distant muffling behind her. Far away and unimportant.

She hadn't heard if any money was taken from the bank. She hadn't heard if any luxury cars from the show had been stolen or destroyed. She hadn't heard how many criminals and villains had been caught. She hadn't heard if their motive was discovered, or their leader. She didn't know if any of the first responders had been hurt. The news just recycled the same footage over and over again.

In one of the clips taken from a bystander's camera phone at the square, Abigail saw a flash of blue goggles and swim trunks. At least Flipps had been wearing them correctly this time. The footage was supposed to show the destruction caused to the area, but Abigail only saw the destruction to one person and the ripples that would affect his family, his peers, his students. She met Cody Perison on his first day at Saves the Day. Abigail bought him a bad coffee out of a vending machine, and he told her he wanted to become a better coach for his middle school swim team and thought seeing how heroes kept motivated would be better than a normal internship somewhere else.

On that day, Abigail had thought him foolish. Looking back now, she thought he was ambitious, determined and brave.

Someone who deserved better than terrible coffee. Someone who deserved better than being sent into an active crime scene alongside those actually trained to handle the situation.

Abigail laughed bitterly, realizing the Media Loss Prevention Team probably kept Cody's death off the news to protect Saves the Day. The media circus about her was just another shield for the company.

The news anchors introduced the next segment of their "breaking" story, and a pre-recorded press conference played on screen. Inferna stood behind a podium, her forced smile as cheap as the polycore podium frame. It was the last time Abigail would wear Inferna's full costume. The stolen mask still hid inside her pocket. She couldn't bring herself to throw it away, even though she knew it was for the best. Best not to be caught with it, and better to forget everything connected to it. The press conference playing above was a package created by the Saves the Day's media team and distributed to the media a short hour after Abigail was fired. It was filmed on a soundstage built on the fourth floor of the headquarters, the background a green screen of the building's front hall.

It was as fake as the news.

The current section of the package airing was Abigail's public apology. The words were still bitter as she watched her silent self mouth them. She was glad the TV was muted, hearing the words aloud might make her sick. Abigail wasn't careless, like she claimed in her scripted apology, she had only been defending herself. She *was* sorry for almost hurting civilians in the chase, and she *was* sorry for the damage that was caused. She would have fully reimbursed the costs but none of that had been instructed for her to say. Choosing her safety over the favorable status of the company hadn't been in her contract.

If she had caught the Flame Villain, things would be different. She wouldn't be drinking alone on a Thursday night. She'd be celebrating with her team after another successful day.

The media only cared about the disastrous outcome. The outlets comparing her "stunt" to the havoc that Volcanic caused two years ago. The explosive combat took place during rush hour on the interstate, destroyed half of a bypass and disrupted traffic patterns for three months. It was the *necessary actions* that almost ended his hero career. It was the storm of bad publicity that had gotten Abigail her job.

But Volcanic had caught his bad guy, so the public damage was forgiven, and the injuries were an *unexpected consequence*. Volcanic was given a medal, a raise, and a sidekick.

Abigail ordered another drink. The current one in her hands boiled as a photo of Volcanic appeared on the television. *Back to solo?* the ticker tape read underneath.

"Want me to get you a glass of ice?" The bartender was trying to be nice, but Abigail didn't care.

"You can change the channel."

"Yeah, I'm sick of the story anyway." He set her new drink down and flipped the station to a game show. "Shame to see Inferna fired like that. She was a cool sidekick."

Abigail toasted her drink toward him before drinking. The liquor was already warming.

"I wonder if she'll branch out," the bartender asked. He picked up a clean glass and ran a dirty cloth over it. "Go to the HRC or become a solo hero instead of someone's sidekick?"

"She can't." Abigail squeezed her glass. "Inferna is owned by Saves the Day. They'll keep her until the contract runs out. Even if the real person doesn't work there anymore."

"I didn't know that." The bartender put the glass and rag back under the bar. "Do you work close to the heroes? Like a lawyer or something? I went to law school, but things didn't work out too well for me."

He ended his statement with an awkward chuckle.

"If I did work for a hero company, I couldn't tell you."

"So you do." The bartender winked at her. "I won't tell anyone. What can you tell me?"

Abigail sighed audibly. "You don't have to work for your tip with me, please go bother someone else."

The bartender wiped a ring of condensation off the bar top before retreating to the other end where a younger couple flagged him. He seemed to forget Abigail's rudeness while making two cosmopolitans.

As Abigail finished her drink, more people filled the bar and the distant muffle of conversation turned into a harsh buzzing. The seats around her filled with strangers and she saw more of the bartender's face than she wanted to. After the second accidental elbow jab into her shoulder, Abigail placed a $10 bill under her glass and left.

Her seat filled before the door shut behind her.

Superhero-employed Abigail took a city bus home to her apartment. Unemployed Abigail would still take that same bus and the same route, but now she felt like an imposter walking to the nearest bus stop. How much of her life, of her identity, had been attached to Inferna? What else would she lose now that she didn't wear the mask? She felt a hundred eyes on her. She felt that each person who saw her knew of her shame. The nameless faces all said the same thing: you failed.

She didn't even sit on the bench once at her stop. Sitting was reserved for winners. She would have to stand. A bus rumbled toward them but not the one she needed. Citizens made their exchange from the bus to the sidewalk, and Abigail continued to wait.

Fourteen minutes later, her correct bus approached the stop. Instead of the usual *whoosh* the brakes produced, the tries shrieked at the sudden demand of stopping 15 tons. Abigail stepped back to allow the bus extra space as it struggled to stop at its proper position. The driver inside waved his apologizes to anyone who saw.

The gentleman beside Abigail did not pay such attention. With his fingers assaulting the digital screen of his phone, and his nose equally obsessed with the message, he stepped closer to the curb, closer to the street, closer to the bus.

Abigail snatched the collar of the man's suit jacket and pulled him away from the street. The bus whizzed past him, the side reflecting his startled expression back at him. Just one more step and it would be him stuck to the bus's front bumper and not the four bicycles. With the once important phone message forgotten, the man turned to Abigail and hugged her.

She stood there unmoving. Behind her mask, nothing had startled her like this man's unexpected hug just did.

"You saved my life!" he shouted, releasing her. "This woman just saved me!"

Abigail waved away the heads that turned their direction. "Please don't make this a big deal."

Her trained Saves the Day media smile floated to her mouth before she remembered who she was. Who she no longer was. She didn't need to smile brightly and bravely in case a camera was trained on her now.

"You're my hero." The man's statement didn't make her feel any better. "Thank you."

"Just look around more often, okay?"

"Sure thing." The man's promise wasn't encouraging as he almost walked back into the bus as he turned around to jog across the road.

Both the man and the bus left and Abigail sighed. If San Arbor's public transport system was on time then her next bus wouldn't arrive for another 45 minutes. She took a seat on the bench.

Sometime later, Abigail's phone buzzed against her thigh. She gritted her teeth. She thought she turned it off after the news of her being fired became public. She pulled the device from her pocket but stopped before powering it down. Flashing across her screen was not a missed call or an unread message.

It was a radar screen.

She had hit him.

The nanotechnology had activated inside the Flame Villain's bloodstream.

He was only eight streets away.

She was not defeated, not yet. She would still have a victory today. He would not get away this time. Abigail raced away from the bus stop and the other waiting passengers. Her legs pumped faster as she neared the place specified on her phone. She tied the red domino mask over her eyes once the area thinned of people.

Her hands burned red when she slid into the alley. The strip of one way road was shaded in thick darkness that only night and tall buildings could create in a dense city. Her flames made terrifying shadows against the walls. Every movement could be him. The radar put her right on top of him.

"I know you're here," she called out. "Show yourself."

"Now, that wouldn't be very smart," a voice answered from somewhere above her. "For you anyway."

"I'm taking you in."

She increased the blaze rotating around her wrists to see further up the walls.

"You?" he laughed. "Doll, you're not even in your cape. Going to make a citizen's arrest?"

Abigail slowly turned to follow the movement above her. Footsteps scraped against the fire escapes. She increased her flames again, but they couldn't reach whatever corner he hid in.

"Volcanic fired you, right? How sad."

"Once I capture you—"

"You'll get your job back? Are you sure about that?"

Abigail gritted her teeth. "It's not about the job. It's about stopping a villain."

"Like you did today?" The voice was close. He was getting closer.

"Scared?" Abigail craned her neck up, scanning all the rungs of the metal canopies above her. "Come down here, and fight me."

A fist struck her stomach as if the Flame Villain had been standing across from her the whole time. Abigail collapsed to her knees and puked out her drink. She was hoisted up by the collar of her t-shirt and shoved against the brick building behind her. The force knocked the air from her lungs. The fire vanished from her wrists leaving wisps of smoke around her.

"I just want to talk," he said calmly. He gave a half-crooked smile. The motion pulled his features across the burn scar crisscrossing over his face. The same burns also wrapped around his hands that gripped Abigail's shirt. She had never noticed them before. "Can't we do that?"

"No!" Abigail managed to yell after gulping enough air to form words and then powered on her flames. She kicked him in the stomach with blazing feet.

The Flame Villain stumbled back and dropped Abigail to the ground. Before she could advance, they were encased by blue flames. It created a tight dome around them, and the alleyway vanished behind it. The air was hot and thin. Abigail's flames weakened without a steady supply of oxygen. Her fists and feet were rendered into cheap night lights.

"I'll let you go." The Flame Villain was unaffected by his fire. He circled Abigail like a shark in a dazzling blue ocean. "But first you have to listen to me. You and I aren't so different. We both have this amazing power, both aren't trusted with it, both have our scars..." he grinned at her, "and we're both chasing something bigger."

"I'm nothing like—"

"You wanted to get stronger, right?"

The little breath that Abigail had left hitched in her throat.

When she didn't respond he continued, "That's why you became Volcanic's little showgirl, so that he'd train you? Teach you? What'd you learn?" Her silence was enough of an answer. "Why not find a new teacher?"

"You're a villain."

"Because you say I am. Because the media says I am. They all lie."

Abigail choked on the thin breath she snatched from the burning air, but it was mostly smoke and heat. She staggered from her left foot to her right. The Flame Villain's marching silhouette turned from one to three then back to one blurry man. He stopped circling her and walked to the center of the dome. She continued to sway.

He sighed. "I'm out of time, aren't I? Getting harder to breathe? We'll work on that another time."

The blue fire vanished as suddenly as it appeared. Abigail dropped to her knees and sucked down the scorched air.

"What did we work on this time?" she asked in a whisper, her lungs burning and eyes watering.

Abigail's back slammed against the wall, forcing the little supply of air she had managed to collect out of her mouth. Her body heated against his hold, but she couldn't turn on her abilities, her oxygen tank was empty. Her vision shook, fear taking over as his hand laid over her scar. She felt the heat instantly. She felt each of his fingers as they pressed into her throat. His face was obscured by thick blue smoke.

"Trust." His cold lips brushed over her ear.

Abigail could barely hear it over the sizzling of her neck. The blue smoke disappeared in a flash and he, the light, and the heat, vanished. Abigail fell back to her knees and covered her neck with her hands. She searched for marred skin, a second handprint next to the first, her neck scorched and blackened like before. But she only felt soft flesh. Her scar was gone.

"The name's Cinder," he called from above.

The alleyway turned cold, and silent as a graveyard.

Chapter Six

Abigail had only ever been a sidekick. For the last six years, she had worn some version of a cape. She was hired by a hero company right after graduation. She only studied Criminal Justice since it was required for any hero to get their license. Her backup plan, the plan her mother hoped had stuck, was using her degree as a detective, or working inside a forensics lab. Abigail never expected to don a mask as soon as she took off her graduation cap. She was a sidekick for so many years she wasn't sure how to just be Abigail. For years she had the same routine. Wake up, shower, dress, breakfast, go to work, save the day, train, microwave dinner, sleep, repeat.

Of course, Inferna had days off. Abigail took advantage of the downtime by cleaning her apartment, stocking up on TV meals, and pruning her melancholy ivy plant growing on the balcony. But today wasn't a day off for Inferna: the sidekick. Today was the first day as Abigail Turner: the unemployed.

Abigail hadn't left her bed all morning. She didn't see the point. There was nothing for her to do outside the apartment, let alone outside her bed. Today, she declared, would be her funeral. To lay to rest her hero dreams, to say goodbye to Inferna, to retire her red mask and golden cape. She had come to terms that her fire producing hands would only heat coffee mugs now. To do hero work without a company endorsing her was a crime. Being a vigilante was as bad as being a villain in San Arbor.

Was there anything worse than a fired hero?

Abigail buried herself deeper under her blankets. She would become an employed civilian. Tomorrow.

Blue boots were replaced with blue sneakers, red skirt with slacks, fireproof cape with a flowery blouse. The business casual look was terrible, Abigail knew it, but half of her closet's contents were already thrown about her room and this was the best she could come up with. She stuffed her mask inside her pants pocket for either luck or courage. She didn't know which she would need more of today. In her hands were twenty copies of her freshly printed resume. She hadn't come up with a good excuse for the six-year job absence since she waited tables in college. Her best plan was hoping the interviewer wouldn't ask about it.

It was just as terrible a plan as her outfit. Abigail ran her toothbrush over her teeth a final time and rinsed out her mouth. She smiled into the mirror.

"Hello, I'm Abigail Turner and I want to interview for any open positions you may have," she rehearsed.

She watched her reflection as she spoke. She watched how her throat moved the skin on her neck when she talked. How freely the skin pulled around her trachea without the weight of the scar. The black handprint was replaced by four baby pink lines, and they had been fading all night. By tomorrow all traces of the scar would be gone. She touched the marks to make sure they were really there. They were warm under her fingers.

She washed her hands. She washed away the events at Saves the Day. She washed away Volcanic. She washed away the Flame Villain. Today was her fresh start. As fresh as the new skin around her throat.

"I can do this," she whispered to herself. "I can do this."

Abigail only heard one "we'll call you if something comes up" that morning, but she knew it was just a polite "no" coming from the old man behind the counter at the hardware store. A third of her resumes had been handed out, and she was pretty sure she was going to be passed over for a high school graduate at the coffee hut she applied at. The electronic store with a "help wanted" sign in the window had her fill out an application while the cashier rang up three customers. They didn't seem impressed with her lack of technical knowledge but liked her smile enough to say they'd be making their decision soon. Another polite "no."

With two resumes left, she stood in front of a goliath. The building loomed over her like a titan in an ancient Greek storybook. She wasn't even sure why she walked to this place. Abigail knew they would never hire a nobody like her; her resume was lighter than a balloon. But something deep down made her want to try. That hero instinct to never give up. The Hero Relief Center was the other hero company serving San Arbor. Maybe they were looking for sidekicks? A phone operator. A lunch runner. A hedge trimmer. Hell, Abigail would scrub toilets if it got her inside the building.

To get back inside the hero world.

Abigail gripped her resume, wrinkling the paper, and walked onto the main floor. The reception area was cooled by the air conditioner, but a bead of sweat still trickled down her back between her shoulder blades. She said a silent prayer that her deodorant was still working. A woman waved to her behind a heavy desk at the back of the open space. She had a corded phone cradled between her ear and shoulder while she picked under a beautifully painted orange nail. The woman looked much more put together in her office outfit than Abigail tried to be. She straightened her shirt while the woman ended her conversation.

"Just had to finish setting up a meeting with the chief of police," she explained with a chipper voice. "What can I do for ya?"

Abigail examined the clean room. The large windows made her feel like she was in a greenhouse. The openness made both her and the woman easy targets, but nothing seemed out of place. "Did something happen?"

"Nothing to worry about," the woman answered. "President Samuels just wanted to thank the force for their work with the incident downtown this week. He's been eating himself up that we weren't able to get there and help. That new ordinance hasn't been too kind to the heroes. Samuels doesn't think the two companies should be separated by districts." The woman shook her head. "You're not here to listen to our worries though, are you?"

"No ma'am." Abigail set her resume on the desk. "I was wanting to drop off my resume. If you had any openings, I would love the chance to apply for them."

"Most people search online for openings," said the receptionist. "I don't think I've received a paper resume in years."

Heat prickled Abigail's cheeks. "I really just wanted to hit the ground running. I thought handing them out would be more personable. More memorable."

Abigail inched her resume a little closer to the desk.

The woman accepted the resume, Abigail noticed from her nameplate her name was Shannon. "I can get this filed for you. We have a database that will connect you to any openings that you're qualified for when they come up. What are you looking for?"

"Honestly, anything." Abigail smiled. "It would be such an honor to work here."

"Among the heroes?"

"To do good, better the city."

Shannon nodded. "Hang on for a minute while I get this in our system, I may have more questions if you're missing anything."

Abigail stepped back. Hanging behind Shannon's desk were three giant portraits of the Hero Relief Center's heroes. They were called the Round Table Knights and vowed to serve San Arbor with the same courage, strength, and chivalry as the fabled Arthurian knights. King Arthur, the team's leader, had been published on the cover of every paper and magazine printed in the city. His handsome face was framed with boyish brown curls. He was the only hero known not to wear a mask. The golden crown atop his head sported sapphires and rubies that matched the colors of his medieval garb. Merlin, dressed in a fitted red dress and pointed hat that dipped past her waist, used a variety of magic like spells to capture their enemies. She was beautiful as she was powerful. The third member of the trio was Excalibur. There were many rumors about who was really under the medieval-styled knight helmet. No one knew for sure. The poster hanging on the wall, as every other one made of the knight, only showed him in head to boot armor.

"Abigail Turner?"

"Yeah?" Abigail peered over the desk. "Is there something wrong?"

"No." Shannon looked up from the resume. "It's just the strangest thing. We had a delivery today, addressed to an Abigail Turner. But we don't have anyone here with that name. The guy who dropped it off said you'd be here. How weird is that?"

"A delivery?" Abigail scanned the empty main floor. Black leather seats and framed portraits looked back at her. "Of what?"

Shannon reached under her desk and pulled out a vase of stargazer lilies. The three blooms were bright white and surrounded by dark green leaves. A blue ribbon tied them together inside the clear vase.

"You're the only Abigail Turner that's come in today. They have to be yours."

"Who sent them?"

Shannon shrugged. "There's a card."

Abigail carefully plucked the envelope out of the blooms, and when nothing exploded, she pulled the card out. She almost dropped it. Her heart hammered violently. Carved in black ink on the blue cardstock was an unsigned message.

You're so predictable, hero. Ready for our second lesson?

"Well?" Shannon prompted, leaning out of her seat to try and read the note. "Who are they from?"

Abigail blinked several times, needing to reset herself. Tucking the card into the front pocket of her slacks, she refocused on Shannon. "No one. I'm so sorry, but I have to go. You should keep the flowers, and thank you for your time!"

Abigail was out of the door before Shannon could respond.

The Flame Villain was here.

Cinder.

He was toying with her now. He could still be close. Hiding, waiting to attack. Abigail would be ready. He wasn't on the public side of the Hero Relief Center. She searched the parking lot, the hedge gardens and as far back down the private side of the building as she could without triggering an alarm. He wasn't there.

He wasn't in the convenience store across the street or in the bank next door. Abigail recovered the card from her pocket. It was her only lead. Printed on the other side of Cinder's cryptic message was an address to a florist shop across town. Abigail ran to the end of the street to a waiting bus. She stepped through the closing doors just in time. If they didn't hit any red lights she might make it before they closed.

Abigail threw herself in the closest available seat to the door. She sat on the edge of the plastic and forced her breath in and out of her nose. She needed to compose herself. She couldn't be caught off guard. Her foot bounced against the floor and, eventually, her heart slowed to an easy pace. The oxygen filling her blood stream calmed her. She knew she could do anything with a full supply of flames.

The sun was a streak of orange light filtering through the single-story buildings when the bus arrived at the south side of San Arbor. They had hit seven out of nine red lights. Abigail's phone flashed 4:49 across the screen. She was hovering above her seat, ready to run to the door once the bus stopped. She double checked the GPS application on her phone. The florist was two streets from the upcoming stop.

She had stopped robberies, she had stopped fires, she had saved lives; she would make it to the florist before it closed.

She had to.

Abigail burst into the florist shop, out of breath and curls sticking to her sweaty forehead, at 4:57. Her deodorant had definitely stopped working by now. The shop was small but charming. The inside was an explosion of colors from the different flowers housed in tall and short pots. A center table was full of pre-made arrangements. It smelled like heaven.

"We're about to close," an older voice from the back said. "Can't do any arrangements until tomorrow. You can buy one from the table if you want."

Abigail walked to the back of the shop where she heard the voice. Her gaze bounced from potted plant to flower vase, her movements careful not to disturb them. This entire shop could be part of the Flame Villain's plan. She was vastly outnumbered if the blooms and leaves were in league with him. She felt the plants knew she could burn them but, with their numbers, they would take her down too.

"Hello," she panted at the older man behind the counter. He was cleaning a pair of gardening shears. Their rusted blades matched his fading red hair. "I have this card but no name. I didn't know if you can track the sender?"

"I don't remember names." The florist didn't look up from his task. "Just the flowers. Do you have the flowers?"

"They're at home," Abigail lied. "But they were lilies. They were white and there were three of them. They were big and star-shaped."

The man looked up with a small grin. "He said you'd come."

"Who?" Abigail shifted her weight to her back foot.

"The admirer. The sender. He said you'd come here to find him."

Abigail swallowed, her mouth drying at the thought of the Flame Villain hiding somewhere in this jungle. Stalking her like a wild animal. She looked behind her. "Is he here?"

The old man laughed. "No. Not him, but he did leave you something. I knew romance wasn't dead. He do this a lot?"

"Do what?" Abigail was still reeling from the word *romance*.

"These little scavenger hunts?"

"It's a first."

"I like them!" the man admitted. "I think I'm going to incorporate them into my business plan." He handed her a small envelope. It was the same blazing blue color as the first. "He told me to give this to you."

Abigail accepted it with two fingers, scared that it would catch fire. *Hero* was scripted in thin ink on the cover of the new card. The florist's mouth moved but she couldn't hear him over the blood roaring behind her ears. She pulled the card out and read the message twice before asking the florist, "How long ago was he here?"

"Came by this morning and set the whole plan up. What's it say?" He leaned across the counter. "Is it another clue?"

"Just an address."

"This keeps getting more exciting." The florist sanded his hands together. "You lucky girl."

"You have no idea."

"Want me to wrap up one of the arrangements on the table for you? You shouldn't meet him empty handed."

"I've already got something for him." *A punch to the face and a trip to jail.*

Chapter Seven

The address written on the card was on the same side of town as the flower shop, luckily. It was the address of a large park, unluckily. Half of Aroma Park was a nature preserve housing dense woods in the center of the residential area making up the majority of the south side of San Arbor. Backyards spilling into the preserve were as much a playground for the forest animals as the jungle gym for the kids who played there. There were shelters for picnics, a walking trail around and through the woods, a fenced-in dog park, and a newly constructed building that taught community classes on gardening, water cycles, and the power of recycling. Tonight, the subject was transferring seedlings from egg cartons to flower beds.

Cinder wasn't at any of those places.

Abigail jogged along a pebbled path that moved adjacent to the narrow, man-made river that ended at the water reservoir several more miles down. The river collected rainwater and was recycled into water bottles (also recycled) and sold at the parks' information center. The system was the winner of a science competition ten years ago. It was named San Arbor's first nonhuman superhero.

Every few hundred yards, a replica footbridge of famous bridges from around the world stretched over the river. Abigail passed the Golden Gate Bridge, the Sydney Harbor Bridge, the Brooklyn Bridge and coming next was the sturdy, yellow Ponte Vecchio. A landmark from Florence, Italy with low arches rising from the water and tall shelters built on top. The setting sun turned the bricks gold.

Cinder was under that bridge.

Abigail saw his duster coat silhouette stretching up the underside of the bridge. His shadow loomed up the length of the entire arch, but he seemed much darker than his own shadow. The river sloshed against the sides as it passed through, unaware of the villain hiding under the bridge. Abigail tied her red mask tightly around her eyes.

She sloshed through the riverbank and ignited her fists once hidden by the bridge's shadow. Abigail imagined a bullseye over the Flame Villain's nose, cocking her arm back and preparing to hit him hard enough to knock him into the water. The river could carry him to the recycling center and turn him into a plastic bottle for all she cared. She'd crush the bottle once the center was done with him.

Just before her fist made contact, Cinder grabbed her arm and flipped her over his shoulder. Her back bounced against the damp platform and knocked the air out of her lungs. Abigail scrambled to her feet, forcing her flames through her hands but the fire only sizzled against the dampness before extinguishing. She widened her stance and prepared her next move. Her flames would return once her breath did.

"I knew you'd solve my riddle." The four feet between them felt vast. He slipped his hands in his pockets, but his smile hid nothing. He was amused, proud of himself. "Why are you wearing that mask? You know I know who you are, Miss Abigail Turner."

Abigail's skin prickled as he said her secret identity aloud. She had taken all the steps to keep it hidden. There was an entire floor at Saves the Day dedicated to it. How had he found it so easily? Who else knew? Who else did he know?

"But the world doesn't know, and I'd like to keep it that way."

"The world sees you as a retired," his grin morphed to shit-eating, "—a fired hero. What do you think they'll do if they saw you with a villain?"

"What do you want with me?" Abigail snatched her mask off and stuffed it back into her pocket. The only thing worse than being seen with him was knowing he had a point.

"To make you stronger. That's what you want too, isn't it?"

"To defeat you," she reminded. "If you know so much about me then you know that's the only reason."

"It's not to save people? Isn't that what you hero types do?"

"I'll be saving a lot of people once I beat you."

"And, when you think you're ready, I won't stop you." Cinder pulled his hands from his jacket and blue flames danced from his fingers to his elbows, mindful of the fabric of his coat. "But do you really want a repeat of the last time? At least learn something first."

Last time had been every time with him. She needed an advantage, and she needed one now. Abigail glanced to the other side of the riverbank. It was empty. She hadn't seen anyone as she ran down it for the last hour. She swallowed hard and looked back at the Flame Villain. As a hero, this would be treason. But Abigail wasn't a hero anymore. Inferna was dead. Learning a new skill didn't make her a villain.

Volcanic wasn't the only one who wielded the blue flame.

"What's today's lesson?"

Cinder took two steps closer. She refused to back away, to give him any more of a victory that he clearly felt he had earned by now. He took another step and another, and then stood toe to toe with her. She had to lift her chin to keep her eyes locked with his.

"Fire burns hotter depending on the color, right?" His voice bounced between the two bridge pillars. It was low thunder, rumbling after a storm. "You burn red, and I burn blue. I burn hotter. This lesson is simple, you can't burn blue until you get hotter."

"I've only ever been red." It sounded like an excuse. Abigail protecting her weaker abilities. She wanted to hide her hands behind her back but forced them to stay at her sides. She would not be ashamed.

"So did I, in the beginning," he admitted. "Raise your hand."

She did so without stepping back. Her right palm was hovering in the little space between them. Her knuckles brushed against the zipper on his coat.

"Ignite it," Cinder commanded.

Red flames sparked to life at Abigail's fingertips and dripped down her fingers into her palm where they gathered into a ball. The cherry-red blaze swirled around itself as if it were alive. The concentrated center of light created a flower bloom of shadows around the pair.

"Make it hotter."

Abigail focused on the burn. She didn't feel a difference in the heat because of her fireproofing. The color didn't change. The tiny fireball still danced between red and orange. She breathed in deeply through her nose and pumped more fuel into the ball. The tiny fire stretched toward her fingers and pushed through the containment.

Cinder covered her hand with his own before the flames could expand past her fingers. The flame snuffed out and black smoke pushed between their encased hands.

"Hotter, not larger," he instructed. "Don't want to blow anything up, again."

Abigail gritted her teeth at his taunt. She yanked her hand out of his and created the flame. The flame raged against her finger-made cage, but she kept it contained. It stayed red. She stayed angry.

"Any other sage advice?" she called after an hour.

Abigail hadn't moved from her spot. The ball of fire hadn't gotten any hotter from what she could tell, her fireproofing still able to protect herself. Cinder watched her as he leaned against the curved wall of the archway. He had been surprisingly quiet the whole time.

"Think of hot things."

Abigail didn't know if he was joking or being serious.

"Think of hated things." Cinder pushed off the wall and stood beside her. "How'd it feel when Volcanic fired you? When he tossed you out like you meant nothing to him."

"I knew it was coming."

"That didn't answer my question, doll."

"It was humiliating."

"Focus on that moment." His voice rumbled. "Replay it in your head until all you can do is burn it away."

Abigail couldn't blame Kenneth, not completely. The deal between them was the only thing that mattered to the number one hero. Abigail hadn't initially accepted the sidekick position of Volcanic when Saves the Day contacted her. She was intimidated by the hero. She didn't want to get pushed around by a man three times her size. She knew heroes like him only thought a sidekick would slow them down. It was Kenneth who offered her their deal. The company was desperate to increase his ratings, and he thought she'd be his best bet for a ratings jump.

The order to let her go came from Kreech. He was to blame. The president held the status of his company over real hero work. Kreech was angrier about the ratings than Flipp's death. If her explosion hadn't been caught on some random cell phone camera, then this would have never happened. She should have burned the phones.

The fireball in her hand crackled, and red sparks trickled to the ground. The orange core was getting smaller as the red grew. As the temperature grew.

"You're getting it," Cinder encouraged. "Go further."

Abigail knew the phone recordings weren't the problem either. If she had destroyed the phones in the explosion, then she would have surely killed their owners, too. That was not hero work. The real problem was standing in front of her. He was grinning as her flame created shadows across his burned face. It made the burn scars grow and shrink with the shadow's movement. This all started with him.

When he attacked that bar and left a horrible scar around her neck.

The fireball popped and turned completely red. A dark red that matched the molten core of the planet. Abigail could smell something burning, something singeing. It could have been her hair, her shirt, the brick around her. It didn't matter. Cinder's grin was the only thing she wanted to burn.

"Push further."

His order was smug, condescending. It was an order from a villain. Everything he said was a taunt, a challenge. The fireball grew bigger, it grew denser, it grew stronger. So did the burning smell. Dark smoke clouded Abigail's vision. It created a wall between them. She commanded the fire in her hands to grow brighter to clear the way.

"Abigail?" Cinder called on the other side of the newly constructed smoke wall. The air was becoming hotter. The fire was becoming brighter. More things caught fire.

Abigail caught fire.

The flames in her hands burst through her fingers. The sheer fabric of her blouse caught easily as a tinderbox. The cheap metal on her earrings melted and dripped onto her shoulders. Her slacks smoldered when sparks fell against the stitching. She couldn't extinguish the flame quick enough.

Two hands pushed through the blaze and smoke and shoved her back. Abigail lost her footing and fell into the water. The only thing she heard was the sizzling of her flames as they extinguished around her. It created tiny bubbles that tickled her skin as they rose up. She kicked to the surface and took several smoke-free breaths. She hadn't realized how strained her lungs had become. How much they craved the cold air. How much her body craved the cold water.

One of the hands that had shoved her hauled her out of the water. The archway was scorched black. Soot dusted the ground and stained her knees where she kneeled against the platform. It coated her hands when she pushed herself up, staining her fingertips black.

Once the roaring in her head faded, Abigail heard laughing. But not from Cinder. The laughter was too high pitched. A group of kids pointed and laughed at the woman who just fell into the river across the bank. Abigail quickly turned her back to them and glared at Cinder. He was just as amused as the children.

"I almost had it." Abigail pulled what remained of her shirt around her. It was charred down the center and now more of a vest.

"Had what, doll?" Cinder teased. "From where I'm standing, it looked like you almost turned yourself into a kabob. Do you catch on fire like that a lot?"

"Never!"

"Next time we'll work on increasing your resistance," he said, ignoring her. "If your body can't handle the heat then there's no point in learning it."

Abigail dripped on the platform. Her skin was burning from where the small blast had burned through her shirt, her lungs were aching from inhaling the smoke, her hand was blistered from the heat. He was right, again.

"If this is going to continue, can we go somewhere more private?" She surprised both herself and him with the question. She wasn't even sure why she wanted to continue.

Cinder tapped his chin. "I think the evil YMCA is open late."

Abigail didn't laugh at his joke, but Cinder did. It was the lighting strike to his low rumble. Bright, fast, and loud.

"If you accept my offer, I'll find other arrangements."

"What's the offer?" Abigail never thought he'd want something in return. A villain just took what it wanted. There were never any negotiations.

"I make you stronger, I teach you my flame, and you owe me a favor."

She glared at him, crossing her arms.

"I'm not going to ask you to kick a puppy or something, Abby," Cinder soothed. "Maybe when you're back to being a hero you give me a head start, you let me run out of this city without a big flashy chase." When she remained silent, he added with a half-crooked smile: "After you defeat me, of course."

"When that happens, you'll be in jail."

"We'll see." Cinder extended his hand to her, and blue flames snaked around his wrist before circling his fingers. "Deal or not?"

The heat was too tempting. The power was too close. She wasn't strong enough to defeat him. She wasn't strong enough to ignore the need to possess the blue fire, either. At least working together, she could keep an eye on the Flame Villain. This was an intelligence gathering mission. She was not becoming a villain.

Abigail shoved her hand in his, and the flames extinguished. "Deal."

Chapter Eight

Abigail awoke the next morning, still unemployed but not jobless.

The grey, hazy light of early morning pressed through the glass patio door and into her bedroom. It was still an hour before she would usually wake for work, but she got out from under the covers. The sheets were warm with sleep and her unnaturally warmer body temperature. Her bare toes chilled when she stepped on to the bathroom tile, however, and she retreated to the furry rug at the sink. She examined her reflection in the mirror. Her chest red from training yesterday, and her right palm contained a collection of tiny blisters. She hadn't burnt herself this bad since she first discovered her fire ability. Her fireproofing developed slower than her flames.

Growing up, she had more fire retardant gloves than most kids had socks. There were several pairs in every room of her home, in each of her parents' cars, her school backpack, a pair stashed under her assigned bus seat. She thought she wouldn't need them any more after her tenth birthday.

Inside the medicine cabinet, Abigail grabbed a half-used tube of snotty-green medical grade burn cream. She rubbed a handful over her tender, pink sternum that received the brunt of the explosion. She glopped a large tablespoon in her hand before sliding a sock over it. The blisters cooled as quickly as her toes had.

The pain of the burns had woken her, but curiosity kept her from returning to bed.

Abigail powered on her coffee pot and gave an offering of bread to the toaster. She searched her junk drawer for a working pen and a pad of paper. An ancient food order was scribed on the front page—apparently; she spent $16.95 on Chinese takeout some time ago. She ripped out the order, poured a mug of coffee, and accepted her warm toast when it popped up. She dumped herself, and her armload of items, into a computer chair and turned on the machine.

She finished her toast and dusted the crumbs into the wastebasket under the desk by the time the old desktop finished booting up and loaded her search request: Cinder. Before leaving the handprint scar around her neck, Abigail had never heard of the Flame Villain. And apparently, neither had the internet. The only thing it kicked up was the definition: *a small piece of partly burned coal or wood that has stopped giving off flames but still has combustible matter in it.*

Abigail tried a new search with *Cinder + Villain + San Arbor* and her results were saturated with numerous news articles of attacks and hero rescues in the city. She tried taking out San Arbor, taking out his name, adding Flame Villain and still, she found nothing of use. It felt like he had been a ghost until he entered her life. She tried a new search: *Villain + Fire + Attack.*

Two eye-catching results came up.

The recent battle downtown, and a news article almost eight years old from New Haines, a city two states away. It was vague, the data collected the bare minimum, but it was enough to make Abigail expand the link. Attached in the digital scan of the article was a grainy photo, but Abigail knew it was him. It was Cinder. In the photo he was running, black and white flames pouring from his body and filling every space behind him. He looked scared. The expression didn't fit the cocky villain she knew today.

ICU Up in Smokes!

The headline was printed in red, using all the color that rendered the photo monotone.

Nineteen people injured, two dead at Tri-County Hospital, Tuesday afternoon when an unknown suspect ignited what police believe to be a bomb.

The attack happened after a man was aditted to the ICU covered in third degree burns. He had no identification and, according to a nurse on staff, was discovered unconscious outside the emergency room doors. The nurse said when trying to insert IVs, the needles melted against his skin.

"I didn't think he was going to make it," Stacy Resto, the nurse on staff, said. "He was covered in horrid burns, and without being able to administer the medicine, there wasn't any hope."

Resto said she went to get a doctor and that's when the bomb went off. Most of the injuries were caused by debris impaling victims, but two were caught in the main explosion and died at the scene.

The bomb's trigger point appeared to be in the room where the burned man was brought, said authorities, but his body wasn't found during the rescue or cleanup operations.

Police believed the man escaped in the explosion and are asking people with information to come forward. Local hero, Helios, has been enlisted to help the police.

Abigail pushed her half full mug away after finishing the article. It didn't sit well in her stomach after picturing the damage and deaths. She printed the article and closed the tab. She opened the paper's main website and searched through their past editions. It was slow work; the city was just as big as San Arbor and saw just as much crime in the last eight years. But none of it had been connected to Cinder.

Numerous front-page articles of past issues showcased the city's hero, Helios, stopping violent crimes and working with troopers to catch escaped criminals. Abigail didn't recognize the hero by his name but by the scowl under his half mask. Kenneth. Abigail grabbed her phone from her nightstand and started punching in his number. She dropped it back on the bed before she hit call. Asking him for help was simply out of habit. She didn't need him anymore. She returned to her desk and grabbed her mug. The coffee bubbled as her fingers steamed around it. She wondered if her feelings of betrayal would ever dissipate.

She checked more issues of the online paper, but Cinder vanished off the pages as quickly as he appeared. Abigail paused, her mouse hovering over the next arrow on the bottom of the page. She couldn't look away from the headline, and her breath faltered as she waited for the article to expand.

Helios' Sidekick Still Missing

Abigail scanned the document. The writer never said what happened to the sidekick, just that Helios had been acting solo the last month. The writer interviewed several people who hadn't noticed the change of line up, or didn't care enough to be bothered by it.

Helios seems different without him. After last night's fire I saw him with his head in his hands. He was ruder to the reporters too. I bet he's sad to have lost him. The op-ed concluded.

Abigail laughed. It was as bitter as her black coffee. Volcanic seemed fine without her. He didn't even try to help her keep her job. Even if he couldn't admit to stealing the tracker, he could have done something. She doubted anyone would see him with his head in his hands now. He wasn't the type to want sidekicks, they just slowed him down. She just slowed him down.

She shut down the website.

Needing to feel like she accomplished something that morning, Abigail found and printed an article from their downtown battle. She dug through past police reports and added her first encounter with the Flame Villain to her printed stack of research. The last thing she pulled up was a report from a jewelry theft dated two months after the bar fire. The small boutique was robbed of its most expensive item: a diamond pendant listed at over $7,000. The store's front door camera captured the thief's entrance; a fiery flash of blue flames. The Flame Villain was in and out in 30 seconds.

Abigail didn't think they were the same villain; the hospital attacker and the diamond thief. Starting from a hospital bombing and then changing to a robbery? Crimes usually escalated, not downgraded. It could have been a different villain at the hospital. Maybe the reporter had the bombing wrong, there were a lot of details missing. It could've been a different person altogether. The photo was blurry after all. Abigail would never align herself with a killer.

She hoped.

Eight days passed since Abigail was fired. The reality of it finally settled in. The small hope that fluttered in her stomach whenever her phone rang hoping it was Saves the Day vanished. Abigail spent her empty afternoons organizing her closet so business casual outfits were first on the rack. Inferna's red mask was rolled tightly around itself and hidden in the lowest drawer of her dresser next to the Christmas sweater and a pumpkin colored T-shirt.

It had been six days since her last contact with Cinder. The reality of working alongside a villain wasn't settling in as quickly as her forced retirement. She should have called the police the second he contacted her. She should let the heroes defeat him. She should not put herself in danger with him. But Abigail didn't think she would do any of that.

Cinder was hers to defeat.

Her burns had healed three days ago. The blisters in her palm were reduced to cute tiny pink circles. They healed just in time too. Abigail didn't think a handful of angry red blisters would win her any points in an interview, like the one waiting for her this afternoon at the tech store. Abigail knew selling phones and extension cables wasn't as exciting as her old job, but she couldn't afford to be picky. Her pantry and fridge were running low on food, her bus pass almost expired. Rent was due soon; according to her bank statements, she had another three weeks to find a new job or change her lifestyle.

Abigail flipped through an advertisement booklet that had arrived with the paper that morning. She studied the electronics section, trying to familiarize herself with name brands, specs and the competitors' pricing. Her kitchen counter was covered in the manuals of her television, microwave and hair dryer that had been collecting dust at the bottom of her desk since the day they came out of the box. Abigail hoped one of the texts would give her enough leverage in the interview.

Time dragged on for half the day until an hour before the interview, then it kicked into overdrive. Abigail kept watching the clock on her phone. It was speeding out of control while her bus was moving in its own time zone. One that moved opposite of what she needed.

She arrived on time, though, and Abigail forced herself to take ten huge breaths before entering the store. She needed this job. She had to play it cool. She took an extra breath just to be sure.

The same man who had her fill out the application greeted her from behind the counter. He wore a dark polo and jeans. Abigail felt overdressed in her pencil skirt and red collared blouse. She cursed herself for not asking about their dress code before leaving last week. She smiled at him anyway.

"Abby, right? I'm Brad."

Abigail shook his hand, not correcting him. She never really liked the nickname, but she didn't think her hopeful future boss would care. "How are you?"

"Good for now." Brad pulled her application from behind the counter and set it on the space between them. "We've been really busy lately. Hope you don't mind us doing the interview out here. I'm short staffed today."

"This is fine," Abigail answered.

"I won't waste your time," Brad began. "This position isn't anything glorious. I just need a jack-of-all-trades employee that can answer questions, stock shelves and ring up customers. It'll feel mundane and boring at times, but you can't let that affect your work. You'd be a cog in our business, and without your hundred percent, we'll fail. Is this still something you'd be interested in?"

Abigail blinked twice and nodded. She had been looking at the collection of baseball cards mounted to the wall behind Brad. "I'm interested."

"Good." Brad looked down at her application. "I noticed you don't have any recommendations, why's that?"

"I took a lot of time off after school to travel," she lied.

"This is a long gap year. Where did you travel?"

"Europe mostly." She'd never been outside the country. "I'm ready to start making a life for myself here."

"At my store?" Brad raised an eyebrow.

"Entrepreneurship is the American dream." Abigail tried to smile, but she felt like the interview was already going down the toilet.

"Why do you really want the job?"

"I'm about to blow through my savings and I really don't want to be kicked out of my apartment." Abigail whined just enough to be cute. She twisted a lock of blonde hair around her finger like she'd seen women in movies do.

Brad made a note on her application that she couldn't read. "How brave would you say you are?"

"Excuse me?"

"Can you act tough?" Brad tried again. "If a robber came in and demanded all the money, could you handle it?"

"I've taken self-defense classes, and kick-boxing," Abigail answered, it was one of the few truths she could tell. "Has that happened here?"

"Only once when I first opened," Brad answered. "But after that attack last week I'm not waiting for them to get me next."

"Them?" Abigail echoed. "Do they know who started the attack?"

Brad shook his head. "No, but a couple more businesses have been getting ransacked ever since."

"If there was a robbery I wouldn't let them get away," Abigail answered his initial question.

Brad scribbled on her application again. "That's everything I need."

Abigail gasped. "Really? That's it? I'm hired?"

Brad cocked his head and laughed. "That's everything I need for the interview. I still have four more today. But I'll make my choice by Friday. If you don't hear from me by then, I hope you still shop with us if you need something new."

"Of course." Abigail forced herself to remain smiling. "Thank you for your time, Brad. Have a great rest of your day."

The bus ride home was just as agonizingly slow. Only, instead of sitting with the excitement of change, Abigail rode back with the disappointment of defeat. Call it a woman's intuition, but she didn't think she was getting the job. She slumped in her seat and her head knocked against the window as the bus hit a pothole. She watched people enter and exit the bus as it stopped along its route toward her apartment complex.

A kid wearing a high school uniform boarded with his arms loaded with a backpack, a gym bag, and an obnoxiously loud cell phone. He dumped his bags and his body into the seat across from Abigail.

Even over the noise of the bus and its passengers, Abigail heard Devon Kreech's voice. It was worse than nails against a chalkboard, worse than a car alarm in the middle of the night, worse than a scream-ing kid in a movie theater. The sound made Abigail want to throw up. She tightened her hand around the handrail on her seat and forced her-self to count the cookie crumbs on the floor next to her shoe.

She lost count when she heard her name. She shifted to better hear the student's phone and the news segment that he watched. She was glad he had forgone his headphones.

"The contract for a hero is very important," Kreech was saying on the tiny screen. "It protects them, their image, and their rights." Abigail rolled her eyes. She currently had more ownership of this city bus than her Inferna identity. "If Inferna wants to return to hero work, it will not be until her post-termination restrictions are lifted, which she agreed to when signing her contract with Saves the Day."

Now that she wasn't working for him, Abigail wondered how Kreech slept at night. Did he ever stop sounding like a snake? He had the answer for anything and always landed on his feet. It was admira-ble, although frightening.

The reporter on the screen asked, "Would Saves the Day end the restriction early if someone else wanted to hire Inferna?"

"What would be the point of having contracts if we broke them simply because someone asked nicely?" Kreech didn't give the reporter time to answer. "I'll tell you what I told them, Inferna will become public domain in two years. If anyone wants the second-rate sidekick they will wait."

The handrail softened in Abigail's hold. She dropped her hands and patted out the embers on her skirt. An impression of her fingers hardened in the metal. She leaned her bag against it hoping the woman next to her wouldn't notice. The student hopped off the bus at the next stop, taking Kreech and his insults with him. Abigail smiled as the bus rumbled closer to her stop. She wasn't wanted at the electronic store, but someone wanted Inferna.

The doorman greeted her with the same smile he'd used the past year. Henry was older, his hair greying under the black cap of his uniform. Abigail knew he had a granddaughter that he loved to spoil with lollipops every time she stopped in with her mom to say 'hello.'

"Hey Henry," Abigail returned his greeting.

"How'd it go today?" he asked with a hopeful glint in his eye. "Did they love you as much as I do?"

"I don't think that's possible, Hen." Abigail didn't have the heart to tell him the truth. She pressed the elevator call button. "I think it's going to be an early night for me."

"Hang on a moment." At his request, Abigail hooked an arm through the open elevator door and looked at him. He was grabbing something from the front desk. "There was a message for you on the phone while you were out."

"From who?"

"Didn't say." Henry handed her a folded notecard.

"Thanks, Henry. See you tomorrow."

The notecard burned against her hand as Abigail was lifted the seven stories to her floor. She refused to open it until she was inside her apartment. Where a locked door could keep her secret. It was written in Henry's all cap print. He said it was a habit from being in the Navy when Abigail had asked, but she heard someone else's voice in her head when she read the message.

How are your burns? Meet me tomorrow. Three o'clock.

Below the message was a new address. It was on the same side of town as the nature preserve, but it was closer to the industrial district. Abigail slipped the note under her keys inside the bowl at the door. The handwritten words spied on her under her keys and spare change.

Abigail retrieved a sour IPA from the fridge and collapsed on her small couch, kicking off her heels under the coffee table. Today had been a disaster. She groaned at the electronic manuals still scattered around her house and at the deplorable interview replaying in her mind. She knew she wasn't going to get the job. She was equal parts disappointed and okay with that. She knew she was built for bigger things than running a cash register.

Her eyes lingered back to the key bowl and her heartbeat quickened with equal parts excitement and dread. She was built for combat. She was built for training. The forgotten burns from last time were like sore muscles after a workout. Proof of her improvement. She handled Kenneth's training without complaint. Cinder's would be no different.

Abigail tossed her manuals into the trash. The blue fire would be hers. She would become strong enough to be a hero. She wasn't a second-rate sidekick. The only thing in her way was the Flame Villain that promised to teach it to her.

Chapter Nine

Abigail didn't sleep well. Her mind cycled through images that chased her deep into her dreams and pulled her awake again, and again. She saw flashes of blue flame so vividly she rolled off her bed attempting to flee them. She glimpsed a burning San Arbor with her at the center. She dreamt of working alongside Volcanic, and for a moment after she woke, she was sure it was true. Her mind warred between turning the villain in and keeping him for herself. She deserved this power, but her city deserved to be safe too. She saw every hour appear on the digital clock across the room. She even saw five o'clock twice. At 6:30 she finally gave in and dragged herself to the kitchen to pour a glass of water.

She knew nothing was making her go today. There wasn't a gun forcing her to the address printed on the notecard, but she knew better than to miss the appointment. She would beat herself up harder than any sparring match if she didn't find out what the villain was planning. Her head screamed at her to reconsider. She knew walking into oncoming traffic had a better outcome, but what waited for her on the other side of the street was too tempting. Not just for herself, but the fate of San Arbor.

She was on an intelligence mission.

Abigail sipped her water. She wasn't as familiar with the residential south side of the city as she was the busy center of the downtown, but she didn't think there was a body of water in the industrial district. Large warehouses and hangers had depleted almost all the land of natural charm and beauty. She didn't know what that meant for their training. If she caught fire again there would be no river to push her into.

Abigail set her empty glass down. She wouldn't catch fire again.

The same thoughts that plagued her sleepless dreams emerged in her head. They could do strength training. She pictured them flipping oversized Bobcat tires. They could do power training, and she imagined them melting steel beams. She had done that with Volcanic once. Abigail even thought they could train endurance by igniting inside a trailer where the air would become too thin. He thought that training method was too barbaric and dismissed it on the spot.

Abigail smiled as she allowed a new image to take shape inside her mind; radiant blue fire expanding from her hands. The flames coating her fists as she fought her way to the top of the hero world. She stood triumphantly at the number one spot. Her sidekick days were over. The blue flames a gold medal around her neck.

It was too easy and felt too good to be that easy so Abigail killed her imagination before it could flourish again.

She showered and washed the training images of herself and Cinder down the drain with her shampoo. Abigail still needed to focus on her main goal of finding a job, and daydreaming about red and blue fire wasn't going to get her anywhere in the business world. She mimicked an outfit she saw in a business magazine that was left on the bus, but she chose sneakers rather than the heeled boots depicted.

Abigail grabbed a freshly printed stack of resumes from the printer and tore out a handwritten list of jobs offering walk-in interviews today. Her notes on Cinder stared up at her from her desk. She closed the notebook. The printed articles poked through the cover. Abigail weighed it down with an empty coffee mug.

Abigail grabbed her keys from the bowl and tucked the notecard into her pocket. She had to stay focused on her current mission. She had to find a job first.

Abigail did not succeed.

She did hand out half of her resumes, sliding several through mail slots of offices that only spoke to her through a speaker box hanging on the door and left one with a hostess desk of a restaurant on the bottom floor of a hotel. She did not stop at any of the places on her open interview list. She didn't know what she would say if they asked her to start that day.

Sorry, I'm meeting a villain for secret training.

Abigail also kept close to the bus line so she wouldn't miss a bus heading south. By 1:30 she was sitting at a bus stop waiting for the next one to arrive. Her sneakers tapped anxiously against the sidewalk. She promised herself she'd try job hunting while on that side of town, too. Play both sides of the market. It had nothing to do with *him*. The florist shop looked like it might need an extra hand.

Abigail arrived at the industrial district without stopping at any store, café, or the florist shop. She threw her remaining resumes in a trash can and found the half-constructed building listed on the notecard ten minutes before three. The first two stories had finished outside walls, and wood studs marked where the internal walls would go. The rest of the stories above her were just steel beams reaching into the blue sky. The only floor was the concrete Abigail stood on. She felt like she was in a silo barn; confined, even with the opened ceiling. Abigail walked through the first floor. Nothing seemed too dangerous, minus the fact she was in a construction zone. Tools and blueprints were stationed on tables, and sections of the floor were covered in sawdust. It looked like the building would house several companies once completed.

"You look disappointed," Cinder called from above. "Were you expecting an evil lair?"

Abigail snapped her head up. He walked across a steel beam like a tightrope. "I didn't know what I was expecting."

He leaped down next to her. "Private enough, though?"

"It'll do." Abigail tugged her suit jacket off and laid it on the table. Taking the notecard from her pocket, she flicked it at him. "How do you know where I live?"

"I know everything I need to know, Abigail."

"And I know nothing about you."

"Let's keep it that way." He winked at her. "Come over here, we've got work to do."

"More resistance training?" She took a stab at one of her theories.

"We need to break your body and rebuild it."

"What?"

Abigail stopped following him. She raised her hands ready to fight. Cinder chuckled, and she glanced around for what he found humorous.

"You've really got to trust me, doll. I did take away that scar of yours."

Abigail reached for her neck out of habit. There was still only smooth flesh. "Why don't you remove yours?"

"Some scars are worth the reminder." Cinder turned around slowly to face her. His green eyes separated by his scar. "Do the fireball again. This time, let it escape your fingers if it gets too big."

"What if I damage the building?"

"Let me worry about that."

Abigail hesitated. Cinder stared. Beside the wooden studs, and the two humans inside, the place was pretty immune to fire damage. When Cinder's eyes became too intense to look at, Abigail created the fireball and watched it instead. It was much easier to look into the burning ball clutched inside her hands. Slowly, unlike before, she forced the flame to turn red. Quickly, like before, it raged in her hands. Sparks flew from her fingers and floated to the ground.

"Let it grow!" Cinder shouted over the crackling and popping. "Release it!"

Abigail sucked a breath in through her clenched teeth and allowed the fireball to grow. She used both hands to hold the flame. It continued to burn red, brighter than before. Hotter than before. Abigail felt the heat crash against her face in waves. It pushed against her fingers until it dripped onto the floor like magma. Abigail compelled more fuel into the fireball, and it expanded rapidly. She turned away as it exploded out of her hands.

The fireball fizzled out against the concrete floor.

"Again."

Abigail obeyed.

She made the fireball until it exploded from her hands and disappeared on the floor. The only proof of it existing was the scorch marks on the concrete. The exercise felt pointless at first. It was failure after failure, and she didn't even know what the end goal was. But, after a hundred fireballs, she saw the change. She could hold onto the flame longer; the heat didn't break her fireproofing as badly. After two hours she was holding onto a three-foot-wide flaming sphere without breaking a sweat. It was still red, but at its core was a dazzling white light.

"How do you feel?" Cinder asked from the foreman's chair he'd found. He wheeled closer to her by kicking the floor. His chin rested on the back of the headrest.

"Good." Abigail grinned, proud of herself.

Cinder placed a scarred hand against the sphere and the flames caressed his fingers. "You're hotter than you started, too."

"I think I can go to blue now."

"Really?" Cinder sneered around the orb looking at her. "You sure?"

Abigail glared at him but nodded.

Without warning, Cinder shoved his fist inside the sphere. The flame whipped around the intrusion. Cinder opened his fist, and his blue flame thrashed inside the orb like a wild animal. He removed his hand, and the blue flame overpowered the sphere. Consuming the white light first before turning the spear purple as it devoured the cherry-red flames. The intense heat charred her fingernails, and Abigail screamed. She dropped the fireball. It exploded when it hit the floor showering everything in blue sparks.

The flames went everywhere.

It engulfed the first floor, the wooden studs, the tools, the foreman's chair. The fire fell over itself searching the floor for more fuel. It screamed into the rafters trying to tear down the metal beams.

And then, the flames were nowhere.

Abigail had never seen this level of control before. She didn't even know it was possible. Cinder coaxed the fire back into his hands like he was calling a child to return to his side. He pulled the flames back inside his body, absorbing them through his hands. Soon all that was left was smoke and ash. He looked over his shoulder at Abigail and waited for her to lift her jaw off the floor.

"Impressive, I know." He flashed his crooked smile. "Still think you can handle the blue flame?"

"Don't throw it at me," she growled, a new plan forming on the other side of her frustration. "Can I take it from you?"

"Can you say 'please'?"

Abigail frowned at him, and Cinder tucked his hands into his pockets.

She twisted the tip of her sneaker against the floor. The white toe cap coated black by the ash. She would have rather burned herself. "Please?"

Cinder removed a hand from his pocket and produced a small flame in his hand. Abigail reached for it but recoiled. An arm's reach away and it was still so hot even after the training today.

"Wait!" Abigail demanded when he started to close his hand, extinguishing the flame. "Let me try something."

Cinder cocked his head, but allowed her a third chance. She lit her pointer finger and thumb in her cherry-red flames and pinched his flame from his palm using her fire as a barrier. The blue flame molded between her fingers and, with wild eyes, Abigail began to command the blue fire around her fingertips.

It slithered between her fingers like she was twirling a coin.

"Woah," Cinder whispered.

His praise was loud enough for Abigail to hear. She glanced from the blue flame wiggling through her fingers to him. When their eyes met, her concentration broke. The flame vanished.

"Shit."

Abigail snapped her fingers together, but only red flames responded. A scarred hand suddenly covered hers and the flames were absorbed leaving white smoke between them.

"Nice job, hero," Cinder's smile was as wild as her eyes.

"Let me try again."

He turned over his hand and ignited the tips of his fingers. The light gave his face a devilish look. When Abigail pinched a piece of the flame, the shadow grew. They stood together in silence. Cinder's flame obediently burning on his fingertips while Abigail's moved wildly between her fingers and palm. After a few minutes, she felt the heat bypassing her barrier. Once his flame consumed her fire, she clenched her fist killing it completely. Ash fell from her fingers as she shook out her hand. Her fingers had the same crisscrossing scars as Cinder's.

Cinder extinguished his flames but left his hand reaching between them. "Let me see."

Abigail lowered her hand into his and blue smoke hid the fascinatingly, unsettling removal of her burns. When he moved his hand away, her fingertips were as pink as her neck had been.

"That's amazing."

"That's everything about me, doll."

Abigail tried to ignore the low rumble in his voice. The lure of a summer storm that promised rain and danger. "What else can you do?"

"You'll just have to stick around and find out."

Chapter Ten

Nice job, hero.

Cinder's voice followed her all the way home. Her fingertips still tingled from the heat. Her mind still electrified from the victory. She had used the blue flame! She knew taking it from Cinder didn't mean she had mastered the power, but it was the closest she had ever been. She'd gotten farther with a villain in one evening than she ever had in the year with a hero.

Cinder followed Abigail into her dreams that night, too.

She was trapped in a sphere of blue fire. The flames encircled her and morphed into a rapidly spinning vortex. The heat was sharp talons ripping the oxygen from her lungs. She was powerless to create her own flames to combat it. The blaze had appeared so suddenly, or had Abigail always been trapped in the swirling fire? She crawled forward, keeping her head as low as possible, toward the center of the twister where something reflected the light. When she reached it, her fingers dipped into a pool of cold water. Abigail fell into the puddle and emerged in a dark ocean. The fire above was a beautiful aurora borealis of blue. The falling cinders created shining bubbles when they fell into the water. Abigail stared at it until her vision turned black.

Nice job, hero.

Cinder sat on the foreman's chair during their next training session, his chin resting lazily on the back of it. The dark mesh left an indention against his chin. His hand extended in front of him, and his blue flame sat idly in his palm. Abigail used her coated fingers to pinch pieces of it away. The flames would dance between her fingers before sizzling out. The blue fire of this size was getting easier to be around, the heat didn't steal her breath as quickly, or burn her arm hair.

She pinched a larger chunk of the flame away and practiced grabbing it from her hand. Her cherry-red fingers morphed the blue flame to purple before changing it to red completely. She gritted her teeth, shook out her hands, and pinched off another piece.

Cinder watched with a strange and quiet curiosity over the top of the flame.

At times she didn't know which burned her more; the flame or his eyes.

Nice job, hero.

The endless horizon was as big as the endless field below it. The dark sky was lit by a hundred-thousand stars, and the dark grass was lit by a hundred-thousand stargazer lilies. The dream smelled so fresh, everything felt so alive. Abigail pinched the flowers' stems and plucked them from the ground and filled a woven basket over her arm. She didn't know what she was going to do with them, but she knew she needed to have them. She couldn't have enough of the stargazer lilies. She plucked more flowers and the stars above her dimmed. Her basket grew brighter.

Nice job, hero.

Abigail's hands were encased in flaming gauntlets that stretched up her wrists. She had flames in the shape of shin guards around her legs, too. She needed all the protection she could get while blocking Cinder's attacks. They danced in the middle of the construction zone. Whenever one landed a blow on the other a burst of sparks raised to the top of the building. As a sidekick, Abigail had only seen the Flame Villain use ranged attacks. He was just as skilled close up.

He expertly dodged every punch and heel kick she delivered, capturing and pulling the outstretched limb until she lost her balance and ended up on the ground. Today's lesson was supposed to be simple combat, but it was more like learning to get off the ground quicker than a flame thrower could scorch her shoes. Cinder readied a punch of his own, and Abigail allowed him to get close to her. She ducked down right as he swung and bounced up with an uppercut that sent Cinder to the floor.

Abigail watched as he lay on the ground. She extinguished her flames when he didn't move. She kneeled beside him when she didn't see his chest rise.

"Cinder, are you okay?" She reached for his throat to check his pulse.

His scarred hand snatched hers. He opened his eyes. "Don't tell me you let criminals trick you this easily?"

Abigail yanked her hand from his hold and stood up. "It's nice to check on your sparring partner if you knock them down."

"We're partners, now?" Cinder chuckled.

Abigail blushed and didn't answer. She crossed her arms and waited. Cinder stood and removed his jacket. The crisscrossing of scars continued from his arms under the fabric of his cut off T-shirt. Cinder stretched his arms above his head, the muscles flexed free of the restricting jacket.

Abigail blushed again.

Nice job, hero.

Abigail was running. Her legs twisted and tangled inside her bedsheets. She wasn't moving fast enough in the dream. The bedsheets binding her sleeping body transitioned over to her dream self. Her arms were pumping so hard against her sides she'd sooner lift off in flight than reach the exit. A beast made of black and white flames chased her down the hallway. Smoke leaked from its mouth and cherry-red eyes. It got closer. The exit sign got farther away.

Heat burned her back before the flames touched her. Her bare feet melted against the floor. Sheets of her footprints were left on the tile.

She kept running but knew she wasn't going to make it. The flame beast was getting too close. The heat from its mouth blistered her skin. Abigail reached for the exit door, she jumped toward it. The hallway collapsed behind her trapping the beast.

A hand reached for her. It was covered in a crisscrossing of black and white scars. Abigail grabbed it, clutching it in case she collapsed through the floor. The hand pulled her to her feet with an agonizing slowness allowing the beast to burst through the building. The dream shook, and the ground around her fell away in pieces. The hand vanished. Abigail fell.

Abigail shot out of her bed like she had been fired from a cannon. She touched around herself and felt only her cotton bedsheets. She shook from the dream and the chills produced from her sweat-covered skin. There was a loud thumping to her left. She turned slowly expecting to see the flame beast ready to finish her off in the real world but only found her phone vibrating against the nightstand. The ringer stopped but started again immediately. An unknown string of seven digits flashed across the screen.

Abigail answered, "Hello?"

"Is this Abigail Turner?" a female voice asked on the other end.

Abigail rubbed a fist against her eye removing the sleep dust and the disappointment of who was *not* at the other end. She blamed her dreams. She didn't have control over them, but she could control how she felt in her waking life. "This is her."

"Hey, this is Shannon from The Hero Relief Center." Abigail placed the cheerful voice of the receptionist. "You left a resume with us about two weeks ago, and a job position just opened up that you qualify for. Can you come in for an interview today?"

"Yes!" Abigail leaped out of bed, falling to the ground as the sheets still held her legs hostage.

There was typing on the other end of the line. "Can you be here at 11?"

Abigail pulled her phone away to check the time, 9:45. "Yes."

"Wonderful," Shannon hummed. "I have you set for 11. See me at the front desk, and I'll send you where you need to go."

"I will! Thank you!"

Abigail didn't care what job the interview was for. It was a job! She could already hear her savings account sigh with relief. Life was feeling good again. Things were getting back on track. Abigail didn't even care that she was picking out another business casual outfit instead of a hero costume. If this paisley printed dress was to be her new costume then she would love it. She would learn to love it. Abigail smashed her feet into a pair of shoes and applied mousse to her hair while she ran out the door.

Getting to the HRC in under an hour would be a heroic feat on its own. Abigail was prepared for the normal villains that would try and stop her, a late bus, or unfriendly red light, but she didn't expect the flashing red and blue lights that stopped the bus completely. She looked out the window to the corner market in question. Its windows were bashed in, and an officer was shouting to the crook inside. She moved to help but stopped herself when she got to the bus door. She wasn't a hero anymore, and she hadn't been called. A *civilian* would only make things worse. She pushed the door open and ran down the street. The bus wasn't going to start moving anytime soon and she wasn't going to miss her interview because someone wanted free cigarettes. The coming police sirens spurred her to run faster.

She needed to be a hero before she could help anyone.

With the lighting fast speed of an unemployed woman, Abigail arrived at the Hero Relief Center with minutes to spare. She used one of those minutes to catch her breath and another to adjust herself in the reflection of the window. She walked in with a smile wide enough to land a plane on.

"Shannon?" she asked at the desk. The same woman from before looked up from her computer. "I have an interview at 11. I'm Abigail Turner."

Shannon stood; her chair bumping against the wall behind her. Her nails had been painted a bright pink and matched her lipstick. "Right on time. I'll take you to the interview room, love the dress."

"Thanks, so um, what's this interview for?" Abigail asked following her. "Any information would be a ton of help."

"It's an assistant job," Shannon answered, her heels clicking with each of her steps. "A lot of secretarial work, but great benefits after the first thirty days. Most of the details will be presented during the interview."

"Okay." Abigail wasn't sure what section on her resume would have triggered "assistant" but she wasn't going to dwell on it.

Shannon guided her through two hallways before pointing to a set of chairs next to a closed door. On the other side of the wall was a collage of the company's heroes and sidekicks. Their Round Table Knights display was the largest, dwarfing the other pictures.

"They should be wrapping up their 10:30," Shannon explained, glancing at her watch. "Have a seat, and they'll call you in."

Abigail's heart tumbled over two forgotten beats. They were already interviewing other people for the position. Of course they were. Just like the electronic shop, this would be a competition. A battle like any other day when she was a sidekick. Inferna didn't lose battles, neither would she.

Nice job, hero.

Abigail rubbed her hands against the front of her dress. She heated them up quickly to make sure all of the sweat had evaporated. First impressions were key in a handshake. Strong and powerful. Abigail needed to be a lion, a fighter, a hero. Abigail needed to be—

"Next?"

Abigail jerked her head to the door. The interviewee before her stepped out of the room with tears swelling in her eyes. A man in a suit had the door propped open for Abigail with his foot. He raised an eyebrow waiting for her to respond.

"Ready," Abigail replied cheerfully, feeling like an idiot. "Abigail Turner."

She stuck out her hand, ready to shake his, but he turned back into the room. She gritted her teeth and followed him. She was already losing ground. Entering the room, she quickly understood the other applicant's tears. Sitting at the table, matching the armored image hanging in the lobby, was Excalibur of the Round Table Knights. Dressed in his hero costume, silver armor and helmet guarding his identity, an emblem embedded on his chest plate depicted a sword buried halfway into stone. A real sword leaned on the side of the table.

Excalibur's signature weapon. The hero wielded that sword like an artist wielded a paintbrush, a chef wielded a knife, Abigail wielded her flames.

"This is an assistant job for you." Abigail finally understood.

"Is that a problem?" Excalibur's voice sounded mechanical as it filtered through his helmet's mouthguard. There was a black cloth behind the slots of the mouthguard. Everything about Excalibur was covered in armor.

"Not at all." Abigail sat in the empty seat across from the hero. She made sure to keep her back straight and chin parallel to the floor. "Abigail Turner. It's a true honor to be interviewing for you, sir."

"Charmed." His cold voice didn't convey the feeling. "List your skills."

Abigail appreciated his quickness to the meat of the interview. She had never been good with small talk. She found the weather boring.

"Dedicated to completing my task, performance won't hinder under pressure, eager and excited to learn new things and adapt myself to your needs and schedule."

"Now your skills that aren't listed." Excalibur tapped the resume he had in front of him.

Abigail swallowed. "I enjoy solving puzzles, I train—work out at the gym, I know a lot about hero companies."

"A fangirl?"

"I do think you're really cool." She batted her eyelashes.

Excalibur snorted. This time his voice did sound charmed. "I don't intimidate you?"

Abigail kept herself from laughing. Compared to Volcanic, Excalibur was a bunny rabbit. "I know under that mask you're just a person like me. You having special powers shouldn't be why people respect you. It's how you act. How you are as a person."

Excalibur leaned back in his chair. The plastic backing whined in protest. "How do you feel about ghostwriting on social media?"

"Is that one of the job requirements?"

"A small portion but equally important."

"I'm fine with it," Abigail answered. "Keeping your ratings positive would be a key factor in your success as a hero in today's world. I'll do whatever needs to be done."

"Last question," It was hard to see what he was thinking, his mask hiding every part of his face. Even the row of open slots where his mouth was didn't allow a viewer to see inside the helmet. "Do you mind making coffee?"

Abigail smiled. "As long as I can get a cup too."

Excalibur nodded and extended his hand across the table. "I like you. Mitch, get Abigail started on the paperwork. And an Excalibur mug from the gift shop."

"Sir, are you sure?" Mitch, the man who let Abigail in, rushed over to Excalibur's side. "We still have several more interviews for today."

"We can keep them for formality's sake, but I won't change my mind."

"Yes sir." Mitch turned to Abigail. "If you'll follow me, miss."

"You will not regret this," she promised Excalibur, her excitement burning her hands.

Mitch brought Abigail to a break room with a collection of vending machines lining half the wall and two copy machines across the room. A table was in the center and stuck between two windows was a bulletin board covered in different colored flyers. The topmost flyer was information about a company softball game. In parentheses under the sign-up information was a rule against using abilities in the game.

Mitch sat Abigail at the table and handed her a stack of seven different forms. They weighed as much as a fat baby.

"Drop them off with Shannon when you're done, and she'll connect you with a start date."

"If I have any questions?"

"You'll figure them out."

Abigail rolled her eyes as Mitch selected a diet soda from the machine and left. She took a sharpened pencil from the cup in the middle of the table and got to work. Some of the forms were the same she had signed with Volcanic and Saves the Day: NDAs, hero conduct agreements, a liability waiver. The others were new beasts all together: an HR statement, tax information, a questionnaire about limitations in a workplace and a code of conduct she had to sign and initial over ten times.

Abigail felt sorry for whoever had to go through all these forms when she finished. She gathered the paperwork into a nice stack and backtracked her way to the main entrance of the building. Shannon was at her desk applying a new coat of pink polish to her fingernails. Abigail's two-week-old lilies were fading to green stems on the corner of her desk.

"Hey Shannon," Abigail greeted. "Mitch told me to bring these to you when I was finished?"

Shannon looked up and carefully collected the stack of forms so she wouldn't mark them with pink polish. She skimmed over the first page, then set all seven forms on a clean section of her desk.

"It usually takes about two days for these to get in the system," Shannon explained, typing on her keyboard. "Then there's a training day where you'll take a badge photo, get a tour of the building, and shake everyone's hand. Can you come back this Friday?" She looked up from the computer. "You'll start officially on Monday, but it'd be nice to get everything taken care of beforehand."

"Friday will be perfect." Abigail felt grounded again. Finally, things were returning to normal. Shannon nodded as she selected the date and confirmed Abigail's appointment. "Thank you again, for getting my resume to the right people."

The receptionist beamed at her. "It was no trouble. If you get any more flowers while you're here, maybe leave them at the front desk again."

It was a joke, Abigail laughed with Shannon, but she hoped there would be no more surprise deliveries. Especially here at her new job. One filled with heroes.

Nice job, hero.

Chapter Eleven

Abigail didn't think her new job would be easy. She came prepared Monday morning with rubber insoles in her dress heels and a to-go cup with the café's strongest brew from down the street. She had chosen her new arsenal of tools to make sure she'd be in tip-top performance on her first day. Whatever this day had in store for her, she would be ready.

But she never thought being an assistant would be harder than being a sidekick.

The moment she tapped her ID badge against the employee elevator and entered the more secretive and private levels of the Hero Relief Center, Mitch ambushed her. He shoved a radio into her hands, causing her coffee to slosh over the cup's sides. Abigail didn't notice the steaming liquid dripping down her fingers.

"You're late." Mitch's bedside manner was soft as a sticker bush.

Abigail was early, she made sure of it. "I was told to be here by eight."

Mitch's large watch face shined at 7:52. He didn't comment on her lack of tardiness. "Don't keep Excalibur waiting, or anyone on this list."

Abigail grabbed the approaching clipboard before Mitch could administer a second attack. The first page was an itinerary. It looked like Excalibur had several meetings this morning. She did not envy him. What kind of meeting lasted three hours?

She hated to admit it, but Abigail asked, "What do I do? No one really gave me a straight answer during orientation."

"You do whatever he needs," Mitch grumbled. "But you do whatever we need first. Like getting Excalibur to the Round Table in an hour."

Abigail tried to smile. "Chill out, we'll be there."

"You've never worked with a hero, have you?" Mitch didn't leave her an option to reply. He tapped her clipboard, mouthed the word *one hour,* and turned down the hallway.

Abigail was painfully aware that she didn't know how to reach Excalibur's office from here. She was on the right floor, at least, level eleven was reserved for the heroes. The floor above her housed the Round Table, the meeting place for the Round Table Knights.

She'd knock on every door if it came down to that.

The elevator *ding*ed behind her, and Abigail stepped out of the way for the coming passengers. Her one small step to the left didn't create the needed space for the man who got out of the car. The armor-clad hero was much taller than Abigail had remembered from her interview. He had to be over six feet.

"Good morning, sir!" Abigail greeted. She made a mental note to return the karmic favor before the end of the day. The universe was looking out for her.

"Hey, Abigail." Excalibur's voice was mechanical as it filtered through the helmet. "What're you doing out here?"

"Waiting for you." Abigail strung the lie together quickly. "I checked your office and didn't find you so thought it'd be best to wait for you here. Mitch is really adamant that I get you to this nine o'clock meeting."

Excalibur made a noise that sounded like a forced breath of air. "Mitch is so crabby. Hope you don't catch his bad attitude. You show up late to *one* meeting and the whole department won't let you forget it. It was only the mayor. We see him all the time."

Abigail's heels clicked as she followed him. When they reached his office, she jotted the room number on the back of her itinerary. He led her into a cramped office about the size of her bathroom. A desk occupied half the space. She was amazed it had even fit in here at all. Her old office had been bigger than her apartment.

"It's nothing special," Excalibur commented. "And it's kind of small, but I hope you like it."

"Pardon?"

"Your office." Excalibur pointed at the desk. Next to the sleeping computer was a coffee mug in the shape of the hero's helmet. "I'd suggest hanging up some photos. And, of course, when nothing's going on, we can have this door open. Give you some sunlight."

Abigail finally noticed the second door across the first. Excalibur pushed it open to reveal a much larger, and much brighter, office. Various weapons hung on the walls like a display at a war museum. The floor was made of interchanging black and white tiles and when Excalibur stood in the center, he looked like a knight on a chessboard.

"This is where they coop me up." He attempted to joke, but it came out cold because of his helmet.

"Want to trade?" she laughed.

"I don't think so. Anything fun on there?" Excalibur pointed at the clipboard.

Abigail checked the itinerary again. "Doesn't look like it, sir."

"Mondays are the worst." He slumped in the seat behind his desk made of glass. "Always have to do administrative stuff."

"Want to make a post about it?" Abigail asked. She tucked the radio between the waistband of her skirt and hip. "After you asked about ghostwriting I dug into your social media, and your views and interactions are lower than the other Round Table Knights. We can rip off *Garfield*?"

"The lasagna cat?"

Abigail nodded. "*I hate Mondays.*"

Excalibur stood from his chair, the sudden motion clinking his armor together. He draped himself over his desk, his hands brushing against the floor looking absolutely miserable. "How's this?"

"That'll work," Abigail stifled her laugh. "Let me grab a camera."

Once the photo was posted, with over two hundred likes in the first half hour, Abigail followed Excalibur to the Round Table. The room looked more like a palace, or an ancient work of wonder, than a corporate boardroom. The interior was designed to mimic old Britannia. The stone walls and floor were lit by observation windows and LED flameless sconces. The large central table had been crafted from a single slate of marble and must have weighed over a ton. It shimmered silver and gold when the sunlight hit it.

Abigail was unhappy to see Mitch waiting for them. Abigail was happy to see King Arthur and Merlin already at the table. They were out of costume, but she recognized them. Merlin's ruby-dyed hair was piled atop her head in a hazardously constructed bun. She was stealing the chocolate candies from King Arthur's snack mix.

"'Xcal, you're actually here on time!" King Arthur chuckled. His laugh sounded like it was stolen from an angel; crisp, light, and friendly.

"Yes, it's quite a miracle." Mitch didn't share King Arthur's enthusiasm. "President Samuels is on his way up. We'll begin momentarily."

Excalibur turned to Abigail and whispered, "This is sort of a hero only meeting."

"I understand." Abigail retreated a step back. "I'll be right outside. Radio if you need something."

That was how most of Abigail's first day as a hero assistant went. As much as she hated to admit it, she felt like a dog walker. She walked with Excalibur to his meetings, waited for him to finish his business, and walked with him back to his office to wait for the next meeting. Mondays really were the worst. So were Tuesdays, for that matter.

Maybe Wednesday would prove more interesting.

Abigail locked her apartment door and headed to the lobby. She thought she'd hate living on the top floor when she first moved in. After accepting her sidekick position with Volcanic, the top story had been the only apartment available in her price range, but the height grew on her. So had the view of San Arbor. The skyscrapers looked like they were burning with the morning sun.

"Have a great day, Miss Turner." Henry smiled at her.

"You too, Henry," Abigail replied before turning to her mailbox.

She had a bad habit of letting the mail, usually junk, pile up until it pushed back through the small slot. After unlocking the door, she found the compartment empty except for one piece of cardstock. It was folded tightly into a square. Abigail looked over her shoulder before retrieving it. She looked again before opening it. The card smelled of woodsmoke and fast food grease. The print was written in the same black ink. Abigail could hear Cinder's low voice in her head when she read the card.

Eight o'clock.

Abigail refolded the note and tucked it deep inside her purse.

"Sign that next one slower." Abigail instructed later that afternoon inside Excalibur's office.

The hero was signing posters of the new promotional photo of the Round Table Knights for a charity event. Out of one hundred he had finished thirty. They would be handed out at the children's hospital next week when the heroes made an appearance. Apparently, that was a reason for a three-hour meeting. It was all the buzz around the company, and Abigail was trying to update Excalibur's social media with an in-action photo.

The hero used a pen as fast as his sword and getting a clear photo was proving difficult.

Her camera flashed, but the image was unusable again.

"How'd that one look?"

"Still too fast." Abigail readied herself for another shot. "Pretend to sign this time but don't really move."

Excalibur was an extremely obedient hero. He paused halfway through writing his name and smiled at her and the camera. The flash fired off, and the camera's display screen previewed a viable shot. Abigail returned to her office, uploaded the photo with a fun caption and details of the event. The post received over one hundred likes when Excalibur finished signing the stack.

"I could use some crime," Excalibur sighed and fell into his chair, the force shook the framed fan hanging on the wall behind him.

"It's been a really slow week," Abigail agreed. She understood his frustration. Not saving the day was like an itch you couldn't reach. "Want me to kick over a garbage can or something?"

"There's not even a lack of crime," Excalibur started. "There's just nothing *big* in our section. Everything since the downtown attack has hit the northern half of San Arbor. The police are handling everything on their own right now, while Saves the Day is getting all the action. It's not fair. Gas station stick-ups and a stolen cart of groceries aren't going to pay any bills over here. I need somebody to do a bank heist, or a villain to bust out of jail, or something."

"I won't rob a bank for you, sir." Abigail swallowed the sour taste in her mouth at the mention of Saves the Day. "I'm drawing the line there."

Excalibur chuckled, his laugh bouncing around his helmet. He gathered all the posters into one pile. "Can you take these downstairs? And maybe bring up a coffee?"

The hero didn't abuse this task from his assistant, but at least twice a day he begged her to bring up a cup. Why he didn't have a coffee pot in his office she never knew. "Sure thing, sir."

Over the two days, Abigail learned the layout of the Hero Relief Center headquarters. The lower levels were for the business side, the middle levels housed the training rooms and hero support development, and the top floor was reserved for the heroes and President Samuels. She rode the elevator down to the second floor, started a fresh pot of coffee in the employee break room, then rode to the fourth floor to deliver the posters to Mitch, who's job title she still didn't know, and then returned to the coffee pot as it finished percolating.

Excalibur took his coffee with such precision it bordered insanity, but Abigail made a cheat sheet and taped it to the wall beside the coffee station. Three-fourths coffee, one-fourth cream, three tablespoons of sugar, and to finish it off, one ice cube.

The kicker was to get it back to Excalibur before it cooled. He could reheat it in the microwave stashed away in Merlin's office, but it wasn't the same. The armored hero could become rather mopey with a bad cup of coffee in his hands.

Abigail carried the drink carefully to the elevator and started her ascent to the eleventh floor. The elevator stopped at every floor in between. The ding from the door opening and closing was making her crazy. She could have gotten back to Excalibur sooner if she'd taken the stairs! Inside the mug, the ice cube continued to shrink. The drink continued to cool.

The final puffs of steam rolling from the mug were fading when the elevator eventually released her. The ice cube had fully melted when she reached the inner office door. She knocked once, and he asked her to wait. Abigail was running out of time. Luke-warm coffee was one thing, cold coffee was unacceptable. She had pulled people from burning buildings! She had to deliver warm coffee! This was her job now.

She looked over her shoulders, and after seeing no one had followed her, heated her hands slowly, transferring the heat from her fingers to the mug. The door opened. Her sparks disappeared. The cup steamed again.

"I have your coffee, sir."

Chapter Twelve

Abigail's stomach was hollow despite the chicken salad she had for lunch a few hours ago. Her leg bounced absently against the bus floor, and the passenger next to her delivered a dirty glare. Abigail stopped the motion and settled for tapping her fingers against her knee. Abigail liked to claim she was a calm person, or at least wasn't anxious. She could handle things that made her nervous without letting the world know.

Maybe she wasn't nervous as the bus rumbled south, dipping in and out of potholes. Maybe she was excited. Looking forward to training with the Flame Villain. She shook her head, there was no way she was excited to see him. She was only using him for intelligence.

The bus let her off, and she walked up the block and into the industrial park. Their building was illuminated by a series of floodlights hanging from a wire stretching the length of the first floor. She placed her purse on the foreman's desk on top of the blueprints and slid her heels off under the table. The floor was cold and bit through her pantyhose. Cinder's black duster jacket hung off the back of the chair.

She slowly turned around and searched the half-completed hallways around her. With no one watching she couldn't pass up the opportunity. She slid her hands inside the pockets of the jacket and removed several fast food receipts deteriorating with grease and a handful of loose change. She didn't find anything dangerous except for his eating habit. She crumbled the receipts back into their misshapen forms and forced them back into the pockets.

She wasn't sure she liked the relief that filled her with the lack of evil evidence.

It just means we can continue training, she told herself.

Abigail found Cinder between two finished walls, the drywall mud still damp. He hoisted his body up vertically in a one-handed headstand. He lowered himself up and down. His naked back faced her, and more burns stretched around his shoulders and ribs, reaching toward his spine like tiny spider legs. Abigail desperately wanted to know what caused the burns. If his fire could burn her, what was strong enough to burn him?

Cinder lowered his free hand behind his back and tumbled forward. The movement was fast, graceful, and landed him on his feet. He cracked his neck and stared at Abigail. She stared back, wanting to win this stare down, but ended up only marveling at his physical appearance. The newly built room seemed to get hotter. His duster jacket hid his true strength. The blue flames weren't his only weapon.

Abigail made a mental note to get physically stronger, too.

"Let's go." Cinder grabbed his shirt from the floor, moving past her and into the more open area of the construction zone.

He lit his hand in blue fire. The floodlights above paled the flame to something you'd find painted in a newborn's nursery. Abigail coated her fingers with her own fire and grabbed the fireball. It morphed into her hand. It was getting easier now. She passed the blue blaze from one hand to the other. She commanded it up her arm and down her other. It twirled in her palm awaiting her next order.

The only thing she couldn't do was summon it.

"You're looking good," Cinder said after she extinguished the flame by closing her hand. "Ready for phase two?"

"What's phase two?"

Cinder shook out his hands and they both raged with fire. The blaze leaped from his skin like a wild animal, it sparked around his wrists like a lightning storm. "Combat. I want to know if you can hold onto me when you can't focus solely on it."

Abigail pressed her lips together. It was annoying how he referred to the flame as *himself*. It was too personal, too intimate, too arrogant. Regardless, she stood across him and consumed enough of the blue fire to ignite both of her hands. She clenched them into fists and the blaze stayed tightly wrapped around her knuckles.

"Ready."

Cinder was on her in a flash. Rain showers of blue sparks crashed against the floor as their fists connected. Abigail had never been this challenged by him before, now or before their deal started. He either had been going easy on her or he was getting his own training. Abigail shielded her face with her forearms as Cinder spun a kick into the side of her head. It knocked her down and he followed with a solid punch to her stomach.

Adrenaline pushed the pain far enough out of her mind for Abigail to kick her blazing feet into his midsection and send him stumbling backward. The blue flames burned into his shirt before scurrying across the floor and back to her fists as Abigail stood.

Cinder grinned at her. He was proud of her. She liked that. She spat a mixture of blood and saliva to the ground.

She leaped at him, keeping her fist tight against her body and sneaking blows into his ribs when he let his guard slip. The flames did little to him, he was immune to his own blaze, but they tore away at his thin defense of a T-shirt. The blue blaze stayed with Abigail, snagging the fabric before returning to her knuckles. She had learned to do this in less than three weeks with the help of a villain. She hadn't gotten anywhere close with Volcanic.

Knowing that this was just the beginning both scared and thrilled her.

Abigail shifted back to avoid his left hook and snapped forward with a quick punch to Cinder's face. When it connected, he grabbed her wrist and hauled her toward him, using her momentum against her. Again. Cinder fought like a trained ballerina danced. Every move effortless and part of something grander. He probably let her hit him just to open up this opportunity. He twisted her arm behind her back and placed his other hand on the back of her neck. Abigail struggled against his hold. His hands heated, his flames moving from his wrist to his fingers, and Abigail froze. The fire vanished from her hands. The force of him and his flame suffocated her. She was panicking. Blue flames filled her vision and she could feel the pain of the burn she knew was coming. His fingers pressed harder against her throat.

Cinder released her and stepped back. "You used to run into burning buildings and you can't face me?"

"You're different." Abigail took a deep breath before she was able to turn around and look at him. "You can actually burn me."

"Only when I choose to." He flashed a blue flame that hid half his smile in shadow. "One day you might burn me."

"What?" Abigail looked between the flames and his eyes. She couldn't tell where his scar started and the flame's shadow ended. "Choose to burn?"

"My flames are always blue, but their temperature isn't always to the max," Cinder explained. "It'd be too much effort to burn that hot all the time."

Abigail took inventory of herself. He was right, or else she would have been covered in burns already. She knew she hadn't been able to dodge all of his attacks.

"Ready to go again?"

Abigail glanced around. The sky above them was black. The floodlights were having trouble keeping the darkness from dripping down to the first level. It was getting late.

No. It *was* late.

"I can't."

"Why? Scared?" he teased, flicking a blue spark at her.

"Work," Abigail answered, turning to the foreman's table and grabbing her shoes. Her pantyhose were ripped, and the sections that housed her feet were missing completely.

"One of those resumes finally stick?"

Abigail put on her shoes, mindful of the blisters forming on the back of her heels. "Yeah."

"Where?"

"I'm not telling." She tried to sound playful.

"You know I can find out." Cinder raised an eyebrow.

"I wish you wouldn't."

"Ashamed?"

The accusation stopped her from leaving. She didn't think it was that. She just had to protect herself. A hero company would absolutely fire her if they ever found out what she did in her spare time. She wouldn't be given a chance to explain, she would probably be hauled off to jail for conspiracy and harboring a villain. No, she wasn't ashamed. She just had to be careful.

Abigail tossed a wave over her shoulder. "See you later."

The crunch of tires against the gravel stopped her. She listened and heard an electronic car lock beep outside the half-constructed building. Two voices weaved around the wall studs. Abigail turned to better hear them as they bounced around the concrete.

"Do you always leave a light on?" someone asked.

"Not intentionally," a second someone answered. "Must've known you wanted to take a look at the progress. Call it builder's intuition. I'll give you the tour, show you the plans."

"I thought it'd be further along by now."

"Safety isn't something you want to rush. We've had to wait for inspections a few times, but everything is checking out."

Their voices grew louder. The shadows that hid Abigail seemed to shrink. She turned around, but Cinder was gone. She cursed under her breath and a dry laugh answered above her. A hand outstretched toward her, blackened fingers tempting her to grab them. When she did, he lifted her onto the rafter with him. Cinder pressed his finger against his lip like she needed the reminder to stay quiet.

The voices circled them. Abigail followed Cinder down the metal beam. He crossed the distance like an alley cat, agile and quick. Abigail was more like a foal still getting used to her legs. Her foot slipped off the edge twice and one of her shoes crashed onto the ground. She righted herself and slipped off the other one, leaving it on the steel beam.

Cinder waited for her on top of the scaffolding. Their escape route leading to the open hole reserved for a window. It was a great plan minus the story drop that waited outside the window. Abigail stepped onto the scaffolding and crouched beside him.

"I'll go first," he whispered, Abigail watched his lips to catch his words. "Do you need me to catch you?"

She ignored his wink. "I'll be fine."

Cinder hooked one leg over the edge, checked behind him, and tumbled down. Behind them, the two strangers didn't hear his fall. The one in a suit was asking about the now empty space they had been training in. The one in work boots didn't have an answer for the scorch marks on the floor.

Leaning out the window hole, Abigail saw the stacked bags of mortar against the wall. It cut the fall in half, but she'd rather have fallen onto the soft grass than the powdered concrete. Before she could talk herself out of it, she pushed off the window and slid onto the landing pad. Grey dust plumed around her, and she clamped her jaw down to keep from coughing. Cinder grabbed her arm and pulled her from the dust cloud.

"Guess my idea wasn't so foolproof," Cinder admitted.

"Who could've known the city could actually work overtime?" Abigail chuckled.

"Aren't you supposed to love San Arbor?"

"I love her people and her heroes—my briefcase."

Cinder raised an eyebrow.

"I need it." Anything in that bag could be used against the heroes at the HRC if the wrong kind of people got it. There was no way she could abandon it.

Cinder rolled his eyes and stepped around her. "That's all on you, doll. Your fault for carrying a purse."

Abigail hooked his elbow with hers and stopped him. "We can still call it training. A lesson in stealth."

Cinder turned around, the dim light from the window opening above flickered off his eyes. "I'm not big on sneaking around."

"Bullshit."

He shrugged with indifference. "We could just burn the thing."

"There are people inside!"

"Your bag, not the building." Cinder explained. "Do you think that highly of me?"

"Lowly," she corrected. "Come on."

Abigail led them to an opening on the first floor. She imagined a large, double door would go into the space and open into a grand lobby. The contractor's desk was at the back of the open room, the floodlight above it was luckily off. Her briefcase, with all its hero company secrets, leaned against a desk leg. Cinder's jacket draped across the chair.

"We can wait until they leave," he whispered behind her.

"I doubt they'll skip the blueprint part of the tour."

Cinder sighed but nodded.

Abigail peered into the space, scanning through the uncompleted sections through the wall studs, and watched the floors for shadows, but she couldn't see the two strangers. They must be on the side of the building with the finished walls. She grabbed Cinder's wrist and stepped over the foundation. Cinder's defiance stopped her like an anchor on a ship.

"We don't need both of us to get caught."

Abigail tugged his arm. "You can cause a distraction."

"I can be *your* distraction."

Abigail saw his point but didn't let him win. "I won't let you take the fall. Don't you trust me?"

Cinder chewed his cheek before saying, "Fine."

Abigail pulled him over the foundation. They ran to the table, keeping their bodies as low to the floor as possible. Abigail never thought grabbing the second-hand bag would fill her with such joy, but she clutched the bag to her chest once she had it. Cinder quickly slipped on his jacket, and when he popped the collar, the snap invaded the quiet patch of darkness they stood in.

Abigail glared at him, smoke escaping her fingertips. Cinder only grinned his sidewise smile. They waited for the strangers to come running, but their pocket of darkness stayed private.

"Let's go," Cinder mouthed.

"Are these shoes?" One of the strangers said.

"Women's heels?" the second added.

It was Cinder's turn to glare. Abigail could only smile sheepishly back at him. She curled her bare toes against the cold cement. The chill froze her, and by proximity, Cinder to the floor.

"I'll do a full sweep tomorrow," the second stranger said. "Make sure there aren't any squatters. I'll show you the plans for the second level. They're back this way."

Abigail glanced down. The white marker on the blueprint was clear as a neon sign. The second floor plans stared back up at her. She looked up at Cinder as the stranger's footsteps padded toward them. She swore she saw him roll his eyes, but his crooked grin returned. He tilted his head toward the only finished room on site: a small closet a few steps away. Abigail assumed it was for the workers to store their belongings when they were here. She followed Cinder inside the closet. He shut the door just as the floodlight above the desk turned on.

Abigail was too focused on how her heart beat against her jaw to notice Cinder's closeness until he shifted around her. Despite his effort, her toes still curled around the top of his boots and his chin continued to tap her forehead. Abigail hated how long the strangers remained at the desk. Her heart returned to normal, and the closet thoroughly smelled of woodsmoke but still the white floodlight spilled under the door.

"What's your family like?" Cinder whispered.

"You're asking about my family?" Abigail kept her surprise as quiet as his question. "Why?"

She felt his head gesture to the door more than she saw it. She heard the strangers laugh and two cans cracked open. "What else are we going to do in here? Unless?"

Abigail elbowed him in what she assumed were his ribs. His chuckle fell from his lips as a breath. She wouldn't deny that similar thoughts hadn't crossed her mind, especially when he removed his coat while they sparred, or the heat she felt off his gaze, but she wouldn't admit it to him. His crooked grin wasn't as cute as he probably believed it was. "Why *my* family?"

"Why not. It's not like we have anything in common to talk about."

Abigail tried anyway. "Did you catch last night's episode of—"

"I don't watch TV."

"What do you—"

"I read."

Abigail frowned and waited to respond until she felt she wouldn't be interrupted again. "What's your favorite book?"

"Are you asking because you want to make sure I read, or because you're curious?"

Abigail found his face when Cinder smiled. His strangely white teeth appeared like magic out of his scarred face. She was curious, but about more than just his favorite book. "Tell me about your family, then."

"I have an evil mom and an evil dad."

"I'm serious," she hissed.

He leaned closer to her. Abigail felt his warm breath on her face. "I asked you first."

Abigail hated that he sounded like they were playing a game. She hugged her briefcase tighter to her. The worn leather was a poor defense, but it was all she had. Igniting in this small space wasn't an option. "I'm not going to tell you about my parents so you can—"

Cinder interrupted her again. "What happened to trust? You trust me to train you, but not to make small talk? You've got to chill out, doll."

She gritted her teeth. "Small talk wasn't part of the deal."

Cinder laughed; it was too loud in their enclosed space. "You need all the help I can give you."

Abigail reached for the doorknob. She didn't need to be insulted by this villain. She had no reason to be embarrassed by anything about herself. She didn't need to make small talk with the criminals of San Arbor. Her only job was to defeat them.

After she became a sidekick, again.

Her hand froze over the doorknob when she remembered the sliver of light sneaking under the door. Two more cans open. Their aluminum sides tapped together on the other side of the door. She stepped back, back into Cinder, and the closet felt half the size it had been. She exhaled her frustration in a deep, hushed breath. Getting stuck in a closet with the Flame Villain wasn't part of the deal, either.

After a minute, Cinder offered into the darkness, "My dad was a professor at a college. Don't know if he's still teaching, haven't been home in a while."

"You could call him," Abigail replied absently.

She could feel the weight of his eye roll, the exhausted sigh that followed filled the space with humid breath. "I would rather not. Being bad isn't something you write home about."

"I can't really tell my parents about the hero stuff, either." Her admission surprised her.

"I figured that'd be the highlight of Thanksgiving dinner."

Abigail didn't fight the sad smile that crossed her lips. She would love to retell her heroic adventures with her family. Get everyone matching Inferna T-shirts and have them visit her at Saves the Day. But it was a foolish dream. She told herself it was to protect them, so no one could use them against her, but she knew the real reason. Saves the Day couldn't afford the chance of a rating drop because of a hero's family. "They don't know."

"What do they think you do all day?"

"Run paper in some big corporate office."

"Kind of what you're doing now." Cinder flicked her briefcase.

"It's better this way."

His crooked smile returned. "So, I know you better than your family?"

"Fat chance."

"You keep thinking that, doll. We're more alike than you'll ever realize."

"And yet you can never tell me how."

"In time."

Abigail furrowed her brows. His cryptic taunts shouldn't mean anything to her. She was still prepared for the moment he would turn on her. It would be in his villainous nature. Abigail shouldn't have wasted time discussing her home life, not when she needed to gather intelligence.

"Can I ask you something?" she whispered. "To test this trust between us?"

"Go ahead."

"Where did you go after you attacked me at the bar?"

Cinder scratched at his face as if trying to remember. "South, I think. Out of the city obviously."

"Obviously," Abigail agreed. "What about before? Where were you before that?"

"Writing a book report about me?"

"I'm just trying—"

Cinder covered her mouth with his hand. She struggled against it, but he only pressed harder. The scars on his knuckles scratched her lips. The small light on the floor clicked off and the strangers began talking again.

"Place looks good, Mike," the first stranger said.

"You'll be doing your law stuff here by the end of summer."

"I'm an accountant, but good."

As the voices drifted further away, Cinder lowered his hand. He cracked open the door and looked into the dim space before exiting the closet. Abigail followed, rubbing her lips with the back of her hand. Cinder somehow left soot behind, and her hand was streaked in black ash.

Chapter Thirteen

The day was a scorcher. The morning temperature already beat the day's predicted high. Abigail fanned herself with a forgotten flyer she had stashed in her purse as she sat on the bench waiting for her bus. The political face wrinkled with each flick of her wrist. The bus was running late, and every heavy car engine gave her false hope of its arrival. If she knew what kind of morning this was turning into, she would have walked to the hospital where she was meeting Excalibur.

Abigail twisted around on the bench to check the bus schedule and spotted something else between the glass and metal frame. The folded blue cardstock would be trash to anyone else. To Abigail it made her hands sweat and her pulse quicken. She pulled the note from its hold and opened the letter.

Let's go again. 7 o'clock.

The greasy smell accompanying the note made sense after last night's discovery. Cinder probably wrote it while eating fast food fries, and she refolded it before sliding it deep inside her pocket. Her bus arrived five minutes later, and the note burned inside her pocket as she boarded.

Abigail never expected to see a children's hospital wing vibrating with as much excitement as it did that afternoon. Even Mitch seemed less of a grouch as he carried the box of signed posters to the central nurses' desk. The nursing staff divided the load and distributed the posters to the children laying in beds and peering through the small door windows waiting for the heroes to visit. This wing had over seventy rooms.

It took all day, but The Round Table Knights visited each room. They were greeted by cheers from the children, bombarded with questions, and begged the heroes for favors. Abigail had counted over thirty piggyback rides Excalibur gave through the hallway.

Volcanic wouldn't have given the idea a second thought. Abigail was pretty certain he hated kids.

The current rider slid off Excalibur's armor and thanked the hero before being ushered back to his room by a nurse. His green gown flapped behind him like a tiny cape.

Abigail followed Excalibur during his next piggyback ride, snapping several photos for the hero's social media. She made sure to grab one of Merlin, who braided a small girl's hair, and one of King Arthur, who selected his favorite crayon color so a boy could give the hero his own autograph. Abigail could see the photos hanging on a wall somewhere on the main floor once they were printed, or on the cover of the weekly entertainment magazine once media got ahold of them.

"I can't believe how many are here this time," Merlin muttered to King Arthur and Excalibur when they regrouped in the hallway. Abigail pretended to go through the digital photos and listened. "It has to be twice as many."

"Most will be able to go home." Excalibur tried to cheer her up. He drank from a water bottle using a thin straw that fit between the slits in his helmet.

"It's the influx that worries me." Merlin smiled and waved at a kid across the hall.

"I read the charts," King Arthur said. "Half of these kids are from the school bus crash."

"The one where a getaway car T-boned into it?" Excalibur asked.

Merlin nodded. "The criminals were fleeing a hobby shop on the north side. Pulled onto the street and right into the bus."

Excalibur added under his breath, "They were originally caught at the attack downtown, but nothing could hold them for more than a couple of nights. The whole crash could have been avoided if we could have intervened at the initial robbery. Or if the holding system worked more in our favor. A crook doesn't turn good overnight."

"The robbery was 'too small for heroes' for anyone to be called," Merlin said.

"There shouldn't be a size category for us." The toxicity in King Arthur's statement surprised Abigail. She pretended to take another picture. "We're able to handle things in far superior ways. If we were given the licenses to patrol instead of being on call, things like this wouldn't happen."

Merlin placed a hand against his forearm. "I know, Arthur, we all know."

"Quinn will make something work," Excalibur said. "We just have to wait."

"Waiting will get people killed," King Arthur whispered.

Merlin cleared her throat and the Round Table Knights looked up. Abigail followed their attention. A police officer walked down the hallway toward them. He was an older officer, his brown hair fading to grey around his ears.

"Hey Chief DaVodi." King Arthur stopped the officer. He had returned to his overly cheerful self. "What brings you here today? Want a poster for Kyle?"

The chief said, "You know my boy doesn't have any more wall space after the last batch of stuff you sent over."

King Arthur smiled. Looking at him through the camera's viewfinder, Abigail didn't think it looked friendly.

"I just didn't want your son to think we didn't appreciate his support," King Arthur said, and Chief DaVodi only nodded. "Just like we appreciate all the good work your boys in blue are doing out there. San Arbor's one lucky city."

If Abigail's camera was a Polaroid, the freshly printed image of King Arthur and Chief DaVodi would have been over saturated with false admiration. Merlin touched King Arthur's arm a second time.

"We've got more kiddos to see," King Arthur said to DaVodi and allowed Merlin to lead him into a hospital room.

"Good seeing you again, Chief." Excalibur excused himself into another room and returned to the hallway with another piggyback rider.

Abigail never found out why the Police Chief came to the event. She kept an eye on him for the remaining minutes he was there. He spoke to a nurse, was handed a paper and left. King Arthur didn't return to the main area until he was gone.

Overall, the event was a huge success for the kids. The children's hospital wing received a large donation from the Round Table Knights and the Hero Relief Center. Abigail snapped her final photo, a group shot of the heroes, the staff, the kids and the oversized paper check, and returned to HQ with the rest of her team.

"Good work today." Excalibur rapped his knuckles against Abigail's desk sometime after they were back at HQ.

"I think all that credit goes to you, King Arthur and Merlin." Abigail happily looked away from the editing software opened on her computer. The blue light was causing a headache between her eyes. "I think you made those kids' whole year being there today."

"It was the least we could do."

"Then why do you sound so sad?"

Excalibur looked like he was considering sitting down in the other chair across from Abigail but thought better of it noting its size compared to himself. "It was the least we could do but we should have been able to do more. To stop the crash all together."

Abigail frowned. "You shouldn't beat yourself up. I know if you could have been there, you would have. That's what a hero does."

"They sure make it difficult."

Abigail nodded in agreement. She faced the same issues at Saves the Day. A hero could only go into action if first called by a first responder. Legally, it was to keep the scene less crowded for the proper personnel to do their jobs. Personally, it was to keep the heroes from over stepping the police and taking control of the justice system. Abigail hated it. No one should need permission to save someone else.

"Are you planning to stay here all night?"

"Just until I finish these edits."

Excalibur leaned against the desk, accidentally shifting it forward a few inches. "You don't want this job to consume all your time. I've noticed I've been leaving earlier than you most nights."

Abigail was touched that he noticed, let alone cared enough to comment on it. "I don't want to fall behind on anything. It's no trouble."

Excalibur was unmoving. Abigail thought he might be studying her through his helmet's covered eye slots. "During your interview, you said you liked training?"

"Working out," Abigail corrected a little too eagerly.

"When was the last time you did that for yourself?"

"I was supposed to go tonight actually." She glanced at the clock on her computer screen. "But I'll be too late now."

Excalibur nodded his head. "Well, if you insist on staying here late, I want to give you access to a training room. Maybe getting your workouts done here can help your time."

"Thank you, sir," Abigail smiled. A hero training room would be soundproof, but even better it would be fireproof. "That would help out a lot."

After uploading the photos, editing them, and getting them sent to their appropriate channels, Abigail returned to her apartment at a quarter after nine. She collapsed on top of her bed, kicked off her heels and requested a pizza from the delivery place down the road.

She left Cinder's note in the bowl with her keys. It stared angrily up at her. Without any way to communicate back, the note stayed angry as Abigail settled in for bed.

The next morning, Abigail flipped the note face down on her way out. She left several hours earlier to make use of the training room Excalibur had given her an access code to, but the stillness of dawn couldn't ease the guilt the note still caused. *It's not like I'm ignoring him,* Abigail thought to herself walking to the bus stop. *And training alone isn't something to be guilty about.*

Three days later Abigail received a new note hidden between two bills in her mailbox. She ran her thumb over the message. The letters were indented deep enough into the cardstock she could have read the message blindfolded.

Did I scare you? 6 o' clock.

She left the bills in the box, relocked the mail slot and pocketed the note. Her stomach sank knowing she would miss this training session too. Perhaps she should leave cryptic messages inside the warehouse for him to find. Or they could share a digital calendar and select dates they both had free.

Abigail sat on the bus with a huff. She scolded herself for feeling this upset. She had her job to focus on, not be on call to a villain. Even if he was helping her more than the heroes. She pulled her phone and the note out of her pocket. She could call in sick, she thought. Meet Cinder tonight and set some ground rules, or at the very least open a two-way communication channel with him. The note weighed heavier than the phone in her hands and she slipped both back into her pocket. She would not choose him over her work. That would be crossing the line.

Besides, she doubted he'd understand her reasoning.

Sorry, I've been working with heroes.

She heard his voice in her head and burned the note under the bus seat, then wiped the ash off on her black pantsuit when the bus rumbled to a stop outside the HRC. Things wouldn't feel right if she did meet him, anyway. They never should have felt right to begin with. A villain training a hero was ridiculous. Abigail could ignore the feelings when she was jobless, but now that she was working with heroes again, spending time with Cinder felt like cheating. Thinking about him made her stomach twist and she didn't know if she liked the feeling.

She didn't like that she wanted to find out, either.

Abigail walked into the Hero Relief Center and found Excalibur waiting for her. He leaned against Shannon's desk and read that week's gossip rag over her styled up-do.

"Hey guys?" Abigail adjusted the bag on her shoulder.

"Hey Abbs." Shannon folded one of the corners down to mark her page.

"Abby!" Excalibur straightened up.

"Anything interesting in there?"

"Yes," Shannon answered.

"No." Abigail imagined Excalibur was blushing under his helmet. "Are you ready to go?"

Abigail checked her daily itinerary on her phone. "I think so, but what's 'supervised backup' and why is it all weekend?"

"You can blame Mitch." Excalibur sounded like the grumpy man he spoke of.

Shannon chuckled while opening her magazine again. "You'll like this, Abigail."

"What do you mean?"

"I'll explain on the way." Excalibur took Abigail's elbow and led her to the exit.

An HRC van waited for them in the back of the building. Unlike the car she and Volcanic had traveled in, this vehicle was unmarked and only the city tags allowing it to park anywhere gave it character. Abigail settled into the back seat with Excalibur, and the van pulled onto the main drive.

"This isn't some secret mission, is it?" Abigail tried to look through the heavily tinted glass.

"Far from it." Excalibur sounded excited. "It's the best weekend of the year. The trade show is finally in town."

"Trade show?" Abigail asked.

"Where people sell all sorts of handmade items."

"I didn't think you liked woven baskets and knickknacks, sir."

His helmet stared at her. "There's a whole floor dedicated to forge work."

"Swords." Abigail connected his vague clues.

"And more! You're going to love it!"

Abigail scratched her head. "I'm still confused, sir. What is it you need me to do? Am I your security guard or something?"

"Don't kid yourself, Turner." Abigail twisted her head and found Mitch eyeing them in the rearview mirror where he sat in the front passenger seat. The privacy divider had lowered halfway between them. "They would never send some assistant to guard a hero."

Abigail crossed her arms and slid deeper into her seat. She could protect Excalibur given the chance. She wouldn't say the same about grumpy Mitch.

"The only thing you're watching is his wallet," Mitch explained. "A hero can't be stockpiling weapons, and Excalibur would buy every sword there if he could."

Excalibur shrugged his shoulders, but didn't deny the statement.

"He can only buy four, understand?"

"Understood."

"There should be a duffle bag back there for you," Mitch continued. "It has some clothes and toiletries. Your room has already been booked."

Abigail twisted around again. "We're staying the night?"

Mitch didn't notice her concern. "Yeah, Excalibur has a speech to give in the morning. Kiss babies and stuff."

Abigail pulled the zipper across the bag and peered inside. The tracksuit was covered in the HRC logo. "I could have packed my own bag."

"Couldn't take the chance of anyone following you," Mitch answered simply. "Excalibur and the identities of those around him can't be jeopardized."

The privacy divider closed before Abigail could respond. She zipped her purse inside the bag and accepted her night time arrangements. It was a good thing she never adopted a pet.

"Don't worry, Abby," Excalibur said across from her. "It is a lot of fun."

"I just wish I could've packed my own underwear," she tried to joke. "Think all the stuff in here is new?"

Excalibur laughed too. "I'd get a new toothbrush from the hotel desk."

The van parked outside the hotel convention center and Abigail had to jog to keep pace with Excalibur as he made his way to the expo like a child to the tree on Christmas morning. His childlike joy was amusing as he examined different blades and talked shop about the weapons with the people who forged them. He paused to take pictures and sign various items from scabbards to t-shirts, and Abigail was again reminded of how human her current boss was compared to Volcanic.

At the end of his shopping adventure, Abigail pulled a luggage dolly behind her with two new swords, one as long as the dolly and twice as heavy, a halberd and a war hammer with a fleur-de-lis carved into the head. Excalibur stopped at the last booth of the row and peered at the swords strapped to the metal walls.

"Sir?" Abigail asked when he plucked one off the display.

"I'm just looking," he promised and returned the sword. "But this one is so cool."

He pulled down the top most blade housed in a fire engine red scabbard. The stall's owner snapped several pictures of the hero as he unsheathed the sword and sliced through the air. The blade was wider than the two he had purchased and slightly curved at the end.

"Mitch said only four."

Excalibur looked at her over his shoulder. "He only says that so I don't scare anyone, but look around. Is anyone scared?"

This late in the day there were only a half dozen vendors left in the conference room. There were even fewer shoppers. None of them looked threatened. One middle aged man didn't even notice the armored hero.

"I'm scared of Mitch," she admitted.

"You should get yourself something to defend yourself, then."

Abigail kept herself from laughing. In a fire fight she'd defeat any of these blades.

Excalibur held the sword toward her. "Try it out."

She sighed but didn't deny him. She held the sword like an oversized butter knife. It was heavier than she thought and fit awkwardly in her hand.

"You look pretty cool." Excalibur pushed the sale on her.

"I'm not buying a sword." She returned the blade to him.

"But what if you did? For me." Abigail only stared at him, so he added in a whisper amplified by his mouthpiece. "We put your name down as the owner, we keep it in my collection, you can use it whenever you want, and Mitch never has to know I broke his silly rule."

Abigail exhaled a laugh. "I don't have that much cash on me."

"I've got my card."

At the end of the day, Abigail pushed the dolly of five weapons and a golden fan that didn't technically count since it was a piece of art to their conjoined rooms upstairs. She grabbed her duffle bag, said goodnight to Excalibur and retreated to her room. The hotel bed was much bigger than the full-sized mattress she had at home and, looking around the posh room, she wondered how much the company had spent on this outing. Saves the Day had bought her lunch once after she and Volcanic stopped a runaway train, but the meal was a marketing gig in disguise. Over the top of her Inferna costume, she was forced to wear the restaurant's shirt and silly-looking hat.

Abigail started to dress down for bed but stopped as the throwaway toothbrush eyed her in the bottom of the bag. She slipped her shoes back on and headed to the main desk for a new one. The employee behind the desk pointed her to the hotel shop, and Abigail scanned the tightly packed shelves for a new toothbrush. She found basic pain reliever, a hairbrush, swimming goggles and overly plush towels. The need for a new toothbrush vanished when she saw a lighter display. The silver Zippos stood like soldiers inside the cardboard box that depicted the flames inside to burn "bluer than an ocean."

Abigail snatched one and flipped the cover up. Brilliant blue fire burned from the spout. The flame called an ache in her chest she didn't realize she had, until she looked for the man who had been the flames only source for so long. But the room was empty except for her and the employee waiting for her purchase. She grabbed a toothbrush, paid for both, and returned to her room where she slammed the lock into place and blocked the joining door with a rolled towel.

She flipped the lighter again, the blue flame catching instantly, and pinched the flame from the base of the spout. It obeyed her command and balanced at the tips of her fingers, waiting for its next order. Abigail twirled it through each finger, her smile and pride growing. She heard a low rumbling voice compliment her in her head.

Nice job, hero.

Someone knocked against her door, and she snuffed the flame sending the room into darkness.

"I'm going to order room service," Excalibur's friendly voice called from the other side of the door. "Want anything?"

"No!" Abigail answered. She hid the lighter inside her pocket, afraid he could see her, afraid he could see who she had been thinking of. "No, thank you."

The Zippo flame was nowhere as powerful as Cinder. It was a soft burn in comparison, the heat not even able to phase Abigail's fireproofing. But still she practiced with it. She practiced each night inside her apartment, too scared to bring it to the training room. Soon she was able to turn the brass knuckles of blue flame into blazing boxing gloves. She wanted to see him, see Cinder and show him her improvements. But after her fifth no show, his letters stopped coming.

Or she stopped finding them.

Her stomach fell when Henry stopped her in the mornings with only a "hello" and not a message. The hooded strangers she passed on the street remained strangers. Her mailbox only received junk mail, and the bus stops were only marked in graffiti. She was realizing the twisting in her stomach was becoming a bad thing.

She could never admit that she *missed* a villain.

Abigail kept her Zippo flame training to the evenings and trained in the Hero Relief Center in the mornings. This would be how she broke the rules now. Not committing treason with a villain. It was better he wasn't distracting her anymore. Now she could focus on her actual mission: become a hero. She would get stronger on her own.

Her cherry-red blaze was all around her as she assaulted training dummies she lined up in a row. The plastic exterior melted and dripped onto the floor. She had been secretly training with the blue blaze for so long she had forgotten how beautiful her own red flame was. Red as a rose, but so much deadlier.

She was becoming deadlier.

Abigail punched her flaming fist into another target. The dummy shattering covered the sound of the door sliding open.

But it did not cover the clapping of two metal gloves.

Abigail spun around, pale as a ghost. Excalibur stood at the door, still applauding. She should have had at least another hour before he came to work. She had planned her illegal training time so well!

"Sir! I... I..." Abigail knew nothing she could say would explain or excuse herself. She sighed a heavy sigh. "I'll turn in my resignation."

"Why would you do that?"

"I lied to you?"

"I wouldn't be a good hero if I couldn't put together a few clues." Excalibur's chuckle was playful. "I had my suspicions."

"What gave it away?" Abigail was able to take a decent breath now but still hid her smoking hands behind her back.

"No one has ever been able to get me a coffee that's still the perfect temperature." He pointed to a small camera in the corner of the room. "And these rooms are monitored. I've been watching for a week now. You've still got your skills, Inferna."

Abigail's heart fluttered as if he'd said her crush's name instead of her old hero identity. She felt like a young girl, getting giddy by just the thought of her alter ego. Her infatuation vanished, and she suddenly felt like a young girl who had broken a vase.

"Are you going to tell?"

Excalibur laughed. "Your secret identity is safe. I had to sign an NDA too. For our public employees. You ever think about becoming a hero again?"

"Everyday. Being Inferna was the best person I could be."

"Well, you're so good at being an office sidekick, I wonder how you'd be as a hero sidekick."

"You better not be pulling my leg, sir."

Excalibur raised his hands. "I'm serious. But it's not a job offer. You're still my assistant. For now."

"I'd be honored to have that opportunity." Abigail smiled; she couldn't help it. She felt like jumping up, shouting, dancing. "If it ever came up."

"You'd be first on my list." Excalibur gave her a thumbs up. "Get cleaned up, you smell like a fireplace. We've got a big day today. A Round Table meeting, I think."

"At ten," Abigail confirmed. "I'll grab coffees and the rundown, and meet you upstairs."

Chapter Fourteen

Excalibur's office was empty the next morning. Abigail peered through the window on the training room door but found it empty as well. She checked the wall clock hanging between two sharpened spears. He should be here. The chessboard flooring seemed endless without him to ground it, the black and white tiles spilling out of the windows and onto the street below. Abigail returned to her own desk and checked her itinerary. She was supposed to bring Excalibur to a round table meeting in an hour, if she could find him.

How hard was it to lose a walking suit of armor?

Abigail reached for her radio to call his frequency when she noticed a bright yellow note card sticking to her pen holder. She traded her radio for it. It felt too thin in her hands. This note card was weak compared to the heavy cardstock she was used to finding. She unfolded it and sighed; the handwriting was all wrong. He hadn't been here.

"Left for a situation at home. I told Merlin she could use you. Have fun!"

The note was signed with a cartoon-styled knight helmet.

Abigail shouldered her bag, attached her radio to her belt, took the note as proof, and left for Merlin's office down the hall. Her mouth dried as she got closer to the closed door. She wished Excalibur would have assigned her to do anything else. She could have dusted all his weapons, hand scrubbed the floors, anything but bother the most intimidating Knight in the building.

Merlin's beauty and intelligence were both as sharp as a serrated knife whenever she appeared in an interview. Abigail didn't think it was just a stage act. The red-dressed woman appeared in San Arbor shortly after the HRC was founded, and she and King Arthur were a packaged deal whenever the company was called to a scene. They were the perfect pair. Abigail remembered the first print posters hanging in every storefront window. King Arthur all smiles, his warm personality matching the half sun background at his back, while Merlin's aloof expression was as mysterious as the half-moon behind her photo.

The first prints were still selling for several hundred dollars online.

Abigail knocked on the office door.

"Go ahead." Merlin's voice was distant on the other side.

Abigail poked her head inside first and was amazed at Merlin's decor. The office looked more like a science lab than a place of business. The extra overhead lights made everything in the room shine. There were no shadows under the tables, or uncertain shapes in the corners. Glass beakers neatly lined the empty shelves that weren't filled with books. Other beakers bubbled colorful liquid atop Bunsen burners. The back wall of the room didn't have the windows like Excalibur's, but a massive periodic table. It looked hand painted.

"Are you just going to stare?" Merlin asked from a glass top desk. She swirled a pink liquid in a flask before slowly pouring it into a boiling one of blue. Purple smoke oozed from the container, and the mixture turned into a solid.

Abigail shut the door behind her. "Excalibur told me I was to assist you while he was gone today."

Hands on her hips, Merlin asked, "And what did he expect you to do for me?"

"Mop the floors?" Abigail regretted her joke instantly; the floor was pristine.

Merlin returned to her experiment. "How much do you know of molecular chemistry?"

"Not a lot." She was careful not to bump into anything as she approached. "Really, nothing at all."

"I'm not surprised." Merlin wrote down her findings in a notebook. "If you did, you wouldn't be here."

"But you're here."

"As the hero who specializes in science."

Both halves of her statement smacked Abigail in painful ways. She'd make Merlin eat half of her words. Abigail would return to her role as a hero, but she didn't know how masterful she could become in the science field. The wall of elements looked more like ancient Egyptian hieroglyphics. Both examples of writing she hadn't seen since high school.

Abigail kneeled to eye the newly formed solid in the flask. Upon closer inspection, it looked malleable. Abigail swallowed the childish need to squish it.

"Are you working on a new spell?"

Merlin's laugh was curt, unamused, and tired. "That's all marketing. Everything I do is pure science. There is no magic word or wand."

"It always looks like magic."

"And that's why I wear the wizard cap."

Her lengthened red cap sat on a lab stool.

"How do your powers work, then?" Abigail asked. She theorized the Knight crafted tiny chemical bombs that exploded into her beautiful attacks. But she had no idea where she hid the bombs; her costumes didn't look like they had any hidden pockets or matching purses.

Being in a different district than the HRC, Saves the Day had little information on the Round Table Knights. Their abilities were the least of their worries when ratings were all that mattered.

Merlin, her pen still scrolling over her notebook, rubbed her pointer finger and thumb together until water dripped from her fingers as if she held a tiny faucet. She opened her hand and rotated it to show it was empty.

The action made her look like a magician, but the white coat reminded Abigail she was a scientist first.

"Water is made of what?"

Abigail fumbled. "Oxygen and—"

"Hydrogen. I force the electrons together and create the water molecule." Merlin set her pen down and wiped her damp hand against her coat. "If the element is around me, I can connect it to others. Change the very build of them."

"Your science teachers must have loved you."

"They all thought I was annoying." A smile flashed across her beautiful face. "I asked too many questions, and they never peacefully got through a lecture."

Abigail stepped closer to Merlin. Her notes were covered in tiny print and detailed diagrams. If the pages weren't lined with blue ink, it could have passed for a published textbook.

"Did you want to be a scientist before becoming a hero?"

"I didn't expect this to be twenty questions."

"I'm sorry."

"Are you allergic to anything?"

"I don't think so."

"Good." Merlin crossed her office and picked a box off the ground. The contents knocked together when she set it on the glass top table. "I can use your help, after all."

Abigail stepped closer again. "What can I do?"

"Hold this."

From the box, Merlin removed a strange contraption. Three cylindrical glass containers were hooked onto a leather strap that looped in the center. The containers were no bigger than a two-liter bottle of soda.

"What is this?" Abigail accepted the contraption. It weighed more than she expected. She cradled it close to her chest so the glass wouldn't knock together. Thin foam membranes protected the containers from each other, so Abigail didn't take any unnecessary risks.

"A belt."

"Not like any I've seen. Are you wearing two pants?"

Merlin rolled her eyes. She grabbed the belt and quickly strapped it around Abigail's waist, the second loop wrapping across her chest. The three canisters ended up on her chest like a baby carrier. "Do you know what hinders me the most?"

Abigail shook her head, adjusting the belt to sit better on her hips.

"Unstable products after a reaction." Merlin returned to the box and removed a tightly sealed glass jar. A thick liquid sloshed up the sides. "Dangerous chemicals in dangerous places. That belt is a transport vessel.

"A purse might be better?"

"I lose my keys in a purse. I don't want to lose something explosive."

Abigail laughed at Merlin's joke until she realized the hero wasn't telling one. "How can I help?"

"Just stand there." Merlin opened the jar. It unleashed a strong stench of industrial cleaner into the air.

Abigail stepped back. "What is that?"

"Caro's Acid. Easy to make, easy to store, but deadly if spilled. It will dissolve any organic molecule it touches." Merlin sounded like she was describing a family pet instead of an acid.

"I don't want—"

"Hush. The glass won't fail, it's not organic. I just want to test the stabilizing on the belt."

Abigail froze while the Knight unscrewed the lid of one of the containers on the belt. "If you're just testing the stability why can't you use water?"

Merlin eyed her dangerously while pouring the acid into the container. "This isn't designed to transport water. Besides, I can split this apart easily if things don't work out."

Merlin twisted the metal cap on the container and stepped back. Abigail felt the solution warm against her skin.

"What do you need me to do?"

"Just walk around." Merlin waved her hand, returning to her notebook. "Tell me how it feels. Be as detailed as possible."

Abigail shifted from her right to her left foot first, slowly gauging how the new contraption felt as she moved. The acid rippled in the container and Abigail tried not to breathe. The last thing she needed was to combust with acid strapped to her chest. She slid one foot across the floor and then a second. It took ten minutes before she took normal steps around the lab. Merlin watched the container and the belt.

"Besides having acid this close to me, I don't feel anything weird," Abigail stated. "The belt is digging into my shoulder, that might be a problem if you put heavier stuff inside. If this is to transport stuff, do you want different containers? I mean, in case the glass doesn't work with everything?"

"Subject is sharper than initially thought." Merlin snickered. "Come here."

Abigail returned to Merlin's side. The Knight touched one of the empty jars and it began to shimmer under her pointed nail. Merlin could call it science all she wanted, but to Abigail, she felt she had witnessed pure magic. The glass container was no longer glass. It was dark grey, thicker than before and when Merlin flicked the container it pinged like metal.

"I can rearrange the atomic structure," she explained. "Change the carbon shape into something stronger."

There was a knock on the door, but the knocker didn't wait for admittance. King Arthur walked in dressed in his golden cape and crown. He didn't give the current science experiment a second look.

"We've got a call," he said with a grin. "Grab your hat."

"What's going on?" Merlin slid out of her white lab coat.

"Store robbery."

"Boring."

"A gun store robbery."

"Where are the police?"

"Dealing with a gunman on the run." King Arthur gritted his teeth. "I'd switch jobs if we could, but—"

"Save it." Merlin stopped his coming rant. "Are you coming?"

Abigail didn't hesitate. "Of course."

King Arthur's grin returned. "You're not scared?"

"Not when I'm with the best hero pair in San Arbor." A store shakedown didn't scare Inferna, and it wouldn't scare Abigail.

King Arthur eyed Merlin who was adjusting her hat. "It'll be a good test run for the belt," she explained.

Red and blue lights flashed across the gun store. The four officers on the call pointed their weapons at the storefront but hadn't breached the entrance. As the driver parked the car, Abigail saw why. The customers and employees were standing in front of the glass door and display windows with their arms stretched above their heads. Not only were they blocking the criminals inside, but they also prevented Abigail from seeing what was happening. The criminals could be setting up a rocket launcher and no one would know.

Abigail jumped from the car, mindful of the canister of acid still on her chest, and approached the closest officer. He had a bull horn at his side, the microphone piece clutched in his hand. She needed to know everything he knew before she could correctly act in the situation. A gun store wasn't the best place for her to ignite, but as long as she kept her flame temperature low she wouldn't set off any ammunition.

King Arthur coughed, and Abigail stopped. She was the only one who had advanced from the car. She turned around and saw the two heroes, dressed and masked for the job. She was painfully reminded that she was only a *secretary*. Her hands heated, and she forced herself to cool down. Abigail stepped aside and waited for the licensed heroes.

"Stay behind me," Merlin instructed. "Protect the belt."

King Arthur stepped around her and addressed the officer. "Tell me everything."

"The call came in about twenty minutes ago," the officer answered. "The caller said there were three inside before the call cut out. Two gunshots reported."

"Is this connected to the loose gunman?" Merlin asked.

"We don't believe so," he answered. "That started across town."

"They had to have taken over quickly," King Arthur said to himself. "That store is an armory, and no one had time to fight back."

"Could have been the shots," Merlin added. "Any demands?"

The officer shook his head. "The criminals haven't responded. That's why you were called."

King puffed out his chest. "You were right to call us. I'll handle this quickly."

Merlin jabbed an elbow into his side. "We'll take care of this. Please have your men stand back."

"And, let me have that."

The officer handed King Arthur his bull horn.

King approached the storefront, raising the bull horn to his mouth. His eyes glowed a brilliant purple when he spoke. "Everyone freeze. If you're inside Pete's Perfect Point Guns and Ammo, step forward."

Abigail watched in awe with the officer as the civilians at the windows took a useless step forward into the glass. Three masked individuals stepped forward too.

"If you're inside the store and holding a weapon, set it down."

The three individuals obeyed again.

"Now, everyone come outside, and if you're wearing one of those cool ski masks walk over to your favorite officer."

Merlin patted the officer's shoulder. "You were right to call us, this could have ended badly."

Once the criminals were cuffed, King's eyes returned to their normal shade of brown. He returned the bull horn and dusted his hands together. Abigail scrambled to take several photos with her camera for the HRC's press page. The hostages were ushered across the street to the comfort of a convenience store while they waited to give their statements. The red and blue logo of the store matched the flashing lights of the police cars.

"Well that was exciting." King Arthur lied while getting back into the car. "At least we got out of the office for a minute."

Merlin fussed with the belt still strapped around Abigail as she sat down. "If you don't watch that attitude of yours, you'll be lucky to get out again. With Quinn being so close you might ruin it."

"Ruin what?" Abigail asked.

King Arthur locked eyes with Merlin before smiling at Abigail. "Classified stuff."

"I understand. Heroes only." Abigail had a feeling it was the same thing Excalibur was stressing over. The car pulled onto the street, and she buckled her seatbelt over the acid container.

"You seemed ready to be a hero today."

Abigail's eyes widened as she looked back to King Arthur. "What do you mean?"

He laughed. "You were about to walk headfirst into that store, weren't you?"

Abigail exhaled through her nose. "I thought you guys were right behind me, I didn't mean to step out of line."

"When you're in the field you become our responsibility, you have to be careful."

Merlin finally ended her inspection on the belt. "Don't mind him, he doesn't want any more paperwork."

"We can't all have assistants like 'Xcal."

Abigail blushed. "Why don't you have assistants?"

"I don't want one," Merlin answered simply.

"Don't take this the wrong way, Abby." King Arthur stretched his arms above his head in the small space of the car. "I'm not in a position to trust the wrong people. Having an assistant is one more person that could damage the company."

"You can take that as a warning." Merlin did little to soothe the air.

"You have it on my life that I would never do something to hurt the HRC or any of you."

Spending the day with Merlin and King Arthur did little to curb Abigail's hero appetite. She knew without King Arthur's interference she could have marched inside Pete's Perfect Point and taken over the situation, mask or no mask. A hero saves people, and seven people needed saving in that store today. How many more people could she save if she wasn't stuck behind a desk? How many more people could be saved if the heroes weren't chained in the backyard?

Abigail stabbed her plastic fork into the take out Chinese food sitting on her coffee table. She hated how scared her world was of change. Even if that change was for the good, humanity would fight against the unknown with tooth and nail. Things wouldn't change until there was no other option. Usually, that option happened when it was too late.

Abigail turned on the television, hoping the noise would keep her mind at ease. There was nothing she could do now. Not until she became a hero again.

The late night sitcom rerun was interrupted by a breaking newscast alert. The flashing red on the screen jolted Abigail from her unexpected nap on the couch. She sat up and rubbed her eyes. The anchor was speaking so fast Abigail only understood every other word. Her eyes drifted to the ticker tape below the anchor, and her stomach tightened.

Vigilante Arrested.

"According to police, Peter Cooper, under the disguise of Victory Man, followed Larry Witman into a house Witman was breaking into," the anchor said. "Witman has been injured after an altercation with Cooper that also injured the homeowners and left the house damaged. Police have arrested both Cooper and Witman. Channel 9's Monica Daniels is at the scene. Monica, tell us more."

Abigail slid from the couch to the floor as the news station changed to the live camera footage. A young reporter waited for her cue before responding.

"The homeowners have been transported to San Arbor Medical with unknown injuries," she read from her phone. "Witman sustained non-threatening injuries and will be transported to County with Cooper. Right now it appears money was Witman's motive, but the investigation is still underway."

The camera zoomed away from Monica as two police officers walked into the frame. They were holding who Abigail believed to be Victory Man. His hand-stitched costume was ripped at the seams and what was left of his mask did little to hide his face. The gun pressing against his back was the scariest thing about the vigilante. His eyes widened when he looked into the camera and he began to shout.

"Something is happening! Something is going to happen in San Arbor. Open your eyes, something—"

The slamming of the police car door silenced him. The camera returned to Monica who took a breath to compose herself.

"Be careful Monica," the TV anchor said from the newsroom. "We will keep updating you on the situation."

Abigail turned the TV off and the living room turned dark. She created a small blaze in her right hand. Without the proper paperwork, her flame was a death sentence. She could only hope Excalibur was serious about her hero career.

Chapter Fifteen

Abigail returned to the endless lily fields in her dreams. The sky above was moving in a chaotic dance of green and blue northern lights. The colors tore into each other. The white flowers were illuminated in whichever color was winning the struggle. Abigail stood on a concrete platform in the center of the currently green lilies. Railroad tracks were newly installed in the dreamscape, they traveled as endlessly as the horizon on either side. She heard the train before she saw it, she felt it shake the platform before she saw it, she felt it whoosh past her before she saw it.

When she finally did see the train, it was miles past the station. Did she miss it? Did it even stop? Abigail jumped from the platform to chase after it. A ravenous need to be on that train drove her forward until the soles of her shoes had worn away, and her feet bled through her socks. Abigail never caught the train.

It was cold. That was the first thought that woke Abigail, stirring her from her endless chase. The cold and crisp touch of night invading the warm bedroom pulled her closer to her mind's surface. The hot hold around her ankles that pulled her from the bed woke Abigail fully. Her head thumped against the floor, forcing her eyes open. The intruder loomed above her. The open balcony door added more shadows to the room. Abigail refused to panic. Red fire scorched her carpet as she stood and reached for the stranger. Her hands stopped inches from his face. His scarred and green-eyed face.

Cinder's face.

"What?" Abigail dropped her arms, but not her blaze. "What are you doing here?"

"Why are you ignoring me? Why have you been avoiding me?"

Abigail slowly stepped away from him, moving so that the bed wasn't at her back. She didn't want anything at her back. "I've been busy, I've had work."

"How are you going to beat Volcanic without me?" he snarled.

Abigail had never seen him this unhinged. This wild. She hadn't thought his cool demeanor would ever allow it. He followed her like a mirror around the room.

"What are you talking about?"

"Getting stronger. How are you going to do that without me?"

"I have been training," she tried to soothe him. "I've been using a lighter."

"What?" Cinder was confused. It took a piece of momentum from his angry sails.

Abigail slowly, with exaggerated motions, reached for the Zippo lighter on the nightstand. She flicked the lid open, and the flame illuminated her bedroom. Just like the hundreds of times before, she pinched the blue blaze out of the lighter and twirled it through her fingers like it was a coin.

Unlike the other hundreds of times before, she was being watched, and her audience did not like the performance. Cinder ignited his fingers and shot a spear of indigo rage at Abigail's hand. It exploded the lighter and, either by perfect aim or by perfect fluke, left Abigail untouched. She dropped the lighter's remains to the floor.

"This is insulting!" Cinder roared.

"I have neighbors!" Abigail stomped her foot. "Please be quiet."

"You replaced me with a cigarette lighter!"

Abigail tried to shush him, but his hands continued to spark blue. Ignoring the dangerous fire, she reached for him. A strange mixture of fear, relief, and frustration tangled inside her brain. Fear that he would cause enough noise for someone to check in and see her with the Flame

Villain. Relief that he had returned, that they could continue her training, that his green eyes were no longer just visions in her dreams. Frustration that *he* was mad at *her* when he never gave her a chance to return a note of explanation.

"Cin, please," she tried again, quieter. "I wasn't replacing you. Let's talk this out."

"Start then."

"Come outside with me." Abigail nodded to the balcony he used to sneak in. If things got heated out there, only her lawn chair and plant would burn. She touched his arm, and he jerked away. "Please."

Cinder reluctantly followed her onto the concrete balcony. Abigail sat on the chair next to a well-watered fern and pulled her legs to her chest. Her skin was speckled with goosebumps before she began to talk. He leaned against the railing across from her. Too far to reach him, but close enough to simmer under his waiting gaze.

"I wasn't ghosting you." Abigail interlaced her fingers around her legs, keeping them pressed against her. "I just didn't have a way to contact you back. And I knew that if I told you then you wouldn't get it. I didn't think you'd understand."

"Understand that you're working with heroes again?"

"You found that out pretty easily."

"You're easy to follow." He crossed his arms.

Abigail shifted in her seat; the plastic chair didn't help relieve her chill. "Can you be any more..."

"Villainous? Yes, I can."

"I want to be a hero," she reminded him. "I want this job."

"I thought you wanted to get stronger?"

"I still am."

"Not with me!"

Blue flames ripped around him, pouring from his arms and neck. Abigail leaped from her chair with her arms up and ready to defend herself.

"Why does that matter!"

"Only I can teach you this!" Cinder growled, extending a burning hand to her. The blue flames were a fatal attraction.

Abigail grabbed the fire, grabbed him. She flinched when the fire burned her without her own blaze as a buffer. She stared him down. "Teach me then."

The fire roared brighter between their hands, louder than any words that could've been said. Harder than any betrayal that one could have felt. Hotter than any stolen glance from training. Reckless, fearless, and intense.

Abigail's fire couldn't catch up, and it couldn't shield her fast enough. Her fingers burned and she screamed. Cinder dropped her hand. She cradled her damaged hand to her chest. Her thumb and the next two fingers were singed black. They should have screamed in agony. She should have collapsed from the pain. She'd seen this level of injury before, but there was only a soft ache. A dull burn.

"Are you okay?" Cinder's question was surprisingly soft.

Abigail pulled her gaze from her hands, flesh marred and twisted to black. "They don't hurt."

Cinder looked down. "I'm sorry."

"No, you're not." Abigail shoved him with her damaged hand.

Blue flames burst from her burned fingers.

Their eyes snapped together, green tearing into blue. Abigail tried again, snapping her charred fingers together, and blue embers sparked from her fingers. She had done it. She could summon the fabled blue flames.

It was only from three fingers, but it was a start.

Cinder took her hand and pulled it close to his face. He examined the burns. Abigail watched him. The burns mimicked his own, criss-crossing around her skin before stopping below the second knuckle. In a second moment of surprising softness, he stroked his finger from the tip of hers to the center of her palm before rotating it over in his hand.

"Interesting," Cinder said after releasing her.

Her burned hand hovered between them. Their feet, his in boots and hers bare flesh, inches apart. They stood as close together as they had under the model Ponte Vecchio bridge at the start of summer. Only, standing on her patio under the light-polluted sky, Abigail didn't feel as threatened as she had then. Their breaths mingled above their hands.

"You picked my lock." Abigail reminded herself with a weary chuckle.

"You weren't returning my calls."

"They weren't phone calls."

Cinder shrugged and tucked his hands into his pockets. "We could meet here if that better fits your schedule."

"We're not setting my apartment on fire."

Cinder looked to the roof above her. "We can train there. Unless you're scared of falling off."

Abigail wasn't scared. Not of him, and not of heights. "Let's check it out."

Cinder's grin returned and he pulled himself onto the roof using the gutter as a handhold. Abigail followed needing to use her plastic lawn chair to get onto the top. The roof was wide open and, best of all, empty of people and prying eyes. This would be better secluded than the active construction site.

Abigail finished exploring the dark roof and found Cinder watching her from the center. He loomed out of the shadow produced from the stairwell room like a monster. Abigail joined him inside the shadow and sparked a blue flame to light the area. He watched the fire burn atop her fingers and after a moment plucked the flame into his hand to examine it closer. When he was finished, he returned the flame but kept a loose hold around her wrist. The flame stayed atop her fingers instead of returning to its original creator.

His eyes shimmered as the fire reflected off them. Abigail wanted to say something, but everything that came to her mind felt stupid and wrong. When the silence got too thick, when his gaze got too heavy, she asked, "Why do you wear that? It's summer anyway."

Cinder looked at his duster coat. "It makes me look cool." When she didn't refute the statement he added, "It's the same reason you wear your cape, right?"

Abigail opened her mouth to defend herself but snapped it shut. "It's also fireproof and the mark of a hero."

Cinder swatted an unknown particle off his shoulder. "Those can be hard to give up."

"What?"

Cinder looked at her. "Do we have a deal?"

"Twice a week." She decided before the rational side of her brain could talk her out of it.

Abigail followed him off the roof and back to her patio. She lingered at the door, and he lingered at the chair.

"Want to get something to drink?"

"Why?"

He looked up from examining the ivy plant. "I'll tell you a secret."

Chapter Sixteen

"What kind of secret?" Abigail asked, crossing her arms. The cooling night air wasn't the cause of the goosebumps this time, either.

Cinder sat down and interlaced his fingers behind his head. "Depends on how good the drink is."

"All I have is coffee." Abigail struggled to think of a drink that warranted a secret. Whiskey would have been better, but she didn't keep that in the house.

"It'll be a bitter secret then."

Abigail spilled the ground coffee on her countertop. She spilled tap water on the floor. She quickly cleaned two mugs sitting in her sink while the coffee brewed. The hot plate hissed as coffee dripped onto it when she prematurely removed the pot to fill the mugs. She tucked the half-gallon of milk and bag of sugar under her arm and brought it all onto the patio.

Cinder didn't move from the chair and only accepted the mug. The other ingredients hung haphazardly in Abigail's arms. She placed them just inside the door and joined Cinder on the patio. She watched him drink the coffee, growing impatient with each little sip. The rising steam tangled with his grin. Abigail curled her toes against the cold concrete floor. When the mug was empty he set it face down on the patio railing.

"The first time we met, when I," Cinder tapped his throat in the same place her scar had been, "you were just in a bad spot. I didn't have any intention of hurting anyone that night."

Abigail's hands sparked angrily with red and blue before she calmed down. She set her half-drunk mug down. "Then why did you do it?"

"Why did you attack me?" he challenged back.

"You were a villain."

"Still am, doll." He added a wink to his confession. "We were made to destroy each other."

She took a step back and regained her composure. "Why haven't we yet?"

"That's a different secret, and I'm not thirsty anymore." Cinder raised from his throne and handed his mug to her. "I'll see you in two days. Don't be late."

Abigail retired back into her bedroom. "Don't cause any trouble on the way out."

The burns didn't hurt the next morning. They didn't pulse when they snagged against the bedsheets, or hiss in the shower. They didn't throb when Abigail knocked them against her dresser, or when she grabbed her keys too tightly on her way out. They didn't hurt, but they looked like they should have. Her fingers were sickening; dipped in some kind of dark acid that dried the muscle and removed the skin.

But Abigail could summon the elusive blue flame so she didn't mind the head turning of the bus driver or the seat changing when another passenger noticed the deformity. Abigail felt powerful.

At the Hero Relief Center, she followed Mitch onto the elevator and tapped her floor destination.

"Jesus, Turner." Mitch's concerned tone was just as sour as his usual one. "What happened to you?"

"What do you mean?" Abigail tucked a stray hair behind her ear, then looked at her hand. "Oh, these. I hurt myself cooking."

"Were you deep-frying cats?" Mitch squinted at her burns before looking away. "Should you even be here?"

"I feel fine. They don't hurt."

The elevator door opened, and Mitch quickly exited. "You've got a stronger stomach than I do."

The door shut again, and within the privacy of the metal box, Abigail snapped her fingers and a tiny blue flame danced atop her fingertip. She wanted to show the world. She wanted to rub her victory in Volcanic's face. She wanted to leap into downtown and declare herself queen. But she knew she couldn't. Not yet. The flame extinguished before the elevator could open again.

Even after a full day of assuring her co-workers that her hand was fine, that the burns didn't hurt, that she had been cleared from a hospital and could work, Shannon still stopped Abigail in the main entrance the next afternoon with a container of herbal burn cream.

"One of the ladies who does my nails recommended this," Shannon explained.

"You really didn't have to." Abigail couldn't read any of the Eastern writing on the lid.

"You don't have to be brave around me, ya know?" Shannon returned to her desk. "You can act tough all you want in front of the Knights, but you can be normal with me."

Abigail winced away from the container horrified, the cream smelled awful. "Thanks, Shannon, but really they don't hurt."

"Keep lying to yourself, but a fire is always going to burn."

Abigail rubbed some of the cream over her fingers to please the receptionist before returning to her office. She had a large list of "to-dos" waiting for her and didn't think the workload shrunk during her lunch break. She updated Excalibur's social media and replied to fan letters. She left the true heart warmers for her boss but answered the fanboy questions and sent them back to the eager kid waiting for their email to *ding* with a response. She had been on that side of the email before and knew how hard that wait time could be.

Excalibur's door opened and the armor-clad giant sat down in the chair across from her.

"Afternoon, sir." Abigail didn't look up from her typing. *Math will be just as important as your gym class. Don't think of solving the problems for a grade, solve those problems for me! If we needed the exact amount of force to cut free a trapped citizen without hurting them then your math class is going to come in handy.* "Need something?"

"Just some words." Excalibur adjusted his sword as it awkwardly pinched against his side in the small seat. Abigail had taken his advice and hung a landscape photo on the bare wall behind him, but it made the space more cluttered than expansive. The painted deer were as trapped as the office's occupants.

Abigail tore her gaze away from the emails, her teal eyes bright and her dreams soaring. "About being a sidekick again?"

"Not quite." Excalibur left his sword alone. "I've been looking into Inferna's file."

Abigail's heart sank.

"You were paired with Volcanic, someone truly reckless and careless. I'm not sure that was the best guidance for someone so young and so…impressionable."

"I was hired to better his ratings. I did a very good job of that."

"Both you and he had an interesting media representation." Excalibur returned to his point. "Only, you were fired because of it."

"Please tell me what this is about." Abigail did not want to be reminded of her broken promise with Kenneth. Kreech's final words threatened to emerge into her memories. Abigail swallowed hard, forcing everything down.

Excalibur reached across the desk, past the computer, past the coffee mug in the shape of his helmet, and grabbed her hand. He handled it delicately, not letting the metal side of his glove touch the burn.

"I don't want you to screw up when you're so close to being a side-kick again," Excalibur said. "This scares me, Abby. What are you doing to yourself?"

"It was a training accident." Abigail told half the truth, sliding her hand from his. She cradled her hand in her lap. Her darkened fingers were as precious to her as a child. "I was trying to get a more powerful flame."

"Did you?"

"Yes!" she smiled, powerless to the intoxicating feeling of the indigo flames under her skin. She stopped herself before asking if Excalibur wanted to see.

"Good." Excalibur stood. "Then this won't happen again. I need you to have a level head. There are no reckless heroes on the Round Table."

"You've got to stop teasing me with that," Abigail grumbled.

"I'm only keeping your goals in front of you. All talks of you returning as a sidekick are off the table until you're healed."

"Yes, sir." Abigail clenched her fists.

Excalibur knocked his metal knuckles against the desk, shaking the pens in their container, and stood. His sword hooked through the armrest, and he struggled in the small space to free himself. Abigail jumped at his delayed exit.

"Sir, can I ask about Victory Man?" When Excalibur looked away from his imprisonment she continued, "I saw the story on the news and before he was arrested, he said something was coming for San Arbor. Do you have any idea what he meant?"

Excalibur gave up on freedom and returned to his seat. "Not in the slightest."

"Could it have something to do with the 'heroes only' thing?" Abigail bunny-eared the phrase she was getting tired of hearing without being in the club herself.

"No, it's not connected with that," he answered after a moment. "I wouldn't take what that vigilante said as fact. You can't trust a criminal."

His words twisted inside her gut as his sword currently had him twisted in the seat.

"But he was just being a hero, like us." Abigail blushed. "I mean, like you."

"Sadly, you can't be a masked hero unless the city backs you at a company." Excalibur tilted his helmet covered head at her, but Abigail could feel the weight of his stare. "You're not getting any ideas like that, right?"

Abigail shook her head. "Absolutely not."

Her ideas were far worse than being an unlicensed hero.

Chapter Seventeen

Abigail climbed onto the roof of her apartment building that night. She turned her plastic chair into a step stool and used the gutter box as a handhold. It was unsafe, but so was everything else she was doing tonight. It was just after ten, and he was waiting for her. The Flame Villain waiting to train a laid-off sidekick.

Nice job, hero.

Abigail zipped up her windbreaker and met Cinder in the middle of the roof. Lights from the passing cars below wouldn't reach this height; neither would the street lamps or soft glow of the hallway lights from the windows. If it wasn't for the moonlight, it would be impossible to see the dips in the roof and spinning exhaust fans. Cinder looked at home with the moon at his back. He seemed to be as endless as a horizon. Untouchable. Uncatchable.

"I have a favor to ask." Abigail stopped him in mid sarcastic greeting. Cinder closed his mouth and raised an eyebrow. She held up her three burned fingers. "I need you to take these burns away, like you did before."

"Why would you want that?"

"Job security."

"You'll lose my flame," he reminded her, like she didn't already know.

"I'll find another way to use it." Abigail wasn't sure whom she was promising: herself or him. "Please?"

Cinder walked to her and took her hand. He peeled the burns off her fingers like they were a gel mask used for a beauty treatment. Blue smoke oozed between the clean skin underneath and the black leathery burn he pulled off. The smoke absorbed back into his hands when he finished.

Abigail slid her hand from his and snapped her fingers together. She only summoned a cherry-red flame atop her pointer finger. She extinguished the flame with a shake of her hand. She sighed, disappointed. The blue fire just out of reach again.

"Thanks."

"What's the plan now?"

"Aren't you the teacher?"

That made Cinder smirk, which made Abigail happy.

"Ever play catch?"

"Catch?" she echoed. "Not since I was a kid."

Cinder created a fireball in his hands. "This will be fun then."

When Abigail played catch as a kid it was an easy game where her father lobbed a softball into the air, and she plucked it from the sky without injury. She would throw it back; most times it rolled to the ground before he scooped it up. She got better at throwing the ball as she got older.

Abigail didn't have the years to get better in Cinder's deadly version.

He launched fireballs like he was pitching in the World Series. Abigail had to do everything not to get nailed in the face, let alone catch one and send it back. The burning orbs snuffed themselves out when they crashed into the roof, bursting into sparks when they crashed into her. Abigail admired his control. The damage to the building was minimal.

"This one's coming just for you, doll." Cinder arced a fireball to her. After nearly an hour of trying, Abigail finally caught one.

She coated her hand in red flames before catching the ball and sending it back. The orb turned purple as it morphed from blue to red in mid-flight. She didn't have time to admire her skills as seven more pitches crashed in a wave of heat against her, pushing her several feet back.

Cinder tossed them lazily, but the force didn't let up. Abigail had to choose between protecting her face or trying to catch them. She chose the defensive route and was pushed further back. There was a break in the assault just long enough for Cinder to toss in an insult with the fireballs.

"Nice catch." She hadn't caught it.

Abigail gritted her teeth and readied herself for the next toss.

A fastball landed against Abigail's chest, burning through the windbreaker and pushing her back.

Only this time, there was no more roof to catch her.

For a moment Abigail was suspended, then gravity pulled her down. She reached up for anything to grab, something to keep her from falling. The gutters were already too far away. It was funny in a way. Seven stories didn't seem so tall when one considers how little time it takes to fall that far. Abigail squeezed her eyes shut. She didn't want to see her own death. Her mangled body smashed against the sidewalk below.

A hand grabbed her before gravity took full control. Abigail's brain couldn't comprehend the sudden change in direction. Instead of falling down she was flying forward, at least until she hit something hard and stopped moving altogether. She opened her eyes. She was back on the roof. Standing up. Being held. Cinder's arms were wrapped tightly around her. Melding their bodies together. He was panting, his chest quaking against her own.

How fast could he run?

No, not run. Rocket. Abigail could smell burning rubber and singed fabric. She noticed that his jacket was gone. It must have burned up.

He had propelled himself to her and was still smoking from it, his body still hot and shaking from the friction. This close, his eyes were as large as the moon. The celestial body was foolish to try and compare to him. He was Unshakeable. Undeniable.

This close it was hard to ignore anything about him. His eyes, his nose, his scars, his lips. She felt them more than she saw his mouth. It pressed against her own with what remained of the energy of his rocket launch. Then, there was fire. A ravenous hunger sparked between them. The heat encased them, expanding around them. Their hands sparked with the desire to touch each other. Hands gripped arms, waists, necks, anywhere to get leverage in this new form of combat. Tongues and flames forced their way inside the other's mouth.

She forgot to be cautious of him. She forgot they were training. She forgot they stood on opposite sides of the law. For the short eternity of their kiss, she saw the wastelands of her dreams come to life.

Abigail trailed her fingers up his bare arms, feeling the crisscross-ing of burn scars as they scratched and tickled her skin. Unable to stop herself, she slipped her hands under his shirt and traced the curves and dips of his shoulders and back. His teeth clipped against hers as he trembled at her touch.

The flames grew between them. His fire bit into Abigail's skin as his teeth bit against her flesh. She didn't mind either. She gripped his shirt, fearing he may escape. In this moment, she couldn't get close enough to him. His fire followed his hands down her body, removing strips of fabric from her windbreaker and the shirt underneath. Every time the cold air threatened to chill her skin the flames returned to chase it away. Abigail was blissful but an annoying and rational voice begged her to stop.

Abigail pulled away first. It was hard being in his embrace. Any-thing she did put her in range of his mouth, and she feared her will to fight her desire was fading. He watched her quizzically, head tilted to the side. He didn't relax his hold on her. Their bodies pressed together as they caught their breath.

"I can't," Abigail finally said. It didn't convince either of them.

"Why?" His voice was as soft as his eyes, fairy-lit in the backdrop of the moon.

"I'm a hero, and you're a villain."

"Don't be a hero tonight." He tightened his arms around her, pulling her even closer against him.

Abigail dissolved back into him. She was a moth to his lantern. He was dangerous, she would get burned, and yet she chased him anyway. Red and blue sparks cascaded around them.

When they finally did untangle, they were breathless, their flames snuffed out from the lack of oxygen. Cinder pressed his forehead against Abigail's and cupped her face with a cooling hand. He rubbed his thumb over her swollen lips, repairing some of the newly left burns. He trailed his hands down her neck and back removing more of the burns he had caused. His eyes never left hers. Her newly healed skin shivered in the summer night.

"Thank you," Abigail whispered, almost too scared to speak in case her voice shattered the dream-like state in which she found herself.

"For what?" Cinder smirked. The blue smoke from his healing touch still billowed around his face.

She snuck a final kiss under his jaw, his own scars tickling her tender lips. When she pulled away, Cinder saw that her tongue had been scorched blacker than the night around them.

"Do me a favor?" he mimicked her from earlier. "Breathe."

Abigail cocked her head, but did as he requested. She pursed her lips, but instead of a puff of vapor misting into the air, a wisp of blue flame escaped her mouth.

Nice job, hero.

Chapter Eighteen

The morning came and went in a blur. Abigail's mint toothpaste, the bitter dark roast in the employee break room, and the sticky honey bun did little to remove the taste still on her lips from the previous night. The Round Table meeting she escorted Excalibur to, the unread emails in her inbox, and the scheduling phone call to get the armored hero on a morning talk show did little to remove the thoughts that replayed in her mind. Every time Abigail closed her eyes, she saw Cinder staring down at her, every time her blouse pulled around her midsection, she imagined one of his fingertips trailing across her skin, every time she spoke, she remembered how his mouth felt against hers.

Abigail shook her head, trying to shake the returning thoughts from the front of her mind, as she still had to focus on today's work. But the memory of Cinder kept stealing her time like the villain he was. After a while, Abigail didn't mind the intrusions. She stared at her computer screen, hidden within the walls of her office, and let her mind rewind the night before. She hadn't been kissed like that since, well, ever. She had never felt the way Cinder made her feel.

The chair across her scraped against the floor as it pulled forward. Abigail clawed into her daydream, demanding to stay as long as she could before reality took control. Excalibur sat down in front of her. His gigantic form filled her vision, and the mental make out session fizzled away.

"Hey, boss." Abigail knew her cheeks would be red. She felt the heat from them stinging her eyes.

"Slow day?"

Abigail refreshed her email and nodded, even though she still had three unread messages. "You weren't wrong when you said you needed crime. I can still do some administrative stuff, but you've got to be going out of your mind."

"You've got that right." His dislocated voice matched his mood. He set his chin in his hand and leaned against the armrest. It looked like a preschool chair with him in it. "It's important that we act well behaved though, have to play everything by the rules."

"What do you mean?"

"Knight stuff, sorry. We covered it at the Round Table this morning, it's been bugging me."

"Anything I can help with?" Abigail offered. "Without knowing any of the details, I mean."

Excalibur sat up. "Yes, actually. I have a new pet project I want your help overseeing."

"What kind of project?" Abigail grabbed a pen and a blank sheet of paper.

"It's one I have to show you." Excalibur opened the door to his office and eagerly removed himself from the tiny chair. "You won't need to take any notes for this."

Abigail returned her pen to the cup containing several others and followed him into his office. Three of the swords he had purchased from the weapons show were displayed on the walls, the blood red scabbard wasn't among them. He led her to his training room. Each of the Knights had specialized rooms designed to best suit their abilities. Excalibur's had more weapons hanging on the walls and enough practice dummies to last a decade of abuse.

Excalibur's ability was less flashy than Merlin's. He was able to master any combat weapon with insane speed, accuracy, and talent with a single touch. Abigail didn't doubt the hero knew how to use every one of the weapons hanging on the walls. She assumed his new pet project was learning a new weapon. Perhaps he needed her to document the training or, and hopefully not, hold the target.

Excalibur pulled a wooden training sword from the wall.

"I didn't know that healing was in your abilities," he commented, twirling the sword at his side.

In a day her fingers had become perfectly healed. Sickening black burns to soft pink flesh. She chewed the inside of her cheek. "Shannon gave me this ointment. It really worked."

"I don't care how it happened. But I'm glad to see your self-mutilation is over. Now, we can continue talking about a potential, future promotion."

"To a sidekick?" Abigail kept her tongue hidden between her teeth. She knew the hero wasn't going to believe her rehearsed lie of burning it on a bowl of oatmeal that morning.

"Nothing's set yet," he said. "I haven't even mentioned it to King and Merlin. But I feel bad watching you do all the boring stuff for me. What if you lose your skills waiting?"

"I train every day. If not here, I do fire practice at home."

"As a licensed hero I'm going to pretend I didn't hear that," said Excalibur. "But, as your mentor, I'm pleased. I was hoping you would accept my offer to train you."

"Really! Seriously?" Abigail jumped with excitement. "Of course, I would! Thank you!"

"Hold on, before you get too excited." Excalibur stopped twirling the wooden blade. "I don't know the first thing about bettering your fire abilities, except giving you a different type of sparring partner, but I was hoping to put some extra meat on you, and if you're willing, teach you how to use a sword."

"A sword would be badass." Abigail grinned. She'd fight with a bag of cotton balls if it meant getting back on the streets.

"I hope your endurance is as good as your enthusiasm." Excalibur sounded like he was grinning. "I won't go easy on you just because you're my assistant."

"I'd be ashamed if you did, sir." Abigail knocked her fists together, igniting them. "Where do you want me?"

Excalibur pointed the wooden sword at the back of the training room where a rack of weights leaned against the wall. Abigail's flames went out. "I was serious about getting muscle on you. You look like a storm could knock you over."

Determined to prove him wrong, Abigail grabbed the 30lb dumbbell off the rack. It was heavier than she expected it, but she didn't change her mind and picked up the matching one. Excalibur grabbed the ones marked with 75 and stood across from her.

"We'll do a few together until you get the form down."

Abigail nodded, the weights already pulling painfully on her shoulders.

"If you need a break or want to switch weights just let me know."

Excalibur started with bicep curls, and several times he stopped to correct Abigail's elbow that bowed too far out to compensate for the weight. Halfway through the second set, Abigail regretted her choice in weight but blamed herself for not focusing any of her solo training on strength building. She deserved the burning in her arms.

Excalibur exhaled loudly after their second completed three set workout. "I think I bit off too much." He set his weights back on the rack and asked, "Can I have those? They're a bit more my speed today."

Abigail didn't think he had any difficulties with his chosen weights. He easily doubled the sets while she struggled to reach ten. She reluctantly handed her weights over. She was grateful for his compassion, but still disappointed with her lack of strength. She selected the 20lbs dumbbells and readied herself for the next set.

***

When Abigail returned to her apartment, she barely made it to her couch before melting into mush. Her arms and shoulders screamed at her. Any movement pulled the well-worked muscles too far and caused her to wince. She knew after the muscles healed, she'd be proud of the growth, and, after more sessions, she'd see a change. But right now, she just wanted to see a tub of chocolate ice cream and a warm bath.

With the freezer bare, she settled for the bath. The tub filled with hot water and rose scented bubbles from the body wash poured in. She undressed, slipped into a robe, and felt her heart momentarily give out when she caught green eyes lurking behind the patio door. Their owner smirked and tapped the glass with a finger.

Abigail tightened her bathrobe knot before sliding the door open a few inches. Cinder grabbed the handle and pulled it over a few more.

"Figured I'd knock this time." He said hello.

"Not tonight," she begged, her arms whining just at the thought of another workout. "I'm all trained out."

"I had something *else* in mind tonight." He snuck a hand through the doorway and rested it against her hip. Abigail felt the heat through the terrycloth.

She flushed, her mind and body jittering at the idea of her constant daydreams coming to life. Abigail forced herself to step away from his touch and close the door a few inches. "Come back tomorrow?"

Her request disappointed herself and him. His usual crooked smile flattened into a pout. She twisted her barefoot into the carpet watching his bottom lip pucker out, remembering how she kissed it this time yesterday. And how badly she wanted to do it again. Cinder leaned in closer, using his foot to spread the door open more. He was inches away, Abigail could feel the heat of his breath, smell woodsmoke; she could almost taste him.

She gripped the patio door handle and forced herself back. She had to do this, she told herself, she had to say no. Any fire would burn, but a slow burn she could control.

His green eyes bore into hers. She felt her resolve begin to trickle through her fingers. With each passing breath it was harder to keep her hand on the door handle and not reach forward and pull him inside.

Cinder stepped back from the door before she lost complete control. Closing it he warned, "Your water's overflowing."

Abigail's eyes widened and she turned to the bathroom. There was no water coming over the tub walls like she imagined, no flooding into the downstairs apartment as she feared. She turned back, but Cinder was gone. She shut the door, made sure it was locked and drew the curtains. Her heart still wasn't beating normally.

Abigail got the hang of being a hero's assistant pretty easily. She had Excalibur's daily schedule memorized and made the proper changes to allow for his habits. She knew to push all ten o'clock meetings fifteen minutes back because the armor-clad hero liked to scavenge the break room for a mid-morning snack. Since he knew her secret, Abigail didn't stress about his coffee anymore. She heated it in her hands before delivering it on his desk. It was perfect every time.

Abigail was not used to the hero training she did with Excalibur every morning. She kicked herself for ever thinking he would be easy compared to Volcanic. After each session, she found a new bruise developing over a rib, a new cut against her arm, or a blister forming on her hand from lifting the weights. Abigail had gained four pounds of muscles since their first day.

Excalibur never removed his helmet, but during their sparring he did opt for gym shorts and an HRC T-shirt. Abigail was thankful he wore padded gloves or else the blow he just delivered would have cost her a front tooth. She wiped her bloody lip across her hand and returned to her fighting stance.

"I didn't get you too hard?"

"Course not. You could hit a little harder next time."

"Abigail." Excalibur dropped his hands.

"I just want to be prepared for when I can return," she explained. "I don't want to forget what a real hit feels like. A villain won't hold back."

"You'll make me feel real guilty if I can't get you hired after all this hard work you've put into our training."

Abigail swallowed. She hadn't considered this not working out. "I'm grateful for the opportunity, either way."

She knew the strength would be useful once she mastered the blue flame. She already knew her endurance was improving; she wasn't getting winded as often as she had in the beginning.

"Let's get cleaned up for the day." Excalibur decided. "I doubt you'll want anyone seeing you with a bloody smile."

"I keep an extra toothbrush here." Abigail set to gather her things at the back of the training room.

He laughed and shook his head. "I have to ask; who's the better teacher?"

Abigail froze, heat rose on the back of her neck. "What?"

"Between me and Volcanic?" Excalibur clarified. "Who's the better teacher?"

Abigail sighed. *Of course, he wouldn't be asking about Cinder. No one knows. No one can know.* "It's been nice not having to dodge Volcanic's fireballs anymore."

"I'll take it as a win for me." Excalibur held the door open for her.

***

When she returned home from work, her second round of training began. Her body didn't mind these training sessions, which were turning more pleasurable than productive as the days progressed. Most nights, Abigail and Cinder didn't make it to the roof. They stayed tangled together on the patio, scorching the walls.

When Abigail's head hit the pillow each night, she was too tired to worry between what was right or wrong. With the success she gained at work, she thought it okay to enjoy her time with Cinder.

Abigail knew she was getting closer to her goal at work. Being trained by Excalibur was definitely a good sign, but spending time with the other Round Table Knights was a flashing sign equipped with bells and whistles. Before, Abigail could only say a quick "hello" when she saw them in the hallways, now they were eating lunch together.

Well, the Round Table Knights were eating a sponsored lunch together and Abigail was updating Excalibur's social media. But she was invited to stay and eat some of the extra food so she counted it as a win.

"I haven't seen 'Xcal warm up to an assistant in a while," King Arthur told Abigail. "What's your secret?"

There were King Arthur posters on almost every teenage girls' bedroom walls and it was easy to see why. The leader of the Knights was too pretty, the definition of homecoming king. He was the bar for the newest hot celebrity, and that bar was high. His brown curls were perfect, nestled under his costume crown, and his eyes were always shining. His superpower wasn't strength, but he didn't lack any while in combat. He commanded any situation like a kingdom.

"She makes a killer coffee," Excalibur answered.

"You're still doing that coffee test?" Merlin sighed. "That got old with the first one."

"Make me something else to test my employees then."

Merlin didn't respond to Excalibur's challenge. Instead, she plucked the last sweet roll from his plate.

Abigail truly felt like she was eating with royalty.

But it wasn't just the heroes she was getting closer with.

Her villainous tutor was gaining a lot of her trust and time as well.

And apartment space.

"Come on," Cinder whined in Abigail's ear late one night. The low rumble in his voice tickled her neck. "Let me in."

Abigail had half her body through the patio door while the other was held hostage by Cinder's hold around her wrist. "And feed you like a stray?" she smiled.

Cinder didn't let go. "You know I can pick your lock."

"But you haven't." Abigail turned to face him. "Which makes me think you won't."

"I didn't want in until tonight." His breath bounced against her lips, and his hand moved from her wrist to her hip where his fingers fit snugly against the bone. "Come on."

"You need a better line," Abigail commented, her pulse quickened at his touch and obvious desire. It mimicked her own hunger.

"I'm burning for you." He grinned at his bad joke.

Abigail rolled her eyes, but his grin was contagious like a plague. And, probably, just as deadly. She laced her fingers into his free hand, kissed him, kissed the barrier she had temporarily made goodbye, and pulled him over the patio door threshold where her bed waited for them like an altar.

They worshiped each other for hours.

Chapter Nineteen

In the quiet morning, Abigail forgot where she was. She forgot who she was laying with. The complexity, the taboo, the thrill of a hero sharing a bed with a villain didn't matter. The only thing that mattered was the warm body pressed against hers, the scarred arm over her waist, the silent murmurs brushing against the back of her neck. Those were the only truths of that morning.

The silenced alarm clock wasn't even an afterthought. It wasn't even real at this point. Its task to wake up a member of the workforce was a lie. It was just as guilty as the hero sharing her bed with a villain. Their trial would begin as soon as the morning sun burned through the sleep dust in Abigail's eyes.

That began at 8:52.

Abigail stretched, yawned, and tucked herself closer to her sleeping companion. She examined his fingers. Nails cut short, scarred divots from past injuries healed to pale pink scratches and the dark criss-crosses of burn scars that started at his palm and continued up his arm. The weirdest part was how soft his fingertips were. How gentle they were when they weren't engulfed in flames.

They were almost as strange as the scar that ran across his face, cutting his features into two halves. One marred and damaged, and the other soft and boyish. She still ached to know what caused it, what was so strong to burn Cinder, and why he refused to remove them himself.

Perhaps they were more alike than she believed. Perhaps he used the scar as a promise like she had. Vowing to keep it until he could defeat whoever left it. She brushed a wild piece of hair away from his eye, and he nuzzled into her touch sleepily kissing the inside of her hand.

Abigail never wanted to leave this bed.

A muted buzzing ended Abigail's examination. She pulled her phone from the nightstand and leaped out of bed noticing the time. She was so late! Abigail silenced the call and ripped into her closet. She tugged on an acceptable outfit, didn't have time to shower, and settled for a quick face wash and teeth brushing.

That's when things got complicated.

Blooming from the collar of her blouse was a bouquet of dark purple marks stretching from her chest to her neck in a possessive display of affection. Abigail paled, and it made the markings more obvious. She swallowed hard. She scrubbed at them with the washcloth but they remained.

Cinder watched her when Abigail returned from the bathroom. Leaning against the headboard with his arms stretched over it. He was the deity the altar now worshiped.

He knew it, too.

"I need you to leave," Abigail said frantically to his reflection in the dresser mirror while she put on a pair of golden earrings. "And take these burns away."

Cinder's reflection smirked as the man got out of bed and met Abigail in the mirror, one body dressed and one just skin. "Those aren't burns, doll."

Abigail's jaw dropped and she touched her bruised flesh. This would not look good at work. Cinder took advantage of her shock and kissed her open mouth. He was clearly amused by the situation and proud of his work. Abigail spun away from him and returned to her closet. She tugged a turtleneck over her head, the restricting collar snagged against an earring.

Cinder laughed and returned to the bed, fluffing a pillow and pulling the sheets over him.

"What are you doing?" Abigail asked, strapping on a shoe.

"Going back to bed. I don't work in the mornings."

"Must be nice," Abigail started to mutter but changed her sentence. "No. No, you have to get out of here."

"Scared your boyfriend will find me?"

Abigail blushed. "I don't have a—"

"Then what's the problem?"

Abigail didn't know. She couldn't form words let alone a proper thought while staring at the naked man lounging in her bed. The way he unapologetically filled the space made her think he belonged there, that he always had. Was it ever really her bed, or was she just keeping it warm until he arrived?

"If you're scared I'll steal something," Cinder joked, snapping Abigail back to the current situation. "Then you'll know the culprit and can get it back. That's hero work, right?"

Hero work.

"Just don't break anything." Abigail put her other shoe on and dashed out the door. She was calling Excalibur before she got to the elevator to lie to him about her tardiness. *Alarm didn't go off, overslept, be there as soon as I can, I'm so sorry!*

Officially two and a half hours late to work, four if she counted the early training session, Abigail raced through the main entrance of the Hero Relief Center. Her heels snapped against the floor, and Shannon eyed her suspiciously from her guard tower of a front desk.

Shannon's comment struck her like an arrow to the back. "Cute sweater! Wouldn't it look better in the fall?"

"I'm behind on laundry." Abigail frantically pressed the elevator button.

"Better hope the others are as gullible as yourself." Shannon snapped a magazine open.

Abigail turned from the waiting elevator and approached the receptionist. "Is it that noticeable?"

Shannon giggled. "Only to me. Maybe Merlin if she even cares, but, come on Abbs, ever hear of foundation?"

Abigail blushed. "I wouldn't have had enough if I tried."

Shannon released a low whistle and fanned herself with the magazine. "From the flower dude?"

"The flower dude?" Abigail shook her head. "No, listen—"

"I won't tell anyone," Shannon promised with a smile. "But you've got to dish to me later. Nothing exciting ever happens here, I'm desperate for anything."

"We work in a hero company, Shannon." Abigail knew they had slow days like any other business, but this was the best job in town.

"For upstairs, maybe." Shannon lowered her attention to her magazine. "Speaking of upstairs, aren't you late?"

"Shit." Abigail raced back to the elevator. "See ya, Shannon!"

The elevator opened prematurely on the second floor, and Abigail was surprised to see Excalibur waiting on the other side. A pang of guilt drilled into her when she noticed the cup of coffee in his hands. That was supposed to be her job, and he had to do it himself because she had been spooning a villain instead of being at her desk.

"I'm so sorry I'm late." Abigail felt like she would start crying. "It will never happen again."

Excalibur stepped into the car and ignored her apology. "It was my fault for working you too hard."

Abigail's face dropped. "Sir, absolutely not."

"Rest is important. I always forget about it. How are you feeling?"

"I'm fine, sir." Abigail blinked several times. She couldn't follow what was happening. "Please, don't feel bad about this."

"I'm canceling training for tomorrow."

"Sir, I am fine, really."

Excalibur raised the coffee cup to his mask, but then lowered it when the helmet prevented his drink. "It's more for me. I may not be up for it tomorrow."

"Doing something tonight?" Abigail asked after he finished laughing.

"Today," he answered and stepped off the elevator on the eleventh floor. "The Knights are meeting President Samuels downtown. Merlin's favorite bar is down there, so we'll probably go there after."

"Is this more about the thing you can't talk about?"

"You're quick," he commented. "These things usually take all day. I don't see why we can't do it over the phone."

"What kind of thing?" Abigail couldn't stop herself from asking.

"Meetings at Town Hall. They always make me wear a dumb suit. Over my armor. It's so restricting, makes me feel like a dress-up doll."

"You must be meeting with someone pretty important, then." Abigail followed him toward their offices.

"It's more like an important issue than a person—" Excalibur stopped and eyed her with his empty metal gaze. "I can't be telling you any of this."

Abigail put her hands up. "I still don't know anything, sir. Just that you don't like wearing a suit."

Excalibur paused, but then said, "I put some stuff on your desk, think you can handle it all?"

"Sir, I'm supposed to take care of you. Whatever you need, I can handle it."

"I'm in good hands then. Take it easy tonight. I'll see you tomorrow."

The mindless work that Excalibur left on her desk gave Abigail's mind time to roam. Her thoughts were drawn back to Cinder like they were the opposite ends of a magnet.

Abigail's mind was a kaleidoscope of memories. Images flashing and morphing into each other. Cinder's crooked smirk. The softness of his fingertips on her thighs. The low growl in his voice when he called her doll. His lips. His eyes. Cinder.

She shook her head. This had to stop. She needed to focus. She took stock of her desk. The mail was sorted. The inbox was empty. The interview set. The action figures approved. There wasn't anything left to focus on but him. A villain training a hero. Abigail sank back into her chair and her thoughts sank back into him.

When the phone rang it sounded foreign. The shrill rings ricocheted off the walls in the small office. Abigail fell out of her seat as she snatched it off the hook before it went to voicemail.

"Round Table Knights, Excalibur's line, how can I help you?"

"Are you stupid or just lazy?" Mitch's sour tone oozed from the handset. "Did you even look at the merchandise you signed off on? I swear, Turner."

Abigail wiggled her computer mouse until the screen turned on and opened the action figure document. "Of course, I reviewed it. What's wrong with it?"

"Try looking at the back of the armor. The plastic's pressed like a dog turd."

When Abigail rotated the image, she couldn't believe the obvious design flaw. Mitch's description was spot on. "Oh my gosh, is there any way to retract it?"

"Not for the first one thousand packaged," Mitch snapped. "Were you even thinking when you submitted this?"

Abigail gulped. "I forgot to check the backside."

"Well get your head on straight and don't let this happen again. And make sure you double-check your interview times. Excalibur isn't going to wake up at 4 a.m. for an overseas call."

The phone clicked off, and she kicked the chair across from her. She was foolish and careless. Something needed to be done. The something was clear enough to figure out, but not as easily executed. She needed to remove any distractions that would hinder her from her work. From her dreams of reaching her cape.

Her heart settled in her stomach.

Chapter Twenty

Abigail half expected to find Cinder still in her bed when she returned to her apartment, the other half expected him to be gone. Vanished into a hidden part of the city. When she unlocked her door and saw him standing in her kitchen, his lower half wrapped in a plush towel and his upper half glistening with water droplets, her stomach flipped with a carnival ride level of uncertainty. She couldn't avoid this, like she prayed she could, if he weren't here.

Cinder's hips pulled the towel open and closed while he prowled around her kitchen. He found a glass in the cabinet and filled it with water. He drank half and then set the glass upside down in the sink. He wiped his mouth with the back of his hand and dared Abigail to move with a sidewise look.

She knew he caught her staring. The room smelled of her rose soap mixed with the campfire smoke that was Cinder.

"I can lose the towel if that's all you can think about." Cinder chuckled and tucked a thumb under the fabric ready to undo the weak knot below his belly button.

Abigail ignored her blush and dropped her purse on the counter. The metal buckles clinked against the countertop with amused chatter. "That's not what I was thinking about."

"What were you thinking about, doll?"

That I wished you would've saved the shower for me too. "That this doesn't feel right." Cinder raised an eyebrow and Abigail corrected, "This shouldn't feel right."

"You mean good." Cinder was smug. "I'd even say amazing."

Not needing the extra heat, Abigail tugged her sweater over her head. The heat returned to her cheeks and to her stomach as Cinder admired his handy work spilling over her tank top from the previous night. He ran his tongue over his bottom lip.

"Stop," Abigail commanded his attention. "I'm serious. This—"

"What's the problem?" Cinder interrupted, rounding the kitchen island and standing in front of her. "We're two consenting adults who find each other attractive. Why *shouldn't* we?"

Abigail only had her same excuse from before. It was tactless and ineffective. "You're a villain and I'm a hero."

"I thought you were only a secretary?"

Abigail knitted her eyebrows together at the insult, and Cinder tossed his head back laughing. When he composed himself, he captured Abigail's face between his scarred hands. His cotton soft fingertips sent waves of sparks through her body.

"Don't talk about work then. We can still just be humans." Cinder's face turned devious hidden in the shadow of Abigail's. "Or animals, depending on your mood."

In her current mood, she wanted him. She wanted to leave her own bruises around his neck. She wanted to knock the towel off his hips. She wanted to worship him back at their altar.

So she did.

The cool night breeze roamed the apartment from the open patio door as it aired out the smell of burnt fabric and sweat. The bedroom was dark except the few candles flickering on the dresser. Abigail sat at the foot of the bed, thoroughly exhausted, wrapped in a bedsheet like it could protect her from anything in the room. She watched Cinder find his clothing from yesterday.

"I have this *business* trip to go on," he said while buttoning his jeans. "Could be a couple of days, or weeks."

"Doesn't sound like business."

"Because I'm lying." He looked at her over his shoulder, his eyes catching the candlelight and raging with the flame. "Do you want to know the truth?"

Abigail shook her head. "No work talk, remember?"

"You could come with me."

Abigail didn't know if he was joking. She didn't know if she seriously was considering the offer.

Cinder pulled his shirt over his head and grabbed his jacket from the floor. "Try not to miss me too much."

"What's there to miss?" Abigail sneered.

Cinder slid onto the porch but poked his head through the opening. "That's harsh coming from you, doll."

She waved him off. "Be good."

His rumbling laughter vanished when he shut the door. The apartment seemed a hundred times larger without him in it, and Abigail a hundred times more alone without him. Her bed still smelled strongly of a campfire.

Apparently, there was a lot to miss about a villain.

She tossed *his* pillow against the wall in frustration, unsure how she ended up here. Abigail was more upset about missing Cinder than ending up in bed with him. Again. The way his eyes scorched hers while alone was all the hint she needed that he desired her too. But, missing him and feeling his absence was something different.

"I'm only on an intelligence mission!" she shouted. She wasn't sure whom she was trying to convince; herself or her lies.

Abigail retrieved her own clothes and filled the empty space with the sounds of the television. Channel 9 was live on the scene somewhere on the north side of San Arbor. Abigail pulled the throw blanket around herself and watched the report. A break-in and robbery at a local jewelry store.

"The three suspects were apprehended four streets over when they ran into—" —the young reporter checked his notebook— "—the Round Table Knights whose jurisdiction begins six blocks to the south."

The scene faded from the young reporter to a grainy video of two people running down a street until they slammed into Excalibur's backside. Abigail watched as King Arthur's eyes glowed fluorescent purple and the criminals froze.

"The suspects were handed over to the police shortly after and are being transferred to the justice center. We have this statement from Round Table Knight, King Arthur."

The scene changed to a well-lit video of King Arthur speaking to a small crowd. A red cheeked Merlin stood behind him and uncharacteristically blew a kiss to someone off camera. "We didn't mean to interfere with the police, or Saves the Day," King Arthur said. "We were just in the right spot and took advantage of the opportunity. A hero's job is to serve their city, no matter what district they're in."

The scene flipped back to the news station interior, then they switched to the equally important weather report.

Chapter Twenty-One

Without Cinder's sporadic appearances in Abigail's life, it was easier for her to focus on other things than imagining him morphing out of the shadows on her patio. It was easier to plan her days without planning his midnight arrivals. It was easier for her to throw herself at work than to think of the work he was doing.

It was easier to burn training dummies at the Hero Relief Center than to admit she was actually missing him. A hero missing a villain, it was absolutely absurd.

And illegal.

Abigail shook her hands out at her sides, and red sparks fell to the training room floor. She did not miss a villain. That's not why she was worried and couldn't sleep dreamlessly since he left. She was only worried about the people that he might hurt during his *trip*. The laws he was breaking, the trouble he would be putting local police or heroes into.

Cinder was a villain and, probably, a nuisance to someone else right now.

Abigail turned another dummy to char.

She lined three dummies in a row and faced the simulated oncoming assault. Abigail sucked in enough air to overfill her lungs, the organs pressed against her ribs, and breathed out a cloud of blue fire. The drastic change of temperature, air-conditioned air to blazing heat, made her teeth ache. The goal was to catch all three targets on fire but only the first sizzled in a slow burn of blue.

Abigail cursed and tried again. Only hot breath shot through her teeth.

"Breathing fire?"

Excalibur stood in the doorway. His signature sword was at his hip. So was the blood red scabbard. The overhead lights bounced off the metal and reflected a bloody wound against the floor.

"Trying to," she answered his question. "It's a lot harder than I thought it'd be." Snapping it from her fingers had been so natural compared to this. Maybe the ability wore off faster as her tongue recycled its taste buds. Her stomach twisted thinking she may need another application from Cinder.

"Keep at it, I'm sure you'll get it."

Abigail appreciated his support but didn't want to focus on her current failure. "You're here early, sir."

"So are you." He entered the room and the door slid shut behind him. "Our training doesn't start for another forty minutes."

Abigail tapped her cheek. "Wanted to work on this a little before we started."

"I can't offer much advice on that," Excalibur admitted. "But I can teach you how to use this."

Excalibur untied the blood red scabbard from his hip and handed it to her. The blade felt lighter now compared to when she first pulled it off the rack at the weapons show.

"I thought you wanted to wait until I was stronger?" Abigail raised an eyebrow. She had only fought against wooden training swords when they practiced. Excalibur never actually let her wield one.

"I think it'll come in handy." Excalibur pulled his own sword from his side. "Plus, I saw it in Merlin's crystal ball."

Abigail grinned at her boss's joke and readied the sword, dropping the scabbard to the ground. She'd never used a weapon before, but how hard could swinging a sword be? She held it in front of her like a golfer in mid-swing. Her hands muddled together at the bottom of the hilt. "Where do we start?"

"Proper formation." He sheathed his blade and stepped beside her, hand reaching for her hands. "May I touch you?"

"Sure."

Excalibur removed her left hand from the hilt and pushed her remaining hand under the guard. "Your other hand is for blocking," he explained. "Only your thumb and pointer fingers will move the blade. The others are for support. Loose hold, heavy swing, got it?"

"I think so."

Next, Excalibur kicked her feet apart until her weight sat evenly between her hips. "All of your strength will come from your hips. A solid base will keep you stable and empower you."

"Got it." Abigail looked down at her feet and made a mental note where they were on the floor. "When do I hit something?"

He laughed. "We're not there yet."

By the end of the three-hour training session, Abigail was drenched in sweat. She hadn't swung the sword a single time and yet her limbs were jelly. They felt worse now than after any day of weight training. When Excalibur ended the session, Abigail collapsed onto the mat, panting. Holding the shallow squat with the sword extended over her head seemed like a joke when Excalibur had first shown her. As time passed the joke became less funny.

"Good work," Excalibur commented. He picked the scabbard off the ground and held it out to her. "Think you can do it again tomorrow?"

"Absolutely." Abigail promised even though her legs begged her not to.

Tomorrow turned into all week. Two hours before the Hero Relief Center opened turned into half of her actual shift. Formation turned to form, form turned to blocking, and blocking turned to attacking. By the end of the first week, Abigail was slaying practice dummies with precision. By the middle of the next week, Abigail was going toe to toe with Excalibur who let her complete a move against him before quickly defeating her. She grew sick of tasting the mat, and learned to dodge his trip attempt with a jump. She learned to block his heel kick to her stomach with a block that uprooted his weight, knocking him back. She learned to evade his powerful downward strike with a quick step back before striking against his sword arm.

By the end of the third week, Excalibur asked her to put on a demonstration for some of the marketing team. He said they were thinking of having him make a workout DVD and wanted to test his teaching abilities. Abigail hoped she wouldn't be cast in the DVD if it did happen. In her mind, she saw herself and Excalibur wearing neon leg warmers and sweat bands as they completed workouts to a funky soundtrack.

When the demonstration day arrived, Abigail did not expect King Arthur and Merlin waiting with HRC Marketing behind the viewing window.

Excalibur patted Abigail's shoulders inside the training room, his hulking form blocking out the window. "Just run your forms and make each swing count."

"You didn't say anything about *them* watching." Abigail peered around him to the viewing window.

"I'm sure they just wanted out of their own meetings," Excalibur said. "Just picture them in their underwear or something."

"I can't do that." Abigail also couldn't stop her cheeks from darkening at the idea of it.

"Then focus on me," Excalibur tried again. "Not in my underwear, I mean. You run your form all the time when I watch. Just think of that."

Abigail took a deep breath and gathered her courage and tried to ignore her sudden stage fright. She finally nodded to him, and Excalibur vanished behind the viewing window.

Abigail settled into her starting stance and moved through the forms. They looked more like dances when Excalibur had first shown her. A choreographed set of movements that showcased the most common attacks and blocks from her type of blade. A broadsword, he had explained during their first week, was designed so a commoner of war could fight without much injury to themselves with little practice. She landed her snap kicks, the contact of her foot against her hand echoing around the room. She kept her balance in the single leg thrusts. Dropped to the ground dodging an invisible attack and sprang up with lightning agility she hadn't possessed last year. She pictured an invisible target with each slice using the blade as an extension of herself.

She gave a bow at the end of the display. Excalibur beamed proudly at his protege. King Arthur applauded, and Merlin whispered something into his ear. They, and the others, were out of the room before Abigail could sheath her blade.

"Did they like it?" she asked when only Excalibur remained.

"I think so." Excalibur sounded sure, but he checked the observation window.

"Did I mess it up?"

Excalibur slapped her shoulder. "Of course not! You did it perfectly. Get changed and meet me upstairs."

"At the Round Table?" Abigail cocked her head. "I didn't know you had a meeting this morning."

Excalibur waved his hand. "It's another Round Table Knight photoshoot. I need you to get my good side."

"I'm sorry I missed the memo." Abigail thought she had been doing a good job at juggling her training and her duties as the hero's assistant. "Did I miss anything else this week?"

Excalibur laughed through the slits in his helmet. "This has been kept under the radar, don't feel bad. I doubt even Mitch knows about it."

"I'll be there in a minute," Abigail promised.

She folded her workout gear into a drawstring bag and stashed it under her desk after pulling on her business casual costume. It was getting easier to find clothes that matched. It made her feel more like a professional. Sucking in a breath, she reminded herself she wouldn't be an assistant forever. She grabbed the camera from her desk and rode the elevator to the next floor.

The air was electric when she stepped into the Round Table. King Arthur and Merlin were waiting with Excalibur and the president of the HRC. They were laughing; an open bottle of champagne was poured into five glasses on the table. It wasn't uncommon for alcoholic companies to want to sponsor heroes. It was uncommon for a champagne marketing ad to be shot at ten in the morning.

Abigail hadn't seen President Samuels in person yet, and promptly straightened her posture before he could look her way. He was a handsome man, older than her and the Knights, and wore a fitted navy suit. He looked more like a high-end lawyer than the president of a hero company. Although, Kreech hadn't looked like a president either.

"Um, sir?" Abigail cleared her throat. When Excalibur looked at her, she raised the camera ready to take whatever photo they needed.

"Put that camera down and come over here."

She walked to the group and Excalibur hooked an arm around her neck, pulling her into their circle.

"You're scaring the poor girl, 'Xcal." King Arthur slapped his fellow hero's arm and the knight released her. Excalibur was the only one of them in his hero costume.

"Sir?" Abigail glanced around them. "What's going on?"

Excalibur took the camera from Abigail's hand and replaced it with the fifth glass of champagne. "Today's the day, Abby. That display you did? It was your audition."

"Audition?"

"For a sidekick!"

Abigail's jaw dropped. It made Excalibur laugh. He used the soft side of his glove to push her bottom jaw back into place.

"Sir? Are you serious?"

"Deadly," King Arthur answered. "'Xcal told us about your history. I thought you looked familiar when you tried running into that gun store. We've gone over Inferna's file and admire the work you've done on the inside of our company. Excalibur has spoken nothing but the highest words about your training. Seeing you in action today makes me confident to have you at our side."

"Well, my side," Excalibur corrected. "You'd be working directly under me."

"I don't know what to say." Abigail's mouth was dry, her heart was speeding. "This is more than I could have ever asked for."

"Will you serve with us, Squire Abigail?" King Arthur asked.

"Yes!"

"One thing." Merlin paused the celebration. Abigail's heart also stopped, the floor about to be ripped from under her. This had all been a joke, a cruel and impractical joke. "Magic is my thing; your flames look pretty magical."

"That's why we've been training with the sword," Excalibur chimed in, and Abigail's heart restarted. "We'll match better this way too, let everyone know exactly where you stand."

"Can I light it?" Abigail asked, referring to the sword.

"A flaming swordsman," the president mused.

"I think that would be acceptable," King Arthur answered for Merlin, whose silence was her only acceptance.

Excalibur knocked his glass against Abigail's. "What do you say? Are you ready for a comeback?"

"Yes, sir."

"Then let's celebrate!"

The bubbly drink didn't help the bubbles already popping from the excitement in Abigail's stomach. The president pulled Abigail away from Excalibur before they could pour a second round of drinks.

"Monday we will go through all the paperwork, and get you fitted for a new costume." He was official even with the champagne flute in his hands. "Unfortunately, your last one is still under copyright with Saves the Day. They wouldn't release Inferna to us. You should bring some ideas of what you'd like to wear, but keep our theme in mind, okay?"

"You talked to Saves the Day?"

President Samuels nodded with a smile. "Of course. Volcanic said some very kind things about your time with him. I think he's a little jealous that we have you now."

Abigail dropped her gaze. "I didn't know how he felt about me anymore."

"Whatever happened at Saves the Day, it sounded like he didn't approve of it." The president took a sip of his drink. "When you were let go, I called to get you on our staff, but they wouldn't release any information. How ironic you found your own way to us? I'm glad to have you on our team and at the perfect time, too."

"What do you mean?"

President Samuels looked past Abigail to the other Knights. "Everyone, I have an update from town hall." The room instantly quieted, and the electrified feeling multiplied. "San Arbor Ordinance Seven Fifty-Nine was passed this morning."

Excalibur reacted first. His *yes* morphed into an excited howl.

"Well done, Quinn." King Arthur congratulated the president with a slap against his shoulder. Champagne dripped onto the floor.

"We didn't have any doubt," Merlin said.

"What's the ordinance?" Abigail asked.

King Arthur answered, "It's what we've been fighting for all along. Patrolling licenses."

"We won't be on-call heroes anymore," Excalibur said. "We'll be able to patrol the city and take care of things in real time."

"There will still be limitations," President Samuels reminded his knights. "There can't be any excessive force to criminals. Or the city. We're entering a six-month testing period, so you all need to be extra careful until this gets fully off the ground. Understand?"

All four Round Table Knights nodded.

"Good, and Abigail?"

"Yes, Mr. Samuels?"

"I hate to ask for you to continue a few of your assistant duties, but please keep an eye on Excalibur tonight."

"Tonight?"

"Hey, Abigail!" Excalibur called from the huddle he formed with King Arthur and Merlin. "We're getting hibachi after work to celebrate, you're coming right?"

"Of course!" Abigail replied, and then to President Samuels, "I'll keep him in line."

Three of the larger-than-life heroes in her city and Abigail was part of them. She had joined their ranks on her own. Not because of a bad deal to better a selfish hero. She was back and this felt like a place where she could thrive.

"I know I said I'd keep your secret, and I'm sorry for telling King and Merlin," Excalibur told her seriously when they exited The Round Table. "I want to show you mine so that we're even."

"What do you mean?"

Excalibur pulled his helmet off. Beneath the hardened steel was the face of someone too soft to wear armor all day. The true face of Excalibur was kind, freckled, and younger than she expected.

"Sir..."

"You'll have to call me a real name tonight." Excalibur smiled. "We're not going out as heroes. Call me Aaron."

"Aaron." Abigail tested the name.

Chapter Twenty-Two

The restaurant was warm, a temperature increase due to eight active grill tops. Chefs entertained customers at each station by flipping food, throwing knives, lighting fires, and squirting shots of rice liquor directly into the mouths of patrons. Every station was having their own celebration: birthday parties, second dates, the release from a week at work, anniversaries, but the most excited group was at table eight who had their second round of beer delivered before their main course was scooped from the sizzling grill top.

The original Round Table Knights felt lifted with the new ordinance taking effect in the next few days. The three of them hadn't been able to stop talking about it. King Arthur had already divided the city into patrol routes. Merlin pointed at the various structures they passed naming off useful elements she could pull into her spells. They'd been the stray dogs of the police force for too long, chained in the side yard until an intruder too dangerous for the police entered the house. They could finally do the job they were built for.

The red tape had finally been pushed aside.

Excalibur lifted his newly filled mug to his comrades. It was still a shock to see him in a T-shirt and jeans, rather than his full suit of armor. Abigail gave him enough double takes in one evening to give her neck a cramp for a week. "I can't get over this! Quinn really did it!"

King Arthur tapped his mug against Excalibur's first. "I told you not to doubt him."

"Like you didn't?" Merlin raised an eyebrow higher than her glass. She told Abigail to call her Mabel while they were in their civilian clothes. Abigail didn't know if she had shared her real name or not. Mabel sounded too soft to belong to such a fierce woman.

"I just got impatient." King Arthur's joyousness didn't falter.

The chef set a large plate of steaming rice, vegetables and steak on the table between them. Excalibur piled a large spoonful on each of their plates. Abigail broke her chopsticks apart and took a bite as the others waited for the food to cool. She didn't feel the burn against her black tongue.

"Let's not forget our other reason to celebrate." Excalibur winked at Abigail. "Congratulations again, Abby."

"I actually prefer Abigail," she said, her *sake* shots giving her extra confidence. "But thank you. And thank you for giving me this chance."

"Just don't get any of us killed," Merlin warned as she blew steam off the chuck of steak stabbed through her fork. "Aaron can be replaced, the meathead, but Arthur and I can't."

Excalibur laughed at her. "I trust Abigail."

She smiled across the table at him, and then asked King Arthur, "How long has President Samuels been working with town hall?"

"With the ordinance, you mean? Quinn drafted the idea almost two years ago, and it's been on the floor for about eight months. There were a lot of people who opposed it."

"Just because of safety?" Even when first responders asked for a hero's help, there were a lot of restrictions and hoops to jump through.

"Because people hate change," Merlin said simply.

"And because people don't want to feel helpless." King Arthur didn't deny Merlin's sentiment. "If it looks like only heroes can stop crime then a new type of fear would be created. I bet Quinn will want us to work closely with the first responders for the first few months. Make sure the media shows us in equal light."

"You're going to hate that." Excalibur reached across the table for the bottle of soy sauce.

"I won't be the problem. If there is one." King Arthur quickly turned to Abigail, his tone very similar to when the chief of police came to the hospital: overly sweet and toxic. "Give any thought to your new identity?"

"I have," Excalibur said with a sheepish smile. "Pendragon."

The others cocked their head at him.

"Because of the fire breath?"

"Fire breath?" King Arthur looked at Abigail, who blushed under his gaze.

"It's really new. I don't have the best control over it yet. I actually planned to read through the legends of Camelot this weekend to get some inspiration for names."

"Sounds like a boring weekend." Merlin stabbed another piece of meat.

"Don't mind her," Excalibur whispered to Abigail. "She can be as much of a grouch as Mitch sometimes."

Merlin kicked him under the table.

Several hours and bars later, Abigail stumbled back to her apartment. The Round Table Knights were surprisingly human under their masks. They were even bad at karaoke. But their alcohol tolerance was still super. If any future battle required a drinking contest, Abigail didn't think she'd be a good sidekick to Excalibur. He sucked down four shots himself after winning the round robin tournament of darts.

Abigail dropped her keys three times before successfully getting her apartment door unlocked. Her kitchen light was on. The yellow glow of the room was too bright, and she slapped her hand against the wall until she found the switch and returned the room to darkness.

The light in her bedroom flipped on in response.

"Hey!" Abigail tried to shout, but it came out in a wave of slurs. She ignited her fingertips and slowly moved toward her room to investigate. She didn't think she'd be so careless to leave two lights on all day. The flames on her fingers were stolen the moment she stepped into her room. They were absorbed into the hand that grabbed her wrist and pulled her close. "Cinder."

"I was wondering where you were." He tilted his head down to kiss the surprised look off her face. "Whiskey? I would have pegged you for a vodka girl."

Abigail liked watching how his lips moved to form words. "Vodka makes me sick."

Cinder released her hand to grab her hip to keep her from swaying. "I think you had enough to do that already, doll. Where were you?"

"Celebrating." Abigail raised on her tiptoes to try and kiss him again, but he dodged her affection and she pouted. She frowned deeper when he laughed.

"What were you celebrating?"

Her frown vanished as her one-track mind focused back on her achievement. "I did it! I'm a sidekick again!"

Cinder squeezed her hips and it focused her attention back on him. "I'm proud of you."

"Want to celebrate with me?" She wiggled her eyebrows.

"Only someone truly evil would take advantage of a woman like this."

"But I missed you."

"And I told you not to do that." Cinder pressed his lips against her forehead. "Let's get you to bed."

"With you?"

"You're making this very, very difficult." Cinder laughed under his breath.

He lifted Abigail over his shoulder like a bag of potatoes and tossed her lightly on the bed. He had her shoes off before she could protest and was throwing a T-shirt at her before she was able to sit back up.

"Put this on," he told her. "I'm going to get you a glass of water."

Abigail stripped off her office wear but did not put on her pajamas. She laid on the bed waiting for Cinder to return. She couldn't believe she forgot what he looked like. Her memories faded his beauty. They had dulled the brightness of his eyes, the darkness of his smile. Her apartment was absorbing his campfire smell again. She breathed in deeply, the bedsheets around her as soft as his fingers. Although he had only been away a couple of weeks, her clouded mind made it seem like years.

Cinder didn't react to Abigail's lack of clothes when he returned. He set the glass of water on the nightstand and tugged a blanket over her. She pouted again, her bottom lip puckered out and eyes pulled together. She was making this *very* difficult for the Flame Villain.

He leaned in and planted a quick kiss against her cheek and hooked his finger around the necklace she wore. The small diamond was bright in contrast to his dirty finger.

"I like this," Cinder admitted.

"You can have it." Abigail tried to sound coy, but her requirement was slurred. "For a secret."

Cinder whispered in her ear, "I'm going to burn this city to the ground."

"What?"

Cinder pinched the necklace chain and melted a link of the metal. The small diamond pendant fell in his hands and he slipped it into his pocket.

"Go to bed," he told her.

Abigail's head throbbed when she rolled over and checked the time the next morning. It was a few minutes after eight. Her mouth was dry, and she drank half the glass of water sitting on the nightstand. She didn't remember bringing it to her room last night; she didn't remember getting home last night either. Her stomach spun as she remembered the last drink she had. It was a shot with Merlin. The bartender set it on fire right before they drank it. She rolled back over, the soft light from the patio too painful to look at.

She also remembered she was a sidekick again, and the thought soothed her hangover. She warranted the coming three hours of extra sleep as part of the promotion, and when she woke up again, she felt more alive and willing to start her Saturday. A hot shower dissolved the remainder of her sick feelings. Her skin absorbed the water like a plant left too long on a windowsill. She'd walked away from fires in better shape than she had walked away from the Round Table Knights. She might need to add some new training topics to her list.

She didn't think the Hero Relief Center would open a stocked bar in one of the training rooms, though.

Abigail stepped into the living room and froze. She didn't expect to see Cinder laying on her couch, fighting off the mid-morning sunlight with an arm extended across his face. He was too long for the couch. One leg hung off the armrest while the second was on the ground. It looked uncomfortable. He shifted to look at her.

"I thought I dreamt of you," Abigail admitted, finally able to say something.

"I only stayed to make sure you didn't choke on your vomit," he said.

"I'm alive, so good job." Her curt response matched his defensive tone. She left him on the couch and hid unsuccessfully behind the kitchen counter. She pulled eggs and milk from the fridge and a large bowl from the cupboard. She wasn't sure why, but she asked, "Hungry?"

Cinder didn't answer her, but he did peel himself off the couch and sat at the island across her chef station. He watched her beat eggs, milk and spices together before dredging bread through the mixture and cooking it on a hot skillet. Abigail managed the kitchen like she was blindfolded, reaching for items and ingredients around her without looking. When there was food in the apartment, she knew a few tricks to make it a meal. The transition from plain bread to French toast was seamless. She set a plate in front of him and offered him a choice of syrup and powdered sugar.

"I didn't know you cooked." He took the syrup.

"Just a few things," she mused, creating her own plate. "I'm better with dinners."

Cinder's response was lost as he tried to speak through a mouthful. Abigail poured them both a glass of apple juice.

"How was your trip?"

"Boring." Cinder swallowed his bite.

"What did you do?" Abigail's curiosity got the better of her, and the question flew out before she could stop it.

"We don't talk about work, remember?" Cinder took another bite and smirked. "You're a hero now?"

"Sidekick," Abigail corrected, then glared at him. She had broken their only rule twice and hadn't even finished breakfast.

"When do you start?"

"No work."

Cinder grinned and devoured his final bite. "How's your training?"

Abigail eyed him and continued eating.

"Come on, that's not work. We do that together."

Giving in, Abigail answered, "I'm learning how to use a sword."

"Going to cut the bad guys in half?"

"If I have to," she warned.

Cinder tapped his cheek. "How's this going?"

"Slowly," she admitted. "I can only breathe out a little puff and then it's gone."

"Does this new job give you days off?"

"I should have the weekend after next off," Abigail answered slowly. "Why?"

He twisted his fork between his fingers and eyed the syrup that dripped back to the plate. "I want to take you somewhere." Abigail's own fork threatened to fall, and he added, "Somewhere to practice your fire breath, calm down. I'm not going to murder you in the woods or anything."

"Why isn't here okay?"

"Oh yeah, the tightly populated city will be great for testing out a new power."

Abigail glowered at him, and he smiled. It was half taunting, half amused, and all sexy. It hung crookedly on his face like he held the fork crookedly in his scarred hand.

"Bring a coat." Cinder took her silence as a yes. "It can get pretty cold on the mountainside."

Chapter Twenty-Three

Abigail compared two pairs of hiking boots in the shoe section of an outdoor store later that week. She had never been camping, let alone exploring some cold mountainside, to have the proper materials on hand. She didn't know what to expect with Cinder's training field trip. So far, her cart had a large weather-resistant backpack, cold weather tent and sleeping bag, thermal under garments, a box of power bars and a water bottle guaranteeing its contents wouldn't freeze.

Once she added the boots, her promotion bonus would be halfway depleted. She settled on the cheaper pair and headed to the cashier station.

Abigail knew she should have declined Cinder's request. Going anywhere with a villain was careless and reckless. Especially one as powerful as the Flame Villain. But Abigail couldn't stop the butterflies that swarmed in her stomach whenever she thought about it. Going away where they wouldn't be interrupted by their erratic *work* schedules, or the fear of being caught together.

She knew this was no longer a self-assigned intelligence mission. She had gathered no useful information on him since accepting their deal. The worst part was she was okay with it. She doubted she'd use any information she'd gather against him anyway.

Abigail tried to rationalize her feelings for the hundredth time that day by reminding herself that since Cinder had reappeared there hadn't been any arson attacks. The rise in petty crime wasn't connected to him since the criminals at the scene were caught. Whatever brought him to San Arbor may not have anything to do with his background. Perhaps that meant he had changed, turned over a new, a good, leaf. Excalibur's words from the hospital fundraising event bubbled into her mind: A crook doesn't turn good overnight.

But it's been months! Abigail chased away her doubt, even though it had good reason to be there. *And, he hasn't tried to hurt me or anyone else.*

Henry met her outside the apartment building when she stepped off the bus carrying the three big bags from her shopping adventure. He grabbed two of them and carried them to the elevator.

"Thanks, Hen," Abigail said.

"Looks like a busy day, Miss Turner." Henry smiled.

"I'm going camping this weekend." She figured she should tell someone before she left. She would have told him the camping site if she knew it. Just in case.

"That sounds fun. I used to camp on a lake when I was little. My dad took me every year. I tried taking my girls there too, but once they started doing their hair and make up the water sports weren't any-more." Henry paused with a chuckle, then pulled a notecard from his shirt pocket. "This was left for you while you were out."

Abigail crammed the paper inside one of her bags. "Thanks, Henry. Have a great evening, okay?"

"You too," the doorman said while she stepped onto the elevator. "And, have fun on your trip."

When Abigail arrived at her apartment, she dumped out the bags and found the notecard next to the power bars. It was the same heavy cardstock and the same black ink as every note before it.

Jolt Station. Friday. 7:45 train.

Abigail hadn't seen Cinder since he left Saturday after breakfast. Now, she didn't think she'd see him until their departure on Friday. Her stomach twisted from the realization, and she told herself it was from not knowing what he was getting into. Even if she wanted to believe he wasn't doing anything criminal, she knew better than to be that naïve.

The same internal battle raged. Her merit as a crime fighter was being tarnished for not hunting down this villain. But, was it really if no one knew? She justified that taking him away from the city for a weekend was civil work. Her stomach twisted again at the thought of being away with him for a weekend. This twist made her blush.

"To train," she said aloud to her apartment to convince the walls, and herself, of their task. She huffed out a small breath of blue sparks, it was the most fire breathing she was able to accomplish right now. "I need to master this before my debut."

To keep her mind off the Flame Villain, she grabbed a wooden broadsword she borrowed from Excalibur and ran through her sword training forms until she could justify going to bed.

Her things for the weekend were packed and waiting by the front door.

Being San Arbor's only train depot, Jolt Station accepted and launched over two hundred trains a day. There were eighteen trains leaving at 7:45 that Friday. Standing at the top of the stairs looking into the station, she didn't think she'd find Cinder before the trains left. The other waiting passengers moved like mice, quickly and numerous.

But then she saw him.

Cinder's face was hidden under the hood of a fur-lined coat. His hands were hidden inside the pockets. His body was hidden inside the shadows of a concrete pillar. He was unnoticeable to the crowd, purposely ignored by the pedestrians who could feel the danger rolling off him. Abigail noticed him by the lean in his body against the stone, the same confidence she'd seen at the downtown attack, the construction site, her bedroom. The danger that rolled off him pulled her close like shadowy tendrils locking around her ankles.

"Hey." Abigail adjusted her backpack straps when she approached him.

Cinder's eyes glowed in the darkness while he looked her over. He twisted one of the braids that draped on her shoulder. "Cute."

She blushed. "You don't have any supplies."

Cinder shrugged. "Everything I need is already there."

"Where is *there* anyway?"

"A secret." Cinder linked an arm through Abigail's and pulled himself out of the shadow toward a train platform.

The moving crowd of mice parted for the pair of walking lions.

They boarded the train, Cinder keeping his head low as he handed over their two tickets. He selected a row of seats at the back of the car, and Abigail stored her backpack on the rack above them. Their train car shuddered as the car ahead lurched forward and pulled the train down the track.

"How long's the train ride?" Abigail asked when the train was out of the tunnel. The city buildings passed the windows in a blur streaked dark blue and white lights.

"Couple hours. Better get comfortable."

"What kind of place is it?" Abigail asked. "How mountainous are we talking?"

Cinder sighed with a smile and looked from the window to her. "Curiosity killed the cat, doll."

"You promised you wouldn't kill me up there."

"And you'd trust me? A villain?"

Abigail didn't answer him. She shoved her shoulder against him and remained against his side while the city vanished behind them. Cinder leaned against the window using his fluffy hood as a pillow. An hour later, Abigail left and returned with an arm full of snacks and two cans of soda. Cinder plucked the mini bag of chips from her collection and stretched his legs into the seat across from them.

Conversations from the other passengers filled the train car with quiet words and muffled confessions. The sounds fell around Abigail like snow, adding to the easy silence between herself and Cinder. Abigail finished her package of fruit gummies and listened to the rumble of the train, felt the rise and fall of Cinder's chest, and soaked in the warmth their bodies produced. Abigail hadn't felt this relaxed in a long time, and it was the result of a villain.

Her mind wasn't planning the next four steps ahead to become a hero. Her body wasn't running itself into the ground to become stronger. She wasn't worried about the media when she would be announced as Excalibur's sidekick next week. She wasn't thinking about the dirty dishes in her sink, the noisy construction down the street from her apartment, or the three request forms to switch her natural gas provider.

Abigail didn't realize she fell asleep.

Three hours later, the train car settled into the lowered platform of another station and hissed. Cinder shook Abigail awake as the other passengers moved to the exits. Her backpack was slung over his shoulder.

"Are we here?" Abigail yawned, blinking his face into focus.

"Not yet," Cinder answered, pulling her from the seat. "Halfway."

Abigail's eyes widened. "A layover?"

Cinder shook his head and pulled her into the aisle toward the open door. "Changing vehicles."

Outside the train, a cold breeze stripped away the warmth her body retained while she slept. Abigail swore her bones began to shake. She didn't think she was able to get cold, but she didn't think she'd been this far north of the city before. She allowed her hands to spark twice to keep them from turning blue. The outdoor station was covered in an inch of snow, and icicles dripped off the roof. The dark sky was endless above them, the only light was the warm fire glow burning inside old-fashioned lanterns.

"How far north are we?" Abigail spun around, absorbing the area. She swore the train took them through time as well as miles.

"Not far enough." Cinder was waiting just inside the station door. "It'll be worth it, I promise."

"And I'm just supposed to trust you?"

"Nothing's stopped you so far."

A bus line was across the station, and four busses were waiting as people climbed inside their metal husks. Thick forest green trees surrounded the station, and a diner sat at the dead end of the loop.

Cinder slipped a twenty dollar bill into Abigail's hand. "Grab us some burgers. I'll get our bus tickets."

Abigail clutched her hand around the money, it had probably been stolen. She swallowed the thought down and walked to the diner. Faded orange and white tiles covered the floor, and the restaurant smelled like pie. An "oldies" station played on the radio, and it made her want to tap her foot. Besides three older diners, the restaurant was empty. She walked to the counter and waited to place her order.

"Hey, can I get two burgers? To go, please."

"Garden? Cheese? Sauce?"

Abigail stared at the young man across the counter like he had spoken in an ancient language.

"Ma'am?"

"I don't know."

"You don't know how you like your burgers?" he stifled a laugh.

"I know how I like mine, it's just my friend's," Abigail admitted.

"I can make it plain," he offered.

"Can you put the extras in a box?" she asked.

The man did laugh this time. "Sure."

With a grease-stained bag of burgers, and a terrible reminder that Abigail knew next to nothing about her "friend," she returned to the bus line and found Cinder lingering in the lamplight uncaring if people saw his face here. His black hair was dusted in snow. He shook it out at her approach. The bus driver ripped their tickets in two when they got on; like before, Cinder chose the seats furthest back. The bus pulled onto the snowy highway and started their altitude increasing journey.

Cinder rummaged through the greasy bag once the overhead lights flicked off and peeked inside the Styrofoam box. He wrinkled his nose when all he saw were vegetables. He returned it to the bag and claimed the fully dressed burger for himself.

"I didn't know how you liked yours." Abigail felt embarrassed.

"I'm not picky when it comes to food."

"What are you picky with?"

Cinder stared at her from the corner of his eye and took a large bite of the burger. His green eyes absorbed the remaining light, shining like precious gems.

"Come on," Abigail pleaded, her voice a whisper in the dim light around them. "I don't know anything about you."

"That's the point. I'm a stranger to you."

"You can't believe that," she protested. "We're taking a trip together and—"

"I'm training you."

"I know my other trainer's real name." She knew it was a low blow. She also knew it was a lie. She stared him down until he answered.

Cinder took another bite, chewed, and swallowed. "I like snow, it's why I come up here."

"You've been here before?"

"A lot of times." Cinder looked away from the window and pinned Abigail with his eyes. "You're the first girl I brought, though, count your blessings."

Abigail rolled her eyes but smiled as she nibbled on a fry. The bus rumbled forward.

As the bus climbed higher on the mountain, the road became more snow covered. When the bus slid on a turn and bumped the guardrail, the driver pulled over and applied chains to the tires. With the extra grip, the rest of the trip was smooth. Streetlights popped up in the darkness, shining through the evergreen trees, revealing a mountain peak looming over them. The bus seemed to sigh when it arrived at its destination: a small village at the base of the mountain, protected by the winter winds by a wall of coniferous trees.

"Last leg of the journey," Cinder said as Abigail did toe touches outside the bus. It was a shorter ride than the train, but far less comfortable.

"By dog sled this time?"

Cinder laughed once at her joke. "Car."

There were just a few cars in the parking lot unsupervised. Cinder walked to the only one not parked under a light post.

"We can't steal a car!" Abigail whispered as she chased after him.

"We *aren't* stealing a car."

Abigail ran the final steps between them and grabbed onto his fist before he could bust through the window. Cinder stopped and opened his hand. Abigail felt the shape of the car key bite into her palm. The cold metal hurt as much as her embarrassment.

"It's my car." Cinder clicked the button and the car's light flashed as it unlocked.

"It looks like it hasn't been touched in months." Abigail ran her fingers over the hood, making a streak in the layer of snow.

"It's been a while," Cinder agreed, creating a small flame to melt the snow off the windshield.

He drove the final twenty minutes on backroads that were treacherous at best. The thin layer of snow that blanketed the well traversed village turned into half a foot once they left the glow of streetlights. It piled at least three feet high on the road's shoulders. Abigail gripped the handle on the ceiling hard enough to turn her knuckles white. She wished these tires had metal chains too. She wished she had opted to walk there. When the mountain road did finally plateau, a log cabin was nestled at the end of a driveway between dense forest trees.

It was the only house she had seen on the car ride. The lower floor windows were filled with light.

"Is someone else here?"

"Afraid to share?" Cinder smirked.

"Making sure this isn't your evil lair."

"I had someone come in earlier to turn the heat up," Cinder explained, turning off the engine. The cold temperature outside quickly claimed the car's interior. "They must have left the lights on."

Abigail grabbed her backpack from the back seat and followed Cinder to the front door. He used the other key attached to the car keyring to unlock it, and let them in. The cabin was much larger on the inside than its humble outward appearance. The ceiling was pitched high above the open layout of the living room and kitchen. One wall was made entirely of windows, overlooking the snow-covered forest. It was furnished in simple decor that looked like it was made of the lumber outside.

The first thing Abigail noticed was the lack of photographs. Or the missing photographs. Slats of sun-stained wood remained where a 4x6 picture frame used to sit, and paled squares marked wall spaces where more photos could have hung. The second thing she noticed was the engraved lines going up the length of the door frame marked with years and initials.

The tallest line, coming up to Abigail's shoulder, was marked with a T and was apparently inscribed over ten years ago. She ran her finger across the line.

"What is this place?" she asked.

"My evil lair," Cinder answered from the kitchen.

Abigail left the door frame and joined Cinder. He unloaded a collection of grocery bags on the counter. There were enough canned and boxed foods to last a week, fresher foods were already stashed inside the fridge.

"You live here?"

"I vacation here," Cinder corrected. "It's nice to get away from everything for a while."

"I thought that was your business trip?"

"This is because of that trip," Cinder muttered. "You said you were good at dinners, yeah? Want to make a deal?"

"What kind of deal?" Abigail allowed the conversation to change.

"You make me dinner tonight, and I make you breakfast in the morning."

"I thought we were here to train." She lifted an eyebrow.

"Tomorrow," he informed. "Tonight, I wanted to do something else."

Abigail wished there wasn't a counter between them as Cinder's eyes burned into hers. They were finally alone after an evening of public transportation. It was the longest time they had been around each other without touching; combat or sex. Hunger pains began to gnaw at Abigail. "What're you hungry for?"

Cinder didn't remove his eyes from hers as he tapped the fridge with his boot. "Why don't you see what's available."

Abigail had watched him unload the delivered grocery bags. She knew everything fresh that had been stored in the fridge. She could easily make spaghetti and meatballs, there was chicken for a casserole, enough colorful peppers for a bed under sausages, but she rounded the counter to check anyway.

She'd use any excuse to get closer to him.

The space was thin between him and the counter, and Abigail enjoyed the contact it forced their bodies to have. She stayed pinned between Cinder and the counter and grabbed either side of his winter coat, the cold zipper biting into her fingers. She pulled him closer so she could kiss him.

So she could kiss him irresponsibly without fear of someone finding out. She kissed him like a lover would. Like someone who missed him would.

Cinder kissed her back with a force he no longer tried to hold back. He shoved her up onto the counter and dug his hands into her hips in fear that she might disappear down the kitchen sink. They didn't need the white bedroom sheets to be their altar. The counter, the couch, the bed in the loft were all holy ground.

With the lights turned off, the inside of the cabin glowed from the moonlight reflecting against the snow. Everything looked frozen under that light, frozen to the core and frozen in time. Abigail watched the snowflakes drift between the tree branches from the loft where she lay in bed. Dinner was left half eaten downstairs, along with their clothing.

She didn't even try to figure out how she ended up here. Just like falling asleep on the train, she felt safe here.

She felt safe locked in a snowy cabin with the Flame Villain who had once scarred her neck in the shape of his hand. Now that hand was tracing shapes on her bare back. She rolled over and captured his hand with hers.

"What made you become a..."

"A villain?" Cinder filled in.

"I wasn't going to say that."

"Yes, you were." Cinder didn't sound upset by her question. "It's just what life made me."

Abigail didn't know what to say. She didn't know what answer she was expecting to get.

"What made you become a hero?"

"I wanted to save people," she answered automatically.

"I think I just wanted to save myself."

Cinder wrapped his scarred arms around Abigail and pulled their bodies together. They couldn't be further from their lives left in the city while locked away in a snowy cabin on a mountainside. Laying in this bed was the most human they could be, and Abigail was content to fall asleep to the rise and fall of Cinder's breathing.

"Were you scared when you got your powers?"

Cinder's question interrupted Abigail's forming dream of snow-flakes falling around a koi pond. Powers were tricky. Most followed a family tree back four generations ago when the supernatural abilities began. The only answer scientists could give the worried population was adaptation; humans were constantly evolving and this evolution gave birth to real world superheroes.

"I wasn't scared. I wanted to be a hero for so long, I thought it was a gift. I was eight, I think."

"You wanted to save people when you were eight?"

"Younger." Abigail smiled. "A hero saved me when I was little. The school bus I was on was going to run off a bridge, and she caught the bus and rescued us. It was so cool. I thought she was the coolest and wanted to be just like her."

Cinder chuckled. It fell into the dark loft as the snow fell outside. "Leave it to a hero-wannabe to be excited by a bus crash."

Abigail gently kicked him under the comforter. "I spent the next three weeks going to school in a cape made out of a bath towel. Were you scared? When you got yours?"

"I was terrified."

Abigail opened her eyes and stared at him. "I find that hard to believe. You use your flames like you've had them all your life."

"I had a good teacher."

"Who?"

"Doesn't matter." Cinder pulled Abigail tighter against him, his chin resting atop her head. "You're going to make a better hero."

More snow fell as the hero and villain fell asleep wrapped in each other's arms.

Chapter Twenty-Four

Abigail awoke the next morning to the smell of grease cooking in the kitchen below. She heard the sizzling of what she presumed was bacon, and the smell intensified. It made her mouth water and pulled her tired body from the bed. The cool air bit into her bare flesh and forced her to return to the fur blankets.

All her clothes were left downstairs. Draped over chairs, laying on the floor, lost under the couch. The thought of searching for them naked on hands and knees did not sit well with her. But, the thought and smell of breakfast made her inch closer to the edge of the bed. She saved lives on a regular basis. Surely she could find a way downstairs.

Her salvation came in the form of a red hoodie hanging on a hook on the wall. She assumed it was Cinder's from the way it smelled of a fire pit and dangled past her knees and hands. New Haines High School was stitched into the front, along with a pair of crossing lacrosse sticks. Her feet slapped against the wooden steps on her way to the main level of the cabin.

Cinder was making bacon at the stove. A grey turtleneck protected him from any grease splatters. He looked too domestic, and it made Abigail absorb the image. He flipped the bacon over with a fork and his fingers, wiping them against his pant leg once completed. He hummed to himself unaware of his audience.

"Morning." Abigail took a seat at the kitchen counter.

"Stealing things are you?" Cinder teased.

Abigail slid her hands into the pockets of the sweatshirt. "I'll give it back."

Cinder chuckled and continued to cook. It was a simple breakfast. Bacon, eggs, and toast that he cooked in seconds using his hands instead of the toaster. He made the plates hastily, piling the food on top of each other and spilling coffee on the counter when he poured it into two mugs. He slid a plate in front of Abigail, set a hand towel on the spilled coffee and sat next to her. Their knees bumped together under the countertop.

"This is weird." Abigail finally admitted halfway through breakfast.

"How?"

"It just feels so…"

"Normal?" Cinder supplied.

"Yeah." She took a sip of the coffee. Her mug had a faded image of a family of cats under a Christmas tree. "Wait no, bizarre. Like, an episode of *The Twilight Zone*."

"I can terrorize the village if that'll make you feel better."

Abigail didn't know if he was joking. "I'll ask you *not* to do that."

Cinder drank from his own mug. His looked like a souvenir from a zoo or animal park. "Mindless crime isn't really my thing, anyway."

"What is your thing?"

Cinder surprised her by giving a serious answer. "I like my crimes to be a bit more organized, they need to have a bigger picture than just stealing money."

"Or setting fires."

"I've only done that a few times," he defended himself.

"Is that what you were doing at the attack downtown?" That incident felt like a lifetime ago instead of a couple of months. Enough things had changed to fill a lifetime.

"I wasn't involved with that, honest." Cinder's willingness to talk kept surprising her. "I was just watching."

"Why did you run?"

"Why did you chase after me?" He raised an eyebrow. "Did I look that suspicious?"

"I had my assumptions."

"You only saw a villain and needed to stop me, right?" He was amused. Abigail could tell by the way half his mouth hooked up in a smile.

"I knew your history." It was a lie. Abigail knew next to nothing about him. Only that he had put that scar on her neck. The first thing to ever burn her. "I knew you were dangerous."

Cinder leaned in close. "What do you know now?"

"That you're still dangerous."

"Think that will change?"

"I have my doubts."

"So do I." Cinder leaned back and covered his mouth with his mug.

"What does that mean?"

"Get dressed, I want to see that dragon breath in action." Abigail hesitated and he added, "Unless you want to go into the snow like that."

The painful thought of landing in the snow without pants motivated her off the chair and to her backpack left by the front door.

The most wonderful thing about breathing fire was the range. Abigail had been a melee fighter her whole career. She could never sling her flames, or get them off her body. If she wanted to burn something she had to touch it. Not anymore. The blue flames flew from her mouth to the target ten, fifteen, twenty feet away. The best thing was it didn't hurt. Her scorched tongue protected her mouth from the heat, her lips seemingly immune to the blaze.

Cinder gave his own lips the credit for that.

Abigail practiced for hours in the snow. Her aim became pinpoint, the breath could be thin as a string or explosive as a bomb. Cinder pulled the fire into his hands once it connected with the targets. All that remained was the melted snow and the smoke coming from Abigail's mouth. She felt invincible.

Finally, she wielded the elusive blue flame.

Abigail launched a celebratory breath into the tree branches above them. A bird shrieked and flew away from its perch just before the fire incinerated the branch. Cinder moved beneath the falling ash and melting snow and absorbed the flames before they could scorch anything else. Abigail watched him. She liked how he commanded the flames into his hands. She hoped one day he would teach her how to do that. She'd make an incredible hero if she could absorb fires before they could burn anyone.

Falling with the embers and sleet, a branch plummeted to the ground. Abigail watched the branch connect with the back of Cinder's unsuspecting head. Watched his body collapse into the snow as his legs gave out under him. She slid into a snowbank running to him.

"Cinder!" Abigail carefully felt behind his neck checking for breaks like she had been trained during a medical class at Saves the Day a year ago. His neck felt solid. "Cinder, can you hear me?"

There was a gash on his forehead hidden under his hair where the branch had cut him. Blood oozed to the surface. She brushed his hair away and pulled his head into her lap.

"Cinder, wake up." Abigail lightly patted his cheek. "Please."

"Don't worry," he muttered, his eyes darted under their lids. "Protect you."

"Cinder?"

"Who's that?" His words slurred together.

"You are," she answered.

Cinder shook his head against Abigail's hand. "I'm wi-, I'm wi-ire."

"Wired?"

Cinder sighed and smiled. "Yeah."

"That must've been a bad whack," Abigail couldn't help but grin, brushing a stray hair off his face. "At least I found your weak spot."

"Silly villain, you can never defeat me."

"Are you the hero now?"

"Always." The fluttering of his closed eyes stopped as he passed out completely.

Abigail pulled her glove off with her teeth and examined the top of his head where the branch had connected. There was an egg-sized bump hidden under his hair. Abigail put her glove back on and made a snowball ice pack to hold against it. The snow kept melting against him.

Abigail kept making snowballs.

It was dark when Cinder woke up. Although he didn't know it when he first opened his eyes. The only thing he saw was Abigail's face above him, her neck glowing with red embers from a fire burning under the collar of her coat. It confused him. Looking past her face he saw the spider web network of the underside of the evergreen trees. They were outside. That confused him more.

"Hey," Abigail whispered. Her breath made a cloud of frost in the air. It was heavy compared to the smoke he had last seen pouring from her mouth. "You hit your head. Are you feeling okay?"

"Why are we outside?"

"I couldn't move you."

"So, you're turning yourself into a popsicle?" Cinder scolded but didn't move. There was a pounding in his head.

"I don't think that's possible with us." She moved his hair out of his face with one gentle touch. "How do you feel?"

Cinder reached for the goose egg on his head. "I can feel this."

"I'm going to help you stand," Abigail warned.

She cupped the back of his head and lowered it into the snow while she stood. He heard her knees pop when she did and wondered how long he had been using her as a headrest. She kneeled next to him and pulled him slowly into a sitting position. He frowned at her.

"I can get up on my own." To prove his point, Cinder rushed to his feet and started to fall forward when his head screamed at him from the sudden motion. The trees spun violently around him.

Abigail tucked her body under his for support. "Sure you can."

Cinder grumbled. It made his head pulse, and it made Abigail giggle. He thought the tradeoff was fair so he did it again.

"Let's get home."

"You going to play doctor?" Cinder was rough, but only to cover the way his face heated when she said *home* like they shared it. Like it was their home. He grumbled again; they could never have a home together. It was a foolish thought. A stupid one. A thought only brought on by a head injury.

"Well?" Abigail prompted.

"Well, what?"

"Do you want me to leave you here for some animal to finish you off?"

"Like they could take me."

Abigail removed herself as his crutch, and Cinder threatened to fall back into the snow. She was back against him before he could.

They stumbled back to the cabin; the noises of their footfalls absorbed by the dense snow around them. Once inside, Abigail set Cinder on the couch and got him a real ice pack from the freezer. She returned five minutes later with a bowl of microwaved soup. She sat on the table across him and readied a spoonful.

"This is pathetic," Cinder protested. "I can feed myself."

Abigail raised an eyebrow and set the bowl and spoon on the table. Cinder tilted his head a painful ninety degrees to the side so the ice pack stayed on his tender head and grabbed the soup. He took a bite that let half the broth dripped down his chin and fixed Abigail with a triumphant look.

"See?"

"Oh yeah." Abigail grinned, getting off the table. "You've totally got this."

"Where are you going?" Cinder asked after another half-assed bite.

"Shower," she answered from somewhere behind him. "I may not be a popsicle, but I'm still freezing."

"You could let me warm you up."

"How about you focus on your soup, Wired?"

"What?" Cinder wanted to look at her but settled for her blurry reflection in the bay window across from him. She was carrying her backpack to the bathroom built under the loft.

"It's what you called yourself," she explained. "I think you were dreaming before you passed out. You said your name was Wired."

"That doesn't make sense."

"It was your dream," Abigail said before closing the bathroom door.

When she emerged back into the main room with warm, pink skin, Abigail found Cinder still on the couch. Finding his gaze staring at her through the reflective window was becoming as commonplace as her hands finding excuses to touch him. He moved off the couch, mindful of his head, and met her in the center of the room. The defrosting ice pack smeared his hair in even crazier directions.

"I'll tell you another secret."

"What's the price?" Abigail knew nothing would be too expensive for her.

213

"I'm glad you chased me downtown."

"I wouldn't count that as a secret."

Cinder shrugged. "I haven't told anyone before. Not even myself."

"What do you think it means?"

"That maybe things can be different."

"Different how?"

He shook his head. "It's bad to ask victims with head injuries difficult questions."

"One easy question then?"

"One." His crooked smile returned.

"Why were you in San Arbor? Why did you come back?"

"That's a difficult question."

Abigail pursed her lips. She weighed the options of dragging a better answer out of him and microwaving her own bowl of soup. The food won, and she turned to the kitchen. Cinder's hand encircled her wrist and stopped her.

"If you're not going to give me an answer, I'd like to eat."

"In a word? I think I came to San Arbor for atonement."

Abigail snapped her gaze to his. "What does that mean?"

Cinder shrugged, then shoved her forward. "I thought you wanted your dinner."

"You'd never tell me, would you?"

"I don't think so. But I surprise myself around you, so you never know."

Chapter Twenty-Five

Exiting the train at Jolt Station Sunday evening was an awful reminder of Abigail's true world. The real world. Cinder pulled his fur hood over his head to hide his face and wore a pair of reflective sunglasses he pulled off a display case while they waited for the train at the bus station hours ago. They had returned to their secrets. The San Arbor cityscape could never know what they shared within the shadow of the mountain peak.

Abigail already missed the Flame Villain as she followed him off the platform to the station's exit. She didn't know when they'd be together again. That uncertainty weighed more in her heart than her guilt of being with him. She knew the road she currently walked down was filled with landmines and red flags, but she wanted to know where it went. How far she would follow him.

That distance felt endless.

She no longer lied to herself. She wasn't going to turn in his file to the Hero Relief Center. She knew she wasn't going to turn him into the police, either. This wasn't a selfish intelligence gathering mission anymore. It hadn't been in a while. Abigail liked this villain.

Cinder waited for her outside Jolt Station. The late summer air in the city was a stark contrast to the snowy winter they had just been in.

"You know how to get home, right?"

The question surprised her, just like he had all weekend, but Abigail didn't mind the delay in their separation. "I got here, didn't I?"

Cinder's half smile returned. "I'll see you when I can."

"You wouldn't have to leave cryptic messages with my doorman if you had my number." Abigail rushed through the sentence so she couldn't chicken out halfway through it. She waited for his reaction.

She waited for his denial. She watched her reflection in his glasses turn from pale to pink.

"I didn't think you'd want a villain saved in your phone." Cinder was deliberate with his words, chewing each one before he spoke.

"It wouldn't be a villain," she countered. "It'd be you."

Abigail hated that she could only see her reflection. Without his lively green eyes she was blind to his thoughts. Cinder finally huffed and opened a hand. She set her phone in his scarred palm. He dialed his own number and let it ring once before returning her phone.

"No late night booty calls." He smirked.

Abigail saved his number affectionately under the emoji shaped like a pile of poop.

The cabin felt like it existed in another lifetime. They had returned yesterday, but the weekend training trip seemed centuries ago, and Abigail felt like she hadn't seen Cinder in twice as long. She hid in a locker room at the Hero Relief Center and allowed her heart to miss the villain while she changed from her day clothes to her new costume. Her new sidekick outfit was finished, and everyone was excited to see her before the grand announcement in a few hours. The media parked outside the building didn't know what was being announced, just that The Round Table was requesting an audience of the people of San Arbor.

Abigail's design had been accepted by President Samuels, and the costume came out better than she had hoped. Her bright red and blue color scheme from before was faded down, but the shape of the dress remained the same. The skirt made with leather pleats that resembled the Nordic raiders of ancient times, her once cute boots replaced with iron greaves, and she wore matching iron gauntlets. Stitched on the front of the dress was the side profile of an English dragon head. Strapped to her hip was the red scabbard that housed her new weapon.

She wanted to send a picture of herself to Cinder but stopped. This counted as work, and it was forbidden to discuss. She grinned anyway; he'd see her on the news. Abigail adjusted the dark red bow, the same color of the mask around her eyes, that clasped her hair behind her head.

Abigail was ecstatic when she stepped out of the locker room. Electricity ran through her as she fought the urge to jump up and down. She was finally back. Abigail Turner, a hero!

"You look great!" Excalibur complimented from his seat in the hallway. He wore a black bow tie attached to his armor. It looked comically out of place around his neck. "I'm glad you took my dragon idea."

"Thank you." Abigail turned around to show off the full design. "What's with the bow tie?"

Excalibur adjusted it. "Is it too much? I thought it would make me look distinguished for the press conference."

"I say leave the ties to King Arthur, but it looks very handsome."

He quit fidgeting with it, the bow tie tilted under his iron helmet. "I'm going to wear it for the announcement today."

"I can't thank you enough for believing in me," Abigail started to gush. "This is finally happening again. I won't let you down, sir. We're going to make an awesome team, I promise."

"I thought it was wrong what Saves the Day did to you. You're just a kid, you're allowed to make some mistakes."

"I won't make them again."

Abigail vowed it on her life. She would not let this second opportunity go up in smoke.

"Want to go over your entrance? It's got to be memorable."

Abigail grinned, "You don't have to worry about that. I've got it all figured out. I think you're really going to like it."

He crossed his arms, but Abigail heard the smile under his helmet. "Keeping secrets from me?"

"A surprise isn't a secret."

The Hero Relief Center always held their press conferences on the front lawn. A platform stage was constructed outside the gardens, the logo of the Round Table Knights projected on the curtain that Abigail hid behind. She poked her head through it and saw the rows of seating were full of interested citizens and the media. The crowd murmured to each other and tried to guess what the announcement would be about.

Abigail hoped they were ready for the performance she was planning.

She took a deep breath and counted to ten before releasing it. Her heart had been pounding since she took cover behind the curtain. She wished Excalibur was waiting in the back with her, but he stood on the stage with the other Knights. She could laugh about his bow tie instead of sweating through her new costume. She counted to ten a second time and knocked her knuckles together. She snuffed the sparks that fell onto the ground with her boots.

This was her rebirth. Her fresh start. Inferna and Saves the Day were in her rearview now.

King Arthur tapped the microphone on stage and quieted the crowd.

"Hello everyone." Abigail listened to his words, focusing on the calm cadence of his voice. A camera flashed at his every move. "I want to turn it over to my good friend, Excalibur. He's been chomping all morning about this."

Abigail's hands sweated, and she rubbed them against her skirt. She felt her heartbeat in her throat.

"There were twenty-five knights who originally sat at the Round Table," Excalibur said. "Yesterday three of them served this city and her people. And today, there will be four. I want San Arbor to meet my squire, my sidekick, Avalon!"

There was a mixture of cheers and murmurs as he said her name. Abigail didn't listen to them. She listened to the crackling of the flames around her wrists. They would provide her worth, not the media lights. She was a new hero now. The same drive as Inferna, but with a clean slate to work with.

She jumped through the curtain and landed with a front flip. She pulled her sword out of the scabbard and across her face where she breathed her blue flame against the blade. The sword caught fire like it was made of paper, and she twirled it at her side.

Excalibur was the first to clap, the first one to shake off the surprise of her mastered fire breathing.

"My squire, everyone," he said proudly into the microphone. "The dragon slayer herself."

Abigail twirled her sword a final time, killing the flame, and stood next to Excalibur who handed her the microphone.

"Avalon, over here, Channel 9 News," a reporter called from the front row. The flashing lights blurred their faces. "Working with Excalibur, how does it feel?"

"Amazing." She smiled. "I couldn't have handpicked a better hero to sidekick for, and for Excalibur to choose me just puts me over the moon. I can't wait to begin working together in the city. We're going to do a lot of good."

"Did he teach you swordplay?" another reporter asked.

"Yes! We've been training together for a while now."

"That *dragon's breath*," another reporter named her new move, "did you learn that from Volcanic or Inferna?"

Abigail's heart lurched forward, but she remained composed in front of the cameras. Even now it was almost impossible to escape

Kenneth. "I figured this out on my own." The lie felt dirty. She hoped Cinder wasn't watching the news. "Want to see it again?"

The crowd cheered, and the camera adjusted to her face. Abigail blew a wide arc of blue fire above her that rained down in beautiful indigo sparks. She ended the performance with a kiss toward the cameras. It formed into a heart of blue fire before shimmering away.

"Were you hired because of the new city ordinance?" a reporter unimpressed by her flames asked when the crowd quieted down. "Is this a call of attack against Saves the Day?"

Abigail paused; his question didn't make sense. "Of course not," she tried to answer. "We would never—"

"Is the HRC concerned with the heightened possibility of fire damage now that two flame users are inside San Arbor?"

"I'm not at liberty to say—"

"Is the HRC increasing their numbers to have a larger presence on the street?"

"I don't—"

"Will you wear body cameras like the police?"

"Is this in response to the surge of crime in the city?"

"Are new laws going to be made to protect citizens and property from damage by heroes?"

"Heroes won't cause—"

A hand on Abigail's shoulder snapped her out of the media storm. King Arthur pulled her a step back from the microphone. He tapped it and the amplified *thump* quieted the reporters.

"Saves the Day and ourselves have released numerous statements about Ordinance Seven Fifty-Nine. I know Quinn Samuels has ensured that the citizens, the first responders and heroes have been rightfully represented in that ordinance. Now, we invited you to our home to celebrate our friend and partner, Avalon." King Arthur smiled at Abigail, and she suddenly felt completely perfect. He turned back to the media. "Avalon is a Knight of the Round Table because we all wanted her to serve San Arbor and work with us. Wanting to better protect this city will never be some sort of challenge against Saves the Day or an endorsement attempt. Heroes are not a marketing toy for sponsors. We Knights will only serve San Arbor."

King Arthur turned himself and Abigail away from the crowd and vanished behind the curtain. The fabric muffled Merlin as she fielded more questions to complete the conference. Arthur released Abigail and sat on the wooden steps that led to the stage. He traced one of the scorched marks left behind by her flames.

"Thanks for the rescue," Abigail said to his back. The silence between them was thick and uncomfortable. "I didn't know they were going to ask about the ordinance."

"They weren't supposed to." King Arthur sighed angrily. "But hungry dogs will always beg for scraps. Hope they didn't discourage you."

"It'll take a lot more than them to do that." Abigail tried to lighten the mood with a laugh, but it came out shaky and unsure.

"When I became King Arthur, I didn't realize my biggest enemy would be the people I was trying to protect." King Arthur pulled off his crown and looked at his distorted reflection in the golden metal. "People can be so self-destructive."

"And selfish." Abigail desperately wanted to get on King Arthur's good side. Even if it meant taking advantage of his melancholy state. "If first responders didn't fear heroes doing their jobs better and sending them out of work, heroes wouldn't have to fight as hard to be able to help."

"You get it." His reflection smiled at her. "But you can never let them hear it. Do you know how the HRC got its name?"

"I don't."

"Quinn wanted to create a group of heroes to give aid and relief to the first responders. His whole goal was to make their lives easier and less dangerous. To give relief to the city's original heroes."

"Was it Quinn who picked the Camelot theme?"

King Arthur returned his crown to his head, his brown curls flattening around his ears with a boyish charm. "That was my condition before joining. I always wanted to be a king."

Excalibur cleared his throat behind them, his head floating between the curtains. "Time to mingle."

"Time to play nice," King Arthur corrected.

Chapter Twenty-Six

Abigail stepped off the city bus and expected to see Henry at the apartment complex's front doors. The retired Navy man had become a permanent fixture in the lobby. His pressed coat and matching hat looked like he picked them up from the dry cleaners every morning. The buttons shined like his permanent smile. But he wasn't at the door waiting for her.

She walked inside and saw someone new sitting at the front desk. He didn't wear the hat like Henry did. This wrinkled hat slipped over the man's hair and was tilted back so it wouldn't fall over his eyes. He was busy playing some loud game on his phone. His thumb clicks created animated gunshots in response.

Ignoring her mailbox that was probably full of junk mail again, Abigail knocked her knuckles against the desk until the man looked up. It took him several minutes, him dying in-game and muttering a curse of revenge against the player that delivered the killing shot, before doing so.

"What?" he snapped, then added slightly more politely, "Welcome to The Phoenix."

"Where's Henry?"

"Who? Oh, the old man?"

"Yes." Abigail tapped her heel against the floor.

"He's dead. I'm just a temp until they find someone who—"

"What?" Abigail asked in disbelief, her bag threatened to slip off her shoulder.

"The guy died," the man said, slower. He handed Abigail a printed piece of paper from the desk. "Heart attack. I guess."

Abigail snatched the paper from his hand. It was printed on her apartment complex's letterhead. She had received similar papers when the complex was steam cleaning the hallways, or when there was a water break, but maintenance always fixed the problems. The letters were just a polite way to stop management from getting calls.

This letterhead wasn't a notice or an apology for any inconvenience. It was an announcement of death. Of Henry's death. Regardless of its name, the Phoenix Apartment Complex wouldn't be able to fix this. Abigail's hand tightened around the paper and wrinkled the edges. Soft red cinders burned from under her fingers. Her heart turned to stone as she rode the elevator to the seventh floor. Her hands shook as she walked to her door, pieces of charred paper fluttered on the carpet. Robotically, she unlocked the door and dropped her keys into the bowl. She didn't hear them clink against the sides. She didn't notice the overwhelming scent of woodsmoke in her apartment. She didn't register that her lights were on. She didn't care that Cinder stood at her fridge drinking from the milk carton.

She let her purse fall from her arm and sat at the island staring at the empty space ahead of her. She knew Henry had a granddaughter. Who would sneak her lollipops now? His daughter would bring him lunch some days, was she the one who found him? Henry had fought for their country, had been a hero, and his heart had betrayed him in the end. He had been her first friend when she moved to San Arbor. Helped her move into her apartment and refused any form of payment for it.

Abigail's life was colder without his smile.

A crooked face appeared in the empty space in front of her. She focused on the green eyes until they started crossing in her vision.

"What's up, doll?" Cinder asked. "Don't you hero-types catch the intruder? Not that there's too much in your fridge to take. You're out of milk."

"Henry's dead." Abigail's mouth dried after she said it. After she admitted it.

"Your doorman?"

Abigail nodded and lowered her head. Cinder's scarred hand pulled the letter slowly away from hers. She tried holding onto it, but the burned edges flaked away in her grasp. Cinder read the letter then returned it to Abigail. She tucked it under her arms. A picture of Henry standing ever-present outside the complex was at the bottom.

"Are you going to the memorial?"

"Am I allowed?"

Cinder touched her hand for a second before pulling it back. She barely felt his soft fingers pull over her skin. "I've never seen a funeral have a blacklist. If he was close to you, then you should go."

"Maybe." Abigail looked back at Henry's picture. She could at least send flowers. Standing with his family and those he served with didn't feel right. She was just his tenant. The thought made Abigail feel like she was stealing something from them. They knew the real Henry. She only knew his smile and hello's. "What are you doing here?"

Cinder's crooked smile flashed, but it didn't have the same playful effect on her. "Had a little run-in with the cops and needed a place to lay low."

"They're not following you, are they?" Abigail barely registered her own voice. It sounded far away as if it was playing from a TV in another room.

Cinder waved his hand. "One of my guys took the fall."

Abigail stood from the island and headed to the bedroom, sliding off a sneaker with each step. "I'm not training."

"I'm not leaving." Cinder's closeness surprised her. She assumed he'd stay in the kitchen. She assumed he wouldn't be here.

Abigail turned to find him leaning against the bedroom door frame. His fingers twitched against his arms as he crossed them over his chest. She collapsed on the edge of the bed. Her heart shook as much as the bedsprings did beneath her. Everything around her felt ready to collapse. The idea of Henry gone shook her. Did she even remember the last thing she said to him?

Abigail glared at Cinder, who stood in the doorway watching her. "I'm tired."

"You're sad." He corrected and sat next to her. "And you shouldn't be alone like that."

"Don't you have something bad to do?"

"Just annoy a hero." Cinder knocked his shoulder gently against Abigail's. "Trust me, have I let you down yet?"

He had a point. Unfortunately. Abigail raised an eyebrow and waited for him to continue.

"Take the warmest shower you can," he instructed. "I'll cook you something."

"Why?"

"You're hurting," Cinder said simply.

He eyed her with deadly precision until Abigail gave in to his demands. She slipped away from the bed and into the bathroom. Cinder watched until she turned the water on before shutting the door and leaving the bedroom. Abigail tested the flowing water and waited for her fingers to turn red from the heat. It took a while, and the small room was filled with vapors.

She stepped under the shower-head and waited for the water to soak her. She felt each water droplet pelt against her skin and the heat it left while rolling down her arms and face. She tasted salt on her lips and didn't realize she was crying. Silently, hidden behind the shower curtain, she let her tears fall. They mingled with the water and vanished below the drain.

The shower either ran cold, or she became numb to the heat before she turned it off and dried herself. The reflection in the mirror startled her. She didn't look very much like a hero with rounded cheeks, sunken eyes, and the snot dripping from her nose. Abigail cleaned herself up, forced the face fluids back and ventured into the main room of her apartment.

She sat at the island. Her fluffy pajama bottoms felt better against the metal chair than the jeans she wore home. Cinder stood across from her at the stove, and he whistled a melody that reminded her of Christmas. He flipped a grilled cheese over in the skillet and the sizzle covered his song before Abigail could place it.

She shook the plastic grocery bag on the counter. She knew she didn't have cheese and doubted she had non-moldy bread in the pantry. "I thought you were on lockdown?"

"It was a necessary trip." He pressed the spatula against the bread.

"I haven't eaten a grilled cheese in years."

Cinder opened three cabinets before finding a plate and set the sandwich in front of her. "My mother taught me how. She called them fire smiles to cheer me up."

Abigail was surprised as he lit a blue blaze against his pointer finger and scorched a smiling face on the bread. "Does the flame run in your family?"

"It skips siblings," Cinder answered coldly, returning to the skillet to make a second sandwich.

Abigail swallowed her bite. The processed cheese stuck against her teeth. "Do you have a brother or a sister?"

Abigail had always wanted a little sister. Someone to play house with and go shopping at the mall for her homecoming dress. Instead, she had a younger brother who left worms in her shoes before school and told her seventh-grade crush she farted louder than the dog. Isaac became a loan officer like their father. He even worked at the same bank.

"I had a brother." Cinder flipped the sandwich, pressing it roughly against the skillet. "Mom made a lot of these the night he died."

"I'm so sorry." Abigail's sandwich fell back to the plate, the apology was a jerk reaction. "When did that happen?"

Cinder started whistling again. He slid the finished sandwich onto a new plate and turned the stove off. Abigail tried to eat another bite, testing the contents on her shaking stomach. What could she say to that? Should she even try? She didn't like her brother, but she wouldn't know what she'd do without him. What her family would do without him.

They would probably do whatever Henry's family had to do.

"Thank you," she said into the quiet kitchen.

Cinder finished his grilled cheese in three bites and piled all the dishes into the sink. He ran water over the top of the skillet, but it had little effect on the burned butter.

"Bath check. Food check." He counted off on his fingers, rounding the island with his scarred arms extended. "Final thing on the list."

"What list?" A germ size grin tugged at Abigail's mouth as he approached.

Cinder pulled her tightly against his chest, his arms wrapped around her tighter than she had felt before. Tighter than their first night on the roof. As he spoke, his chin rubbed into her damp hair. "I've lost a lot of people already. I know how this works."

Abigail relaxed against him, her skin and heart softening from the hot water that melted her tears. As she exhaled, Cinder tightened himself even more. She didn't feel like the rabbit caught in a constrictors' coils, though. The sturdiness of Cinder's chest held her together, the steady beat of his heart below her head kept her mind from sinking. Woodsmoke filled her senses, and she was okay with that. She nuzzled into him, and Cinder tightened his hold once more.

Abigail reached across the bed the next morning but found it empty. She reached to her nightstand and found it full. Henry's death announcement cut her finger. The sudden pain distracted her for only a second until she remembered what the letterhead said. She reached out again and silenced the alarm waking her for work. She could only hope that work would keep her busy. She needed to stay busy today. She ignored her desire to sleep for ten more minutes and got dressed.

Avalon's outfit was hanging safely at the HRC, and she couldn't wait to get into the costume. Behind her mask, where people she knew didn't die without warning. When she thought about it, the coming sirens at an accident were a comfort. They herald death, but also hope. She'd bet on hope every time.

She opened the bedroom door and froze in the doorway. Cinder was still there, trying to scrub a skillet clean in the sink. From the bead of sweat on his forehead it looked like he'd been at it for a while.

"Good morning," she said approaching the counter, kicking her discarded shoes from yesterday along the way.

"I made you breakfast." Cinder didn't look away from his task.

Abigail eyed the plate on the counter. "Another grilled cheese?"

"It's all you had."

She didn't argue with him. She wasn't about to pass up homemade food. She picked at the crust when she finished. "Tell me about your brother."

"What do I get in exchange?" he set the skillet on a towel to dry.

Abigail checked the time on the stove. "What do you want?"

"Tell me about Volcanic."

She scrunched her nose, disgusted at hearing the name so early into her day. It felt like she could never escape the hero. "What do you want to know?"

Cinder leaned his cheek into his hand. "Is he as strong as they say? Can he rocket like me?"

Abigail hesitated and finished eating the torn away crust. She hesitated again and drank a cup of water. "He's the top hero in San Arbor, of course he's strong."

"You worked with the guy, tell me something good."

"He's fireproof, completely." She lied. "Nothing can burn him or slow him down. I'm pretty sure I saw him melt down an entire concrete floor. Are you wanting an autograph or something?"

"Could you do that?" His sarcasm was as sticky as the processed cheese. "I just don't see how someone so strong needed a sidekick."

"PR reasons mostly," Abigail answered. "Have you seen him interview? The guy's not the friendliest."

"He was using you?"

"It was in the contract."

Cinder straightened. "Sometimes I think you heroes are worse than us. If I'm going to screw you over, you know it's coming."

"Is that my warning?"

He smiled his handsome crooked smile. "Is that what you want?"

"I want to know about your brother."

Cinder sighed. He picked up a damp spoon and watched his reflection as he spoke. "He was a good kid. I don't know what you want from me."

"How old were you when he died?"

"I was fifteen when he was hit by the car. He was eleven." Cinder took a breath, glanced up and added. "He was walking home from school when it happened. Died on the way to the hospital. Mom had to make the ID there. I've hated hospitals since."

Abigail replaced the spoon with her hand and squeezed his fingers. "Don't you have people to save?"

She wanted to save the person in her kitchen the most. She wanted to know if that tragedy was what set Cinder on his path. She wanted to be a hero because someone had saved her. Did he become a villain because someone couldn't save his brother?

"Not until eight-thirty." Abigail pulled her hand away. "Don't you have candy to steal?"

Cinder grinned but it didn't reach his eyes. "No work talk."

Chapter Twenty-Seven

Abigail didn't realize she'd been lying to herself when she said she'd be happy to just scrub toilets at a hero company. She'd been lying to herself when she happily accepted her business casual wear over a hero costume. She had been lying to herself for months, forcing herself to feel content by just being a hero assistant. Patrolling the streets was where she was most happy. Her life was full again now that she wore a costume. She felt like she had purpose now that she was helping people. She couldn't be happier, even if she was taking a punch to her gut on a Wednesday afternoon.

She doubled over, the impact folding her in half. Her sword threatened to fall from her hand, but she steeled her resolve and gripped the handle tighter. The criminal in front of her was a low life. He smelled like the gutter he must have crawled out of. He and his no-good buddies tried to hold-up a city bus. Excalibur was taking on the four inside, while Abigail chased this one down the street.

"You only get one chance to turn yourself in," she warned.

"I ain't getting taken by some B-lister."

Abigail's sword sparked to life as a cherry-red blaze jumped from her hands to the blade. She tackled the criminal to the ground and used her knees to keep his hands pinned against the asphalt. She lowered the flaming sword toward his face. The temperature was low, but he didn't need to know that.

"Do you surrender?"

The criminal's face shifted in response. His skin morphed to rock. The veins of sedimentary stone shimmered in the fire light where there had been wrinkles a second ago. Abigail inhaled and added fuel to her flames. Even with his stone face, sweat sprouted from his forehead. For extra intimidation, Abigail's next statement was punctuated with blue smoke as her dragon's breath sparked in her mouth.

"How certain are you that you can withstand the heat?"

"Not the blue," begged the man, turning his head to the side. "I'll go with you, just please not the blue fire."

She grinned. Barely a week and her power was already known in the city. Abigail flipped the man over and cuffed his hands together with a zip tie.

"Your first mistake was trying to rob that bus," she scolded while she led him back to the scene. "Your second was insulting me and the Round Table Knights."

She pushed him back to the street where an officer waited.

"You'll want a dampener for this one." Abigail explained eyeing the regular cuffs in the officer's hands. "He can morph his skin to stone."

The officer returned his cuffs to his belt and removed a black collar from the inside of his squad car. Abigail took the collar from him and snapped it around the man's neck. The remaining pebbles that marked his skin like pimples vanished. Once her captive was secured inside the squad car, she joined Excalibur at the bus. He was checking IDs and returning wallets and purses the criminals had attempted to take.

"I have to say it's nice to have someone do the chasing," Excalibur joked loudly for the camera phones to hear.

"I'll chase them down so long as you do the heavy lifting," she replied.

"We'll call you if we need anything else," an officer interjected before returning to his patrol car.

The police drove away with the criminals, and the bus continued on its route. Excalibur and Abigail waved to the passengers before moving down the street to patrol another section of San Arbor. Abigail cracked her knuckles above her head as they walked.

"I don't remember it being so busy," she admitted when they were far away from the scene.

"It's different now that we can react in real time. Now, nothing is considered 'too small' for heroes."

"Still. I feel like we've stopped more tiny crimes than the city's had in months."

"Crime has been on the rise for a while now," Excalibur confirmed. "Nothing catastrophic, thank goodness. But it's still concerning. The ordinance couldn't have come at a better time."

"I wonder if more baddies have entered the city, or if the ones already here are just getting braver."

Excalibur shrugged. "Could be both, hard to tell."

"I'll do some research when we're back to HQ," Abigail decided, chewing the inside of her cheek. "Scan the databases for anything new."

"You can take the assistant out of the office," Excalibur laughed. "We have people who can do that, you know."

Abigail shook her head. "It'll be easier this way. I know what to look for."

"And what's that?"

"I'm not sure yet."

After returning to the Hero Relief Center when their patrol was finished, Abigail exchanged her hero costume for a computer desk. The Round Table Criminal Database was a collection of crimes the company had stopped and investigations that they were part of. It also had a direct link to the police station to view all active cases. The integrated system was developed so hero companies couldn't hide any information from the police on shared cases.

There was still a level of distrust between the heroes and the first responders. Abigail was hopeful that the barrier would dissipate in time. They were all on the same side after all.

According to the database, crime numbers had risen seven percent in the last month. It was a thirteen percent rise from last year. The numbers were small, but still too large for a hero to be proud of. The recent crimes were all simple, Abigail scratched notes into a blank sheet of paper. In the month since the ordinance had passed there was a nine percent increase of crimes being stopped before the criminal could escape the scene. No one had been seriously hurt either, and the heroes and police forces were able to come on the scene in minutes. The response time was something to be proud of.

Response time.

Abigail pulled up a map of the recent attacks in the last two months. Almost all occurred around city bus stops surrounding the main downtown artery. The red dots flashed on the locations making a ring around one downtown building. Town Hall.

Abigail printed the report. Next, she printed the list of caught criminals in the last two months, along with the list of known criminals who had evaded capture in the last year or been recently released. She would cross check them. There may be a connection that could point to the person behind it.

Abigail grabbed the files off the printer. They were warm and smelled of ink. She fingered through the stack to make sure she had everything. Halfway through she paused, her breath becoming a hostage in her windpipe. A pair of grey eyes burned into her. The photo was black and white, but she knew the brilliant shade of green they were supposed to be. The photo was older. Cinder looked younger but just as deadly. The photo was taken from a street camera, and he was looking right into it. His scarred face was unmistakable. He was unafraid, uncaring, and his taunting half smirk didn't reach his eyes.

Name: Unknown

DOB: Unknown

Location: Unknown

Wanted: Arson. Burglary. Person of interest with connection to attack on Murphy's Pub. Considered dangerous.

Abigail pulled the sheet from the stack. A red spark from her finger caught the paper on fire and she dumped the ashes on the carpet, rubbing them into the fibers with her shoe. She hadn't stopped to think twice about the action. She would keep Cinder off the Knights' radar. He was changing after all, wanting to atone for his past misdoings. Abigail turned away from the printer and searched for Excalibur to show him her findings.

She knocked against his interior office door. The tiny office outside that used to be hers was now empty. There would be a new assistant to the armored hero soon, and Abigail would get her own knight-sized office once an unused room was cleaned out of forgotten office equipment and extra chairs. Excalibur's helmet sat on his desk when he called her inside and he didn't bother to put it on when she entered.

"What you got there?" He eyed the stack of papers in her arms.

"I think the criminals are planning something." Abigail set the stack on his desk. "I think there's a pattern. I think someone is testing response times to Town Hall."

Excalibur pulled the printed map from the top of the stack. "Are these recently targeted places?"

"Yeah." Abigail sat in the chair across from him. "All the crimes that we've been stopping have been petty. Big enough to make someone call the police but small enough that the perpetrators aren't staying in jail for long. If this is something bigger then it could mean that whoever is pulling the strings doesn't want to lose their numbers."

"What else do you have?"

Abigail separated the stack in two piles. "A list of criminals, the ones who have been caught and others that are still active. I wanted to see if they had any connections. If I remember right, after Volcanic came to San Arbor there haven't been any gang activities, but what if one is starting?"

"You could be onto something," Excalibur commented. "What can I do?"

"Can you help me write up a report to take to King and then we can take it to the police too? If we all work together then it could help our partnership and stop whatever may be happening."

Excalibur pulled the stacks of paper across the desk to him. "You write, and I'll check these guys out."

Four hours later, the knight hero and his squire delivered their work to President Samuels and King Arthur. Samuels was excited to send the theory to the police, King Arthur was not. If the hero had his way, they would overturn the city and shake the criminals from San Arbor's pockets. Samuels assured that working with the police would be the best option. For now. They just needed to wait for Police Chief DaVodi to go over their findings.

Being a hero required a lot of waiting around. After work, Abigail decided to do something productive instead.

Her kitchen shelves were empty, and her fridge was costing more money eating up her energy bill than keeping the expired milk cold. She had put off her grocery run for too long. Abigail rode the six blocks east to the bargain market while typing a list of things not to forget on her phone. Her last item was ice cream.

The bargain market was on the back side of a neighborhood with abandoned buildings taking up a lot across from it. Abigail found the discounted grocery while she was unemployed but stuck around for the savings. She assumed the low property value made the groceries cheaper. While she stepped off the bus, wrangling her phone back into her purse, Abigail stepped into someone.

The stranger was built like the abandoned buildings: tall, dirty, with a foundation that knocked Abigail back a step.

"Watch out girly." The man grabbed her arm before she fell completely over. A dark red tattoo wrapped around his forearm. "Someone'll snatch you up if you're not watching."

Abigail didn't register the threat. She didn't register the tightening grip around her wrist. She didn't register the silver shine of the knife sticking from the man's belt. She could only register the other man standing next to him.

"Leave her alone," Cinder ordered with a sigh. "You can't make me late again."

"You're no fun." The first man released Abigail's arm with a toss.

"You better get out of here, doll." Cinder's voice was cold. She knew it had to be; they couldn't know each other on the street, but she still fought the desire to reach across the short space and touch him.

They stood unmoving until the bus pulled away, and Cinder crossed the street with the other man lagging at his heels. They entered the largest of the abandoned buildings. Two spirals were built on the roof, but half of one was crushed and pieces drifted onto the sidewalk in a waterfall of dust.

Abigail forced herself into the grocery store. Forced herself to get a cart. Forced herself to follow her list. She forced herself not to run recklessly inside the building, chasing Cinder into the shadows that may cause him harm. She was at the checkout line when her phone buzzed. The smiling pile of poop on the screen sent an electrical current through her body.

You looked good in your costume. I want to see you tonight. Ten.

Abigail replied with a simple thumbs-up.

Chapter Twenty-Eight

Cinder arrived promptly at ten that night. He slipped through the unlocked patio door and locked it behind him. The high collar of his duster jacket replaced the soft fur of the coat he wore in the mountains. The sharp edges and hard shadows maintained his villainous persona. Abigail pulled her legs off the couch giving him space to sit next to her. Cinder eyed the romance movie playing on the television, sat a plastic bag on the coffee table, and joined her. The couch sagged in the center pulling the two closer together.

Neither of them spoke, but the small space between them was alive with chaotic energy. The space needed to be filled, but who would move first? Who would admit defeat first?

Abigail reached for the takeout bag on the table. It smelled of fried chicken. The smiling face on the bag was happy to see her. Their knees knocked against each other in her reach. Cinder snatched the bag before she could and only delivered his signature half smile in return.

Abigail kissed it off, and he returned the food to her lap.

"Long day?" she asked him, claiming a chicken leg and biscuit before allowing him in the bag.

"Business meetings all day," he joked. "Yours?"

"Stopped some bad guys, the usual."

"They're calling you Dragon Slayer now."

Abigail sighed. "We're trying to stop the nickname."

Cinder raised an eyebrow, his mouth too full to talk. Half a chicken leg hung between his lips.

"All of my sidekick names have been so dark," she explained. "Fire Killer, Dragon Slayer. I want something a little lighter. Something that sounds a little bit friendlier."

Cinder swallowed. "I'd pick the friend who can kill monsters. What's a better friend than that?"

Abigail laughed. It was so easy around him. "The Center is going to release a new T-shirt print with Excalibur and me. They want to show off that we both use swords."

"That sounds stupid."

"Welcome to the marketing side of hero work." Abigail chuckled. "Can you imagine if the bad guys had publicists and marketing teams?"

"Instead of fighting in the streets we'd be fighting in ball courts. Wouldn't be as fun."

Abigail pulled a napkin from the bag. "If you say so."

Cinder changed the subject. "What were you doing on the east side of town today?"

"Buying groceries?"

"Isn't there a store down the street?"

Abigail knew he knew the answer. It was the same store from which he acquired the grilled cheese ingredients. Cinder probably walked by its neon yellow door sign every time he came over.

"They're cheaper there. Afraid I'm going to see something I shouldn't?" The collapsed church flashed in her mind. The way its shadows swallowed Cinder whole was nightmarish.

"I'm afraid you're going to get yourself hurt."

"You're worried about me?"

"Yes."

Cinder's response surprised Abigail. How easily he admitted it surprised her even more. She smiled, dropping her gaze to the honey packet she was trying to open in her lap.

"I'll pay the difference if you shop here instead."

"I'll send you the bill in two weeks."

He bumped his shoulder into Abigail's, a bad habit he picked up from her. "I'm adding stuff to the list."

"That's not the deal," she joked. "I'm not doing your shopping for you."

"I bring a girl dinner and she can't even pick me up some peanut butter."

"What were you doing there?" Abigail asked, referring to the church.

"Just because you're bad at not talking about work, doesn't mean I am."

"Come on. I won't tell anybody."

"Isn't it against your hero code to withhold information from your team?"

"I'm pretty sure *we're* against hero code." Abigail ripped the honey packet open. She wouldn't turn Cinder in, she knew that as well as she knew her flames. But if she couldn't prevent other people from getting hurt it would be worth nothing. "Tell me."

"No way, *hero*."

"What are you plotting?" Abigail smeared a line of honey across his cheek.

Cinder wiped it away with his thumb before wiping off the smear across her mouth with his own. "I'm not conversing with the enemy."

"But this is fine?" She returned his honey-flavored kiss.

"This is perfect," he admitted in a whisper. "Way better than I could've hoped."

"What do you mean?"

"That's another secret." Abigail opened her mouth, but Cinder stopped her. "One too expensive for your bad coffee. And, if you must know, I'm cleaning up some things over there."

Abigail picked apart the rest of her dinner. "You're restoring that old church?"

"Yes."

She shouldn't have believed him, but she did. She could pull records tomorrow about the church's history and find the restoration company and that would prove his story.

When the movie switched to a commercial Cinder asked, "Did you go to Henry's memorial?"

She shook her head. "I sent flowers."

Cinder knocked his knee against hers again. "He was a good guy. Never said anything about me snooping around the mailboxes."

"He caught you?" Abigail asked with a grin.

"Just once," Cinder defended. "Said he'd give the note to you himself."

They finished their meal. They finished the crappy movie. Abigail fell asleep pressed between him and the couch. Cinder was gone when she woke in the morning. Her apartment smelled of woodsmoke.

Chapter Twenty-Nine

Abigail had gotten used to seeing Shannon behind the reception desk when she came into work. It was easy to feed off her energy; her brightly painted nails always matched her mood, and even if Abigail didn't care about the drama of the Who's Who of San Arbor, she could enjoy Shannon's eager and outlandish speculations. Abigail was not used to seeing Mitch waiting for her in the HRC lobby. Avalon's costume was slung over his shoulder in a clear dress bag. He already looked annoyed with her.

"Morning Mitch." Abigail offered him a wide smile that he did not return. "What's going on?"

"I didn't think you'd be more trouble as a sidekick than you were as an employee."

"What's that supposed to mean?"

"The chief of police is upstairs waiting for you." He shoved her costume at her. "Whatever you and Excalibur cooked up last week is making a lot of people talk. Do you know how much I have to do now? Get to the Round Table."

"I've got to stop and change." Abigail cradled her costume and flattened out one of the leather pleats where Mitch had manhandled it too roughly. "Tell them I'll be there in ten minutes."

"There's no time. Change in the elevator and get there now."

Abigail didn't want to fight with Mitch. His grouch level was already reaching double digits, and she didn't want to be around if it got any higher. An explosion from Mitch could put Volcanic's flames to shame. She successfully changed into Avalon's dress in the elevator, using the reflective surface to straighten her mask and bow before it opened on the twelfth floor. The door to the Round Table room was open and she quickly walked in and took her seat next to Excalibur.

Chief DaVodi stood across the table from them. He looked just as annoyed as when Abigail saw him at the hospital. President Samuels sat on the same side as the chief with an untouched pot of coffee steaming between them.

"Is this everyone?" The chief asked.

"Yes, Chief DaVodi," King Arthur answered politely. "You may begin."

Chief DaVodi adjusted his reading glasses and opened his notebook. Merlin leaned over King Arthur's shoulder to get a better look at the documents. Abigail recognized them as her and Excalibur's report. A television monitor across the room displayed a city map with the same red marks as the paper map did. The dots were an unsettling ring of red around Town Hall.

"We didn't connect this together like your team did," DaVodi admitted in a sour tone. Excalibur tapped Abigail's boot as a secret high five under the table. "Good job figuring this out. We've seen this type of quick hits before in larger cities. In those situations, the criminals were testing the response time of first responders. If this is their plan, then their target would be inside the ring."

The television monitor zoomed into the map and focused on the town hall building.

"We can assume that this is the target, as it's the only point of interest within that section, but we don't know the motive yet." DaVodi pulled his glasses down his nose. "Or the timeline that they're working under."

"Increasing our presence could help keep the criminals and villains away," President Samuels suggested from his seat. "We can mobilize at your command."

"Say the word, Chief," King Arthur interrupted. "My team can take care of this without you and your men needing to lift a finger. Let us squash this problem."

"We're here to listen to Chief DaVodi," President Samuels reminded, giving King Arthur a hard stare.

"We have a better approach that we would like your team to help with," DaVodi said. "We were tracking known criminals' movements the last few weeks but were unable to catch them in any act. But, with the list of potential suspects you sent over we believe that this location is being used as a base of operations. There are enough of the suspects acting within the location to warrant a search. If we can take the base, we can find someone who knows what's going on."

"Or, even better, a nice big poster with the villain's plans printed on it." King Arthur was grinning.

DaVodi wasn't as hopeful. He pointed a remote at the monitor and the image changed to a mugshot of the men Excalibur and Abigail caught during the bus robbery. Several other images appeared on the screen of the same men entering and exiting a run down building.

"This is the building that we've been tracking the activity to," the police chief explained. "Since receiving your report, we've had the location under tight surveillance."

"Where's this building?" Merlin asked.

"On the east side," DaVodi answered, and the monitor changed to reveal an aerial shot of the building.

Abigail's mouth dried as she stared at the twin spirals coming off the building, one of which was breaking apart.

"We are ready to raid today," DaVodi continued. "Our men will be in place in three hours. We want to hit this place fast and hard."

"We'll be there," King Arthur promised. "Tell us what you need us to do."

"Protect my men," said DaVodi. "I don't know what kind of people they'll have in there so we're asking for your support in case they're villainous."

"We're the Knights of the Round Table," Excalibur boasted. "No one will get past us. Right, Avalon?"

Excalibur slapped Abigail's back, and it reconnected her brain wires enough to agree with him.

"We'll send a bus for you." DaVodi closed his notebook.

"I'll walk you out." President Samuels stood from his seat. "Thank you for meeting us here."

King Arthur waited for the door to shut behind the chief before shouting, "Finally! This is what I've been waiting for."

"I'm even looking forward to it." Merlin grinned and poured herself a cup of coffee.

"I didn't think you could be excited about anything, Mer," Excalibur teased.

"I'm excited for the day someone pops your jaw hard enough to keep you from talking for a week."

"Ouch," Excalibur feinted. "How about you, Abbs? Ready for your first real mission?"

"I think I'm going to be sick!" Abigail pushed herself away from the table and ran out of the room.

King Arthur laughed. "I remember my first takedown. I think I threw up too."

Abigail locked herself inside a bathroom stall. Her hands shook so violently she almost dropped her phone in the toilet when she pulled it from her pocket. She had to retype her message four times because she kept pushing the wrong buttons. She still couldn't breathe right after hitting send, and a traitorous pit grew inside her stomach.

Get out of the building! The one across from the grocery store. Please!

***

The public gardens that encircled the front half of the Hero Relief Center usually calmed Abigail. The bushes moved in the summer breeze like a perfectly crafted meditative video. She was not calm as she stood with the Round Table Knights now, however. Two hours had passed, and she hadn't gotten a response to her warning. The warning that could have cleared out the entire building by now. The warning that could have given the criminals inside enough time to rig an explosive trap. Abigail swallowed hard. She had locked her phone in her desk and had no way to check it again. She had no way to take it back.

She looked to each of the Knights and the two dozen heavily padded officers that stood with them. They would all be in danger because of her. They could all die today because of her. She gripped the hilt of her sword until her nails bit into her palm. She couldn't tell them anything. She would just have to work twice as hard to protect them now.

This was the bed she made, and she would lay in it. She would die in it if it came to that.

Chief DaVodi stood at the front of the group. He was going over their plan of attack, but to Abigail his voice was lost over the blood roaring in her ears. Someone pinched her upper arm.

"Don't be so nervous." Merlin instructed next to her, pinching Abigail a second time. "You're making me antsy."

"Sorry," she answered absently.

"This mission is going to be easy," Chief DaVodi said. "I've only asked the heroes to be with us today since they were the ones who gave us this lead. And because we don't know what's waiting for us there. They take the lead once we're inside, got it?"

DaVodi's officers nodded.

"Let's load up."

The mission was easy on paper. Lead the police force through the building. Protect them while advancing through, stop any threat, find any information concerning the recent attacks, the suggested town hall attack, or the theorized crime gang.

The mission was harder in action. The old building was falling apart. Floorboards were missing, broken glass littered the ground, and the only light came from the officers' flashlights and that could barely break through the floating dust motes that created a smokescreen.

Abigail stood at Excalibur's side. Her sword burned blue as they led their squad through the ancient church. The front of the building was all open space, with tall ceilings and faded stained glass. Abigail felt she was being watched. Judged by the heavenly depictions above, judged by the police force who had to put their lives in her young hands, judged by the hero at her side who didn't know she had tipped off a villain.

Her burning blade lit a path through the dust clouded room, but it didn't shine any light through her clouded mind. Every corner they turned down she expected to find Cinder waiting for her. His fists burning blue as her blade. She would either have to defeat him or let him run, unless he chose for her and burned her squad to ashes.

King Arthur and Merlin had taken their squads deeper into the church as planned, while Excalibur and Abigail cleared the main level. The congregation room had two rooms built behind the altar. There was a door on either side of the raised platform housing a pool of green water. The tub was lined with so much grime Abigail figured the last baptism had to have been over a decade ago.

Excalibur gave her a hand sign to separate their group. Abigail to the left and himself to the right. As planned, they kicked the two doors down at the same time. Abigail created a ball of red flame in her free hand to help fill the new room with additional light. It looked like it was once a classroom. Desks were still pushed into a back corner. A giant of a man appeared in front of her, stepping out of the shadows. She tried to evade the metal bat the criminal wielded, but the crack against her side rang in her ears. If her costume was any less professional, her ribs would have broken.

"Get back!" she yelled to the police officers behind her. Her arms combusted into cherry-red flames, and she blocked the second attack with her sword.

The blade's sharpness didn't beat the bat's brute force. The weapon pushed Abigail back a step. The giant man didn't seem to have any powers outside his massive size and strength, but Abigail's only job was to protect the police behind her so she wouldn't take any chances. She couldn't let this man reach them. She would not fail. She couldn't.

On the third swing, Abigail caught the bat against her blade. Before it could push her back, she filled the space between her and the criminal with the hottest blue flame she could muster. The bat softened under the intense heat, and Abigail's sword pushed through it like butter. Her blazing blade continued past the bat and into the criminal's stomach. The man cried out in agony, stumbling away from the sword. His wound cauterized itself as the burning blade slid out of his stomach.

Three officers behind Abigail fired their tasers. The potent electrical current knocked the criminal out. They cuffed the giant and continued through the back door on the other side of the room. It released them into a dark hallway leading deeper into the ground. Abigail smelled the musky scent of cold and damp earth. Her flames created better light in the tunnel which lacked the dust of the main floor, but her breath still caught against her teeth at every corner. If she hadn't seen Cinder this far down did that mean one of the other heroes had?

"We're coming up on squad A," an officer announced. He watched a radar device in his hands. Each squad had a tracker embedded in a similar device. "Through the door on our right."

Abigail propped the door open to see inside before moving in. King Arthur spoke to someone hidden just beyond the door. His eyes glowed a royal purple as his power activated. King Arthur could've become a politician, using his power of sway to get whatever he wanted, but he became a hero instead.

"Are these all the papers you have?" he asked.

"Yes," the person answered, powerless to lie to King Arthur.

Abigail led her squad in. Scanning the room, she only saw the criminal King Arthur was controlling. A dark red tattoo wrapped around his forearm. The relief she felt almost knocked her off her feet. The room was absent of Cinder and his woodsmoke smell. Abigail breathed a little easier.

"What was the target?" King Arthur asked.

"The mayor," the criminal answered. He stood rigidly with his arms bound tightly at his sides by an unseen force. "And the city revenue. I was going to take the city hostage."

"And do what with it?" King Arthur flipped through the various documents that were set out on a table.

"Either take it over or burn it down."

"And you were the leader?" King Arthur asked, his eyes glowing brighter with each word.

"Yes."

King Arthur smiled and set the documents back on the table. "Chief DaVodi, he's all yours."

Chief DaVodi emerged from the back of the room and properly cuffed the criminal. He began reading him his rights as he led the criminal out through the tunnel.

"Good job everyone," King Arthur said to the men and women in the room, his purple eyes returning to normal. "Let's clear out the building and get back to HQ."

Abigail joined up with Excalibur. He had a few dents in his armor but was otherwise okay. He gave her a thumbs up. She didn't deserve it. Abigail helped drag the captured criminals to the waiting police van. She checked each of them but never found Cinder.

The broken church loomed behind her. It's judgmental glare a hundred times stronger.

Chapter Thirty

Abigail paced her apartment. Her feet dragged through the thin carpet leaving a track of worrying footsteps between her kitchen and her bedroom. Kitchen counter to bedpost. Over and over again. She felt she could've walked halfway across the country by now. But her mind and heart were worn out more than her legs.

Countertop to bedpost. Countertop to bedpost. Countertop to bedpost.

She had jeopardized everything today. The lives of the Round Table Knights, the police force. Her life. Her job. She threw it all away just to warn him. She knew things shouldn't have gone that smoothly. She knew other villains should have been waiting for them. She knew there should have been an ambush waiting if anyone else saw her message. She knew Cinder should have destroyed any evidence before they got there. The raid should not have gone that smoothly. Which only meant one thing, what came next would be rougher than hell.

Countertop to bedpost. Countertop to bedpost. Countertop to bedpost.

It was almost midnight when Cinder arrived. Slipping through the patio door like he had a hundred times before. Abigail waited for him like she had a hundred times before. Instead of her heart soaring at the sight of him emerging from the shadows, it fell. It fell like she should have fallen off the roof months ago.

"Thanks for that heads up, doll." Cinder approached her, but Abigail turned away from his waiting arms. She couldn't get pulled into him. Not tonight. Not again. "Hope you were able to catch whoever you needed."

"I shouldn't have done that," Abigail said. "It was against the rules to tell you."

"I'm glad you're bad at breaking them." Cinder smirked. "Or did you want to put me in cuffs?"

"You don't understand. I can't do this."

Cinder took another step toward her, and Abigail stepped back again. "What are you talking about?"

"I can't—we can't be like this anymore." Abigail gestured between them, hoping her hands explained what she couldn't. What she was too scared to say.

Cinder dragged a scarred hand through his hair. "Come out and say it."

Abigail swallowed hard, forcing down the emotions that were going to spill over. Her voice still cracked. "We can't be together."

"Don't start that crap again," he growled. "You know I'm different."

"Different how? What was all that today?"

"I'd say a victory for you." Cinder tried to step closer to her, but Abigail backed away. The apartment they had been inseparable in was now vast and cavernous. "I left everything there for you to find. You got the bad guy, good job."

"You were part of it?"

"I was leading it!"

I like my crimes to be a bit more organized. "You were going to kill the mayor?"

Cinder gaped. "What? Abby, no. I just needed to—"

"I can't do this!" Abigail interrupted in a desperate shout. Her fingers sparked as her emotions forced their way out. "I can't love a—"

"A villain?" Cinder spat the word like it was poison. "But you did. You do."

"A murderer," she corrected.

Cinder pointed at the desk in the corner of the room. "Murderer? Because of that?"

Abigail hadn't moved the notes she started collecting when their 'arrangement' started. The news articles, the notes, all of it detailing what little was known about his criminal life. The two versions of him filled the room, and it was hard for Abigail to breathe. The villain responsible for the attack on the hospital, and the man responsible for the sidekick's heart.

"You have no idea what that is." A bolt of blue fire scorched the notes, and Cinder lowered his hand.

"It looks like you bombed a–"

"Volcanic left me there to die!" Cinder's statement knocked the wind from Abigail's lungs. She backed against the wall like she had been shoved into it. "He's a real killer, and you buddied up to him just fine."

"What?"

"You weren't his first sidekick, Abigail!" Blue flames raged up Cinder's arms burning his coat, but he didn't care. His dark scars twisted around his body. "Be glad he only fired you in the work sense. I got the full force of it."

Abigail was silent. Her legs wobbled, and it wasn't from her endless pacing. What Cinder said didn't make sense. She knew what the words meant on their own, but strung together in that sentence, they sounded alien to her. She could only stare at Cinder. His blue flames ate away his coat and dropped smoldering pieces onto the floor.

"Your scars." She watched his face twist under the markings in question. "They're from him?"

"Everything is from him."

"What do you mean?"

"I was going to use you to destroy him."

"What are you saying?" Abigail had never felt this breathless.

"I was going to burn his city to the ground. Have his little sidekick beat him with his own curse." Cinder stomped to the patio as his fire grew around him. "I was stupid to ever trust you."

Abigail chased after him and reached through the flames grabbing his wrist before he got to the door. "Cin, wait, please, tell me what happened."

A burst of blue fire erupted between their connected skin. It was hot enough to burn and Abigail was forced to let go. Unlike before, her burned fingers pulsed in pain. The patio door curtains smoldered in the heat.

"This is over." Cinder's voice was too cold compared to the fire raging around him. It chilled Abigail to her core. "Don't follow me."

Chapter Thirty-One

Abigail slid down the patio door, her aching hand finding solace against the cold glass that her heart couldn't. The burns were superficial, her fingers bright red instead of the haunting blackness. She twisted away from the glass, away from the patio that contained too many memories, and crawled on top of the bed containing only slightly less memories of Cinder. She needed to sleep. She needed to wake up tomorrow with sunshine and new beginnings.

She needed to wake tomorrow and discover this was all a dream.

Abigail did not sleep.

Tossing and turning against the mattress, she couldn't escape the woodsmoke scent that clung to the sheets, the pillows, to her. Eventually, she passed out as her mind warred between Cinder's accusations and his departure, but she didn't count it as sleep. Sleeping was meant to be peaceful. A recharge from the day before. She wasn't supposed to wake up two hours later with red eyes and a hurting heart. Abigail's pillow was damp from the tears that snuck past her closed eyes.

She wrapped the heavy quilt around her shoulders and wandered to the kitchen. The blanket dragged behind her as a cape. The burden of a hero. It erased the remaining pieces of ash that Cinder's burning coat left on the carpet. Abigail spotted the dirty skillet on the counter where they had made grilled sandwiches and teared up again.

She turned her back on the kitchen memories and stared at the memories still clinging to the bedroom. She resumed her pacing, her computer desk keeping her pace as the burned remains of her notes trickled to the floor. Countertop to bedpost. Countertop to bedpost. Cinder to Volcanic.

Abigail hadn't known much of Kenneth's past.

She knew he had an ex-wife. Kenneth hadn't seen her in a long while. He didn't like to talk about her. Or the boy in the picture on his desk.

A boy with stunning green eyes and wild black hair.

She barely knew anything about Kenneth's present. The number one hero ranked at the very bottom of personal connection, but Abigail didn't believe he could do something like... She wasn't even sure what Cinder had accused him of. Trying to kill his sidekick? It didn't make sense. Nothing made sense.

Abigail slowed her pacing. Staying still wasn't in her power set, and she refused to do so now. She may not know of her ex-partner's past, but she knew his routine. She knew the 5 a.m. run he'd be getting ready to take through his neighborhood.

The quilted cape fell from her shoulders, and Abigail exchanged her current clothes for something more suited for a marathon. The woven sneakers were light on her feet. She'd join Kenneth whether he liked it or not.

She would either run off her frustrations or run into answers.

The community park on the backside of Kenneth's neighborhood was dim. The rising sun hadn't chased the gray of night off the plants, sidewalk, or street lamps yet. The light posts were slick with dew. The fountain in the center of the duck pond remained dormant. The ducks floated sleepily on the water's surface. The park was silent and still. The peace of it caused a bead of sweat to run down Abigail's spine. Something hunted in the sparse trees on the side of the running trail.

Abigail didn't think it was her hunting Kenneth, either.

Around a bend, a glare of orange light blinded her through the trees and Abigail assumed it was the sun beginning its ascension. As she turned the corner her assumptions were wrong. A flash of blue devoured the defensive flames summoned from Kenneth. He knelt in front of a tree several yards ahead of her. An indent of his body contorted the tree's trunk with a painful looking divot. The low hanging branches above him smoked with glowing embers. Without his mask he looked human. Kneeling across his opponent, he looked weak.

Across from them, two trails of indigo fire circled Cinder's arms like venomous snakes. The air snapped with chaotic energy as the temperature raised. The crooked smile Abigail believed to be as trademarked as his blue flames was gone. The glare raging beneath his scars resembled that of a man who never learned to grin. Never learned to laugh. Never knew love.

Abigail's attention was pulled off Cinder as Kenneth called her name.

"Abigail, get back!" Kenneth returned to his feet. "That man's dangerous."

Cinder barked. "I'll show you dangerous, old man!"

Cinder unleashed his twin flames as powerful flamethrowers toward Kenneth who rolled to the side avoiding a direct hit. Smoke sputtered off his back as his shirt melted but, with a flash of his own orange flames, he snuffed the blaze. Abigail knew Kenneth's next move from their time training together. Apparently, so did Cinder. Kenneth pitched a baseball of fire toward Cinder's feet causing him to dodge to where a second fireball would have made contact.

Abigail had fallen for the trick too many times in their early partnership.

Cinder didn't.

Launching himself forward, Cinder used the first fireball as a springboard and dove headfirst at Kenneth. The second fireball rolled painlessly off Cinder's chest.

Coating his fists in flaming gloves, Cinder walloped into Kenneth's midsection for a long six seconds before Kenneth shoved him off with a giant wall of flames between them. Cinder reached through the fire anyway, and Abigail saw the flames enter his scarred skin.

Abigail ran to Kenneth and pulled his hulking form out of the way just as a jettison of blue and orange flame obliterated the tree directly behind Kenneth's former position. The fire wall dissipated, and Cinder's hateful eyes scorched them both.

"I told you not to follow me." Cinder's voice remained cold despite the inferno around them.

"Who are you?" Kenneth demanded.

A burst of blue flame around his wrist explained the rage that billowed inside Cinder better than any words could. He glared at Kenneth, and Abigail felt the heat of his gaze where she stood. His hands were engulfed in flames, and the light obscured his face until he absorbed his own fire. The area became still again, but the predator no longer hid in the tree line.

He stared down his prey with enough firepower to level a city block.

"Figures you gave up your memory when you gave up on me, Helios." Cinder spat Kenneth's old name. Sparks flew from his mouth with each word.

Recognition shimmered in Kenneth's eyes, but he didn't speak. Instead, he readied another attack. The orange glow of his flames were dull and dim compared to the forest burning blue around them. "Cover me," he told Abigail. "We're taking down this villain today."

Cinder exploded.

Blue fire fumed out of every piece of Cinder. Even his eyes smoked in the rage. He tore after Kenneth, barreling at the hero like a deranged beast. All the sensibility that made Cinder cunning had evaporated. All the planning that made him deadly was replaced with reckless rage. Kenneth didn't know how to handle reckless and was unable to deflect the shot that connected to his shoulder.

Thankfully, Abigail burned with a similar recklessness. Burned with similar blue flames.

Igniting her hands with her Dragon's Breath, she side stepped around Kenneth and snatched Cinder's wrist, twisting him away with his own momentum. Cinder stumbled but turned his attack on her. His fists glided off her cheek without impact. She grabbed his other hand.

"Cinder, this has to stop," she pleaded.

His fire flashed between their hands with enough heat to break through her barrier. Abigail held onto him until the pain forced her hands to release him. "Stay out of my way."

Cinder shoved Abigail to the ground and leapt toward Kenneth. She jumped back to her feet but was too late to stop the deadly blast of blue fire that consumed Kenneth. The light blinded her, the heat scorched her, the snap of the sound barrier deafened her. She still ran for him.

Without her senses, Abigail found Kenneth by touch. Crawling on her hands and knees until she felt him on the ground among the ash and broken foliage. Her sight returned, and she wished it hadn't. Kenneth was alive, but she didn't understand how. One side of his face was charred beyond recognition. Boiled fat oozed where his skin should have been. His gums were too exposed and made his mouth appear skeletal.

The scent of burning flesh choked Abigail.

Cinder loomed above them. Body shaking with adrenaline. The trees around him burned. He looked at home within their blaze. Flames, his own and those feeding off the carnage, caressed him. He looked far from finished. Kenneth wouldn't survive another attack.

Abigail lowered Kenneth's head to the dirt and stood between her former teachers. She had trained her whole career to defeat the Flame Villain. She never imagined she'd be doing so as tears evaporated off her cheeks.

"Cin, don't make me do this."

"You think you're finally going to beat me?" Cinder was able to laugh, but it sounded awful. It was raw, hurtful, unhinged.

"No." Abigail knew it was true. She felt his deranged heat chew through her fireproofing an arm's reach away. "You're going to let me win."

The blue flames crawling around Cinder dropped momentarily as he looked at her with confusion. They snapped back to life as he said, "He's a monster. He deserves this."

"You'll become one if you do this. I know you're better than this, Cinder. I know you're better than him." The oxygen grew thin and she whispered, "I know you."

"I don't think you do."

Fire erupted between them. Abigail was barely able to protect her face before the force knocked her down. She scrambled to cover Kenneth's dying body with her own. All around her the fire snapped viciously. The trees cracked and broke apart. Abigail felt the heat of the flames as her fireproofing weakened. She wasn't sure she'd be able to outrun the blast. She knew Kenneth's damaged body wouldn't survive the hit.

But the finishing blow never came.

Beside her, a smoldering ball of blue fire tore into the ground inches from her and Kenneth. But it had missed them. Cinder didn't miss. Abigail looked around, and inside the inferno she saw a black silhouette running away. The blaze hid its fiendish creature.

She needed to run after him like she needed to breathe. Each second the distance between them grew, the more cracks splintered inside her heart. As she stood to chase him, a weakened hand encased her wrist.

"Abby." Kenneth choked on her name, blood and soot trickled over his bottom lip. "Call for back up."

His good eye, if she could call it that, was swelling shut and she had lost sight of the other one buried below the char. His hand slipped from her wrist.

A hero saves people, and right now this hero needed her more.

Chapter Thirty-Two

Kenneth Jinkins, a brute of a man, was displayed on the other side of a window wrapped up in gauze and kept alive by fluids pushed by IVs.

Volcanic, number one hero in San Arbor, had been defeated.

Abigail Turner, sidekick, stood helplessly on the other side of the window clutching a box of chocolates to her chest.

She didn't know if she would have recognized him as Volcanic if she didn't know before coming in. Not because he was out of costume, the green hospital gown was too small for him, or because his face was obscured with bandages, but because of how fragile he looked hooked up to the hospital machines. Heroes were ultimately human under their mask, but Volcanic was the type to never take his off. Sometimes, it was like Kenneth had been the actual mask.

More tears ringed her eyes, and she wished she would run out of them already.

They had been in the hospital for hours after paramedics picked them up. Kenneth was in the ICU far longer than any of the other patients wheeled into the ER after him. Abigail refused to go far from his room while white coated doctors used their own superhero-like abilities to bring him back. She only agreed to give her statement, that she found this man in the middle of the forest fire, when the officer agreed to take it down outside the curtain around his bed. She only agreed to be treated after Kenneth was transferred to the zoo exhibit he now laid in. Doctors recommended she go home and give him time to rest. She recommended they keep their opinions to themselves.

A rolling cart of goodies passed her hallway sometime between dawn and noon, and she procured the chocolate box she now suffocated in her arms.

Abigail was a terrible sidekick. A terrible hero.

She couldn't save anyone.

A fuzzy reflection joined hers in the window. Glancing up, Abigail saw red hair and a freckled face. It chased away her heavy emotions for just a moment, but Abigail was grateful for it all the same. "Hey boss," she whispered, certain if she gave her body the chance she would burst into sobs.

"I was worried when you didn't come in today, even worse when you didn't answer your phone. But, after getting the report I knew you'd be here." Excalibur wrapped an arm around Abigail's shoulders and pulled her into him. "Talk to me."

Not feeling his armor shocked her system. The small reset allowed her mind to detach itself from the events of the last 12 hours.

"He hates flowers," she tried to explain the chocolates.

"I'm sure he'll love them when he wakes up," Excalibur smiled. "What did the doctors say?"

"Third degree burns, but they should have been much worse. His fireproofing stopped a lot of the damage. They've been impressed with his numbers, but I'm not sure what numbers they mean. A nurse switched the breathing mask for just a nose tube thing."

"All good signs, what about you?" Excalibur touched the gauze around her forearm.

"It'll all heal."

"The attacker must have had some heavy fire power to burn you guys."

Abigail nodded, returning her gaze to Kenneth who slept on the other side of the glass.

"King and Merlin are searching the city right now. I'm headed out after this."

"I'm coming with you!"

"No, you're not. King's orders." Before Abigail could lash out with protest, Excalibur added, "You're too close to this, Abigail."

"But my powers are better suited for this." Abigail couldn't say how she truly felt. That she needed to find Cinder before anyone else.

"You're better suited to be here." Excalibur pointed at the glass. "When he wakes up, he'll feel a lot better having you here for him."

"I don't think you know him like I do."

"You're right, I don't. But, waking up alone in a hospital after an attack would shake anyone up. I don't think a hero ranking stops you from that."

"Maybe you're right."

"SAPD handed the investigation to us. The threat is too high for them to do on their own. I know you already gave your statement, but I'm hoping you can tell me more. Anything that can help us figure out who this villain is, and where they may have run to."

Abigail's heart seized and she repeated what she told the officer. "The villain was already fleeing when I arrived. I didn't see his face."

"But you know it's a guy?"

"It could have been the Flame Villain."

"That would explain the fire." Excalibur nodded. "Why were you over there, anyway?"

"Running. Training."

"There are closer places to run near the HRC and your house."

"I liked the area." Abigail sighed. "'Xcal, I feel like I'm the one under investigation here."

Excalibur grinned. "Sorry, Abbs. That wasn't my intention. When he wakes up will you see what he remembers?"

"Will you update me with your search?"

"You'll be my first call." Excalibur squeezed her shoulders a final time before leaving the hallway.

***

The clock on the wall kept track of the hours, but time felt frozen as Abigail waited. She watched nurses come and go from Kenneth's room without offering any information to her. The cart full of goodies circled back, and Abigail grabbed something sweet and sticky to keep her blood sugar and energy up. The longer she watched Kenneth sleep the stronger the need to shut her own eyes overcame her.

Sometime later, a hand shook her awake and Abigail jumped to her feet, wiping drool off her chin. A white coated doctor waited for her to compose herself.

"He's awake now."

Abigail didn't remember how being tired felt. Her body energized, and her eyes darted around the doctor to find a way into the room. A way to Kenneth.

"But still needs his rest. You can see him, but only for a few minutes. Okay?"

"Yeah, sure."

The doctor opened the door and Abigail bolted inside as if she were running inside a burning building. Her eyes widened, and she froze mid step. The door shut behind her. The glass had somehow hidden the worst of Kenneth's injuries. Seeing him unobstructed solidified that he had indeed been defeated. That he was just human. Vulnerable.

"Stop." Kenneth's voice was hoarse from the smoke inhaled during the attack. "Don't look at me like I'm broken."

Abigail slowly lowered herself into the chair next to his bed. The bearish hands that taught her how to throw a punch without breaking her pinky finger were charred.

Abigail swallowed hard. "I brought you these."

Kenneth took the box from her and lifted the lid. He grabbed a piece filled with raspberry cream. He usually saved them for last. They were his favorite. "Did you catch him?"

"He got away. I decided to save you rather than chase after him."

"Police hunting him down?"

"The Knights are. SAPD handed over the investigation. We have a better chance of detaining the villain." Abigail's mouth soured.

"Are they good to you over there? The HRC?"

His question surprised her. "They are. They're hoping you can remember something from the attack that will help them find him."

Kenneth rested the chocolate box on his lap. "You were there. You saw who it was."

Cinder. "The Flame Villain. But why did he attack you like that?"

Kenneth fished for another raspberry-filled chocolate square. His hands were covered in a crisscrossing of burn scars.

"What happened to your first sidekick?"

Kenneth choked on the chocolate.

"Kenneth, please," Abigail begged. "Tell me what happened."

"You don't know what you're asking—"

"I need to know. You need to tell me."

"Why?" He pinned her with his one visible eye. It was harder than steel.

Abigail knew she played dirty. "Because you didn't make me strong enough to stop him. You owe me this."

Kenneth put the lid on the chocolate box and drummed his fingers against the top. Abigail's heart matched the fast pace.

"You reminded me a lot of him when I first met you," he said softly. "You were both too eager for the job. Too ready to jump into danger. It's why I didn't like you. I kept seeing his face."

"Who?"

"Tommy, but his code name was Wildfire. We worked together about ten years ago. It was a different city. I'm surprised anyone here knew about him outside Kreech. Did he tell you?"

Abigail shook her head. "What happened to Wildfire?"

"He jumped in the way," Kenneth answered bitterly. "I nailed him with a flame big enough to level a house. He wasn't as fireproof as you. I was surprised he survived at all. The building was collapsing, the support beams were failing. I carried him out. The first responders were busy with the collapse and carting off the arsonist, so I got away without being seen.

"I took him to the emergency room. I put him on the gurney and left." Kenneth glanced from his hands to his ex-sidekick, the steel beam of his eye wavered in something. Sadness? Pity? Regret? Abigail couldn't place it. All she felt was the heat coming from her hands. "I couldn't look at him anymore, Abigail. I couldn't look at the boy that I charred, I couldn't be there if he didn't wake up."

"But he survived." Abigail's words were shaking. *I'm Wi-ire.* "He didn't blow up that hospital, he was scared, the flames poured out of him. He couldn't control it."

"If he didn't die then then he died in the blast he caused. Whoever walked out of that hospital wasn't Tommy anymore."

"You left him there to die!"

"And he damn near killed me! Killed us!"

Kenneth's heart monitor jumped. They were both quiet as the beeping returned to normal. Abigail's phone buzzed inside her pocket. She let her voicemail answer.

"He had red fire like you," Kenneth added sadly. "Before that day. I don't know if my blast supercharged him or something."

"Did you know?" Abigail ignored him. "When he first came to San Arbor did you know it was him?"

"Not until this morning."

There was a knock at the door.

"Abigail." Kenneth grabbed her wrist as she stood. "Do not go after him, understand me? He's dangerous and he will kill someone. Leave it to the heroes."

Abigail only understood one thing. She pulled her hand free of the hero's weak grip and turned her back to Kenneth so he didn't see her cry. "I am a hero."

When Abigail stepped out of the hospital, she thought she was finally out of tears. She wasn't ready for the voicemail that waited for her like a landmine.

This is where your end of the deal comes in, doll. I want my head start. If you know what's good for you then you won't chase after me. Goodbye, Abigail Turner. I'm sorry I hurt you.

Chapter Thirty-Three

Abigail didn't feel the cold snap of AC against her skin when she entered the HRC. She didn't register Shannon's polite greeting from her desk. The elevator didn't shake her as it normally did during the ride to the top floor. Abigail was numb to the static shock the metal door left on her hand. Remembering to fill her lungs every ten seconds took her full attention. Each inhale threatened to cut her loose.

She was lost. Not in the building, but in her mind, in what she needed to do. Abigail didn't know what she even could do. Kenneth was laid up in a hospital with burns so severe she didn't think he'd recover; she doubted his bandaged eye would see properly once the gauze was removed. Her heart broke when she thought of him, but not for him. The heaviness in her chest was reserved for the boy who had suffered the most at Kenneth's hands.

The same man that was now a villain running for his life for taking what he thought was owed to him.

Abigail collapsed in her seat at the Round Table. She couldn't blame Cinder. She knew she'd try to do the same if she had been in his scarred shoes. The same need for retaliation started her on this path. She could never blame Cinder.

As her throat tightened, she pulled the closest folder over to her for distraction. She recognized King's organized handwriting and read through his report on the raid, except it didn't make sense anymore. The tattooed man hadn't been the leader. Taking the Mayor had never been Cinder's intention. Abigail chewed the inside of her cheek. She didn't think any crook would take the fall for something that large. Especially after Cinder left them as easy targets for the Knights to find.

Abigail was too deep into the report to hear the elevator chime outside or the approach to the Round Table. She missed the knock against the door frame and the body sitting in the chair next to her. The same hand that had given her comfort weeks ago made her drop the folder in fright when it cupped her shoulder.

"It's just me." King Arthur's voice was peaceful. "You don't have to be here. You can be with Volcanic."

"I couldn't," Abigail declared. "I need to do something helpful. Have you found him?"

"Not yet."

Abigail swallowed her relief. "Any leads on where he went?"

"I was hoping you got some information from Volcanic."

"I wish I had." Abigail desperately wished she had any clues on Cinder's location. Just so she could send the search in the opposite direction. "He was totally blindsided by the attack."

King Arthur squeezed her shoulder, then lowered his hand. "Let me know if I can do anything for you, Abigail. I know this isn't easy for you."

She didn't acknowledge the understatement but tapped the report. "Can you talk to me about this? It doesn't make sense to me. The guy you arrested; he didn't seem big enough to pull something like that off."

"So, you caught that?" King Arthur's perfect smile dripped in guilt. "I used him as a proxy. Made him say everything I wanted to hear."

"What? Why?"

"Quinn needed us to have a solid victory. A raid like that would boost the success of the new ordinance. It was a win for everyone."

"But you were lying."

"No one got hurt," King Arthur reminded her. "Sometimes you have to play a little dirty to get the bad guy. You understand, right?"

"I guess so." Abigail lowered her eyes, the words on the report blurred together. "Are we going to investigate who the real leader is?"

"If we need to, but if they were smart, they would have fled San Arbor after our display." A muffled voice escaped from the earpiece hidden under his hair. King Arthur tapped it and listened. "I have to go."

"Is it him?" Abigail grabbed his arm before he could stand. "The Flame Villain?"

"Just a report of a stolen car. Something to check out though." King Arthur removed her hand and stood. "Go home, Abigail. I don't want you here or on the street until we have more information."

"Yes, sir."

Abigail waited ten minutes for King Arthur to leave the building before she descended the elevator herself. She couldn't go home, not yet. Not without trying to find him before the heroes could. She hailed a taxi and arrived at the justice center where the tattooed man was being processed before being transported to the San Arbor prison. She flashed her hero license at the door, received the mandatory pat down, and waited behind a glass divider for Chester Rose.

The spiraling tattoos around his forearm made sense when he sat across from her and pulled the phone from the wall hook. The rose blossoms tangled together in thorny vines. Even in an orange jumpsuit, shaved head, and missing knife at his hip, the man still looked dangerous.

"You my lawyer?"

Abigail shook her head. "You'll get one once you're transported. But, after a confession to the Knights, I'm not sure how much good one will do."

Chester spat. "That confession was a filthy lie."

"I was hoping you'd tell me more about that. What's the truth about what was happening?"

"Why should I tell you anything?"

"To get it on record," she offered. "If it was a lie, wouldn't you want to nail the guy who's really behind it? Do you have any idea where he could have gone?"

"You think you can catch him?"

"I'd like to find him."

Chester leaned back in his chair. "Do I know you?"

Abigail regretted not coming in costume. "Tell me about the real guy in charge."

"I think I do recognize you." Abigail swallowed as the man leered at her through the glass. "You're Cinder's girl, aren't you?"

Abigail's mouth dried.

"He made it very clear that none of my guys were to so much as look at you. Almost tore my head off the day you bumped into me."

Abigail tucked a curl behind her ear. "He was your leader."

"He was wild," Chester answered. "Made my crew triple in size and attack the downtown just to prove we were serious."

"Was he paying you?"

"Not exactly. He kept us supplied, but the real payoff was going to be taking the mayor."

"You wanted to kill him?"

"Cinder said I could do whatever I wanted with him and San Arbor after he set the place on fire. If you're half as crazy as your boyfriend, I'd love to see what you're made of." Chester laughed.

The light above Abigail flashed twice, letting her know their time was almost over.

"Do you have any idea where he went? Why did he abandon the church?"

Chester's laugh stopped. He gritted his teeth together. "That coward hung me out right before those heroes came in. Knocked me in the back of the head so hard I wasn't waking up until it was too late. He started getting weird about everything."

"Weird how?"

"I don't know, almost like he wasn't as committed as he made us be. I know he had several chances where he could've snatched the mayor, and he let him go. He could've set San Arbor on fire without us, but something kept stopping him."

A guard appeared behind Chester and made him hang up the phone. A second guard escorted Abigail back to the main lobby. Cinder's final request replayed in her mind. For once she was glad she was good at breaking the rules. Good at ignoring Cinder's request not to follow him, and ignoring the Knights' order to stay away from the situation. She'd check the cabin first, already trying to remember the name of the mountain village.

The bus to Jolt Station just arrived when her phone rang. Excalibur's number flashed across the screen.

His voice interrupted her greeting. "We need back up at the Federal Reserve. Something is robbing the place. Something big."

"The Flame Villain?"

The squeal of sirens and a scream from someone on the other end of the call interrupted the conversation.

"Doubtful. This thing looks like it's covered in vines. We could really use that Dragon Breath."

A hero saves people. Abigail made that promise not only to herself, but to her city, and to one intern that wanted to be a swim coach.

The bus doors slid into place. Abigail still stood on the street as it rumbled away.

Nice job, hero.
"I'm on my way."

Chapter Thirty-Four

One year and eight months later

The Hero Relief Center announcement stage was rebuilt on the lawn between the hedge gardens and a newly constructed fountain resembling a sword hilt trapped in a boulder. Two hundred chairs faced the stage under a canopy of string lights. The media's cameras and lights were aimed at the microphone. The tapes already capturing the coming event. The usual water and finger sandwich station for basic press conferences had been replaced with the best catering service in San Arbor, and bottles of champagne were chilling inside buckets of ice.

Something big was about to happen.

President Quinn Samuels stepped onto the stage and tapped the microphone. The crowd took their seats and watched the man with eager eyes. He had retired his courtroom suit for a black tuxedo. He looked like he was hosting an awards ceremony. The media had only seen the president dressed this nice for three other Hero Relief Center press conferences.

"I won't waste your time; I can see you eyeing that buffet spread from here," Quinn opened. "I have the greatest honor to introduce you to *all* of our Round Table Knights."

King Arthur emerged from behind the curtain first, waving to the crowd. Merlin followed him with a dress covered in sequins that reflected the lights around her. Excalibur came next wearing a black bow tie attached to his armored collar with Velcro. Abigail entered last. A smile as big as the moment plastered on her face. She wanted to look cool, like Merlin, but she couldn't stop the smile. Her fingers sparked in response.

"I would like to formally announce the newest Hero member of the Round Table Knights: Avalon, the Dragon Slayer."

The crowd cheered and more cameras flashed. Abigail had finally done it. She was a hero. She looked at the crowd, at the faces of the citizens of her city. She promised each of them, and all the others in San Arbor, she would not let them down. She was going to be the hero that caught the bus now. Someone San Arbor could depend on. Someone to inspire others to become heroes themselves.

Her gaze stopped on a face she almost didn't recognize. For the past few months, the face had been disfigured by a burn scar that should have marked the man for death. Baby pink flesh covered the majority of his face. With the scar now removed, Kenneth finally looked like the hero she remembered and trained under. But, instead of the scowl, the retired hero was grinning. He raised a water bottle, toasting her achievement.

"Everyone, please enjoy yourselves tonight," the president concluded. "We want to celebrate this night with you. A full media package will be released tomorrow morning."

That promise didn't stop the hungry press from swarming Abigail when she stepped off the stage. Her teammates left her to the sharks and used the commotion to head straight for the party starting behind the rows of seating. The gauntlet through the media was as much hero work as stopping the bad guys.

"Avalon, over here!" one of the media members shouted. "Give us a quote, how does it feel?"

"Amazing." Abigail stopped and smiled for their camera. "I'm honestly speechless, dreams really can come true."

"Will you take up your own sidekick?"

"Maybe one day?" Abigail wasn't sure about that one.

"Is there anyone you want to thank?" Another reporter crammed themself to the front line.

That was an easy one. "Of course, everyone at the HRC who believed in me. Excalibur for training me and letting me sidekick under him. This team is amazing to work with." There were two more people she needed to thank, but on the air she couldn't. Avalon belonged in a different world. A world outside of retired heroes from the defunded Saves the Day company. Outside of broken promises to a villain. Even after all this time, his crooked smile kept her up at night.

A few more cameras flashed, and a few more microphones pushed themselves forward.

"Will the Hero Relief Center accept more heroes?"

"We will answer all questions at a later date." President Quinn Samuels snuck in to rescue Abigail. "Please, enjoy the party we have set up here. Our team will send the full package to you in a few hours."

Quinn pushed Abigail behind him and distracted the sharks long enough for her to find her team at the buffet table. She had been smelling the food since hiding behind the curtain while the guests arrived. She loaded a plastic plate with tiny puff pastries and fingerling potatoes. She took one big bite before being handed a champagne flute.

"Avalon, how does it feel?" King Arthur mimicked the reporters.

"Only one word," Abigail raised her glass to the three heroes. "Excelsior!"

King Arthur laughed and tapped his glass against hers. Merlin rolled her eyes but smiled. Excalibur forgot protocol and lifted Abigail into a hug, spilling her drink against his armor.

"I am so proud of you," he said, setting her down.

"One group photo, please?" a small voice squeaked behind the heroes.

The young reporter shook behind his camera. He looked like today was his first day.

"After this, you better find a quiet corner to hide in, or else you'll never finish your meal," Merlin offered her sage advice to Abigail in a whisper.

"Thanks," she whispered back.

The heroes clinked their flutes together a second time and shouted *Excelsior*. Abigail snatched something that looked like a salad presented in a rolled sheet of parmesan cheese and vanished inside the hedge gardens. She plopped herself onto a bench past the first curve. The food was just as good as it smelled, but before she could finish a full puff pastry a voice called to her.

"Excuse me? Could I get a selfie, just real quick?"

Abigail swallowed her bite, and her annoyance, before turning around.

She watched him morph out of the hazy glow of the string lights behind him, his green eyes fairy-lit from the backdrop. He got closer, but still she didn't believe it. She couldn't believe it. His face looked so soft without the crisscrossing of burn scars that had covered it before. It probably felt as soft as she remembered his fingertips being. His hair was slicked back away from his face. His face that he didn't need to hide anymore. Without the mask of scars, he was a new man in San Arbor.

Abigail would never forget the green eyes or the half-crooked smile currently painted across his lips. She saw that face everywhere. In her dreams under the endless sky, in the craters of the full moon outside her window, in the hooded faces of San Arbor.

"Hey, doll."

His voice still rumbled with the force of a starting thunderstorm.

Abigail was off the bench in a heartbeat. She had him pressed against her in another. She didn't care who saw it. She kissed him so hard that she felt the flames begin to catch in her throat. She tried to fill two years of missing Cinder in a single moment.

Cinder chuckled against her lips, and she pulled away just enough so she could speak, her arms still wrapped tightly around his shoulders.

"How is this even possible?"

"You're still easy to follow." The threat was so strange spoken from his charming face. "You didn't even change your locks after I left."

"You always just picked them." Abigail shook her head. "How are you here?"

"It's a long story. One that doesn't need to spoil this moment." He tightened his arms around her. "You saved me that night, too. I didn't want to be a monster."

"Cinder—"

He stole the name off her lips with another kiss.

"You made it pretty clear you would never be with a villain," he explained, leaning his forehead against hers. "So, I became a hero too."

Cinder pulled a badge from his suit pocket and offered it to Abigail. She ran her fingers over the metal. It was as real as he was. The badge was shaped like a fireman's helmet. *Thomas Sanders* was engraved under the symbol.

"I transferred to San Arbor about two weeks ago." He was smiling. "I guess being able to absorb flames is a pretty good skill to have."

"Do they know you're powered?"

"I don't want anyone to know. Miss me?"

Abigail kissed him again. The feeling of his scarred lips fading as his soft ones replaced their memory.

"You removed your scars."

"I was tired of holding onto them. I'm done with it, Abbs," he promised. "I don't want to hurt anyone anymore. I just want to be here. With you."

"I don't even know what to call you now."

"I was hoping *boyfriend* for starters."

She lowered her gaze. Despite his suit, he wore an old pair of sneakers. She stepped away from him. His fingers left goosebumps as they trailed down her arms, letting her go.

"I need to know what happened." Abigail named her price. "Two years ago. Explain it to me."

She expected him to fight her on the answer. She expected him to make a joke or distract her with another head-spinning kiss. He sat on the stone bench, wrung his hands together between his knees and took a very deep breath.

"After the accident, it took years for me to gain control over myself. For months fire would erupt from my skin without warning. I had to stay away from everyone I knew. I had to isolate from people. But it didn't always work. People were hurt because of me, of these blue flames.

"I was so angry, Abigail. Angry at myself for not being strong enough to contain them. Angry at the world for letting this happen to me. But most of all, I was angry at Kenneth for leaving me to die. I didn't care that he hit me with the blast, that was my own fault. But my own partner left me to die."

Abigail squeezed herself next to him, but kept her arms crossed tight across her chest. She needed to hear it all. She didn't dare stop him with a touch.

"Soon I did regain control, and I tried to fit back into my old life. My parents were so relieved to see me. For a while it was nice, us being a family again. But it didn't make me any less angry. It burned me every moment of the day, and the only way I could feel better, feel normal, was burning things. It's cliché, but being reckless made me feel whole. Alive.

"People labeled me a villain before I knew what was happening. I didn't realize burning dumpsters and stealing cars would mark me for one, but everyone agreed I was dangerous, and I left my family. I couldn't risk my parents getting hurt because of me.

"I ran for a while. I think I saw both oceans before I realized what I thought would fix me. I needed to hurt Kenneth the same way he had me. But, I couldn't burn him like he did me. It had to be something more. I needed to take away everything he loved.

"I planned to burn down San Arbor once I found he was transferred here. He only loved one thing, being a hero. After seeing his new side-kick I knew using her to defeat him would be perfect justice. I wanted to turn you against him." He waved his hand as if clearing the air of smoke. "But we know how that turned out."

"I don't." Abigail refused to let his story end there.

"Being with you started making me feel normal. Without all the fires and recklessness of stealing. At the cabin I really thought we could have something like that together. I wanted to try and have something like that together. I changed my plan, I backed out of the raid and left evidence to pin it all on that Rose guy."

"Then why did you attack Kenneth that night?"

He wrung his hands together again, struggling to find his next words. "I overreacted. I felt like all I would ever be was a bad guy. To the world, and to you. No matter if I wanted to change. I felt like Kenneth had taken everything away again.

"I am glad you stopped me." He captured her gaze, finally looking away from his hands. "I mean it. You're right, I'm not some monster."

"I don't know if I can forgive you. Or trust you again." Abigail didn't know a lot of things at the moment.

"I understand—"

"But, I would like to get to know this new you."

"I guess that means you have to call me *stranger*." He tried to joke, referring to his earlier statement.

She shoved his shoulder and they both laughed. His sounding like the lightning strike in the storm, and hers the joyful hum of the electricity.

"I searched for you after you left," Abigail admitted.

"I didn't want to be found," he replied simply. "Especially by you, not until I could become this. Become better."

"Did you?"

He nodded. "Ask me why I wanted to be a hero, why I became Wildfire."

"Why?"

"I wanted to prove my flames weren't dangerous. But I didn't do a good job of that."

Abigail twisted her fingers through his. "There's a lot that happened that wasn't your—"

"Those are excuses. I'm going to make up for my mistakes. I will be a hero, for you and for me. But the kind that doesn't wear a mask. I want to leave that all to you."

Abigail kissed him again.

"Does this hero gig give you any time off?" she asked, breathless. "There's this cabin in the mountains I'd love to take you to."

Acknowledgments

First and foremost, I must thank my agent, Nancy Rosenfeld, and publishers, Kurt and Erica Mueller for believing in me and my story. I hope I make you proud.

Most importantly, I must thank my husband Charlie because without our D&D games, Abigail would have never been created.

A huge thank you to my earliest readers and cheer team; Kenzie, Larissa, Rachell and Allison. You'll never know how much your support made this dream happen.

This book would not be as strongly written without the help from my friends at The Central Cincinnati Fiction Writers group. I am excited for you all to finally read this story. Mark, your wisdom is as unfathomable as your friendship.

To my family at the Western Hills of Kung Fu and Tai Chi. When you taught me broadsword you were also teaching Abigail. Thank you for making us badasses.

It may be cliché to thank you, the reader, but I am grateful for you taking a chance on this book. I hope you follow Abigail and Cinder through the rest of their story.

About the Author

Jordan S. Keller is a Cincinnati based writer whose love for stories started at a young age when she preferred to write in a spiral-bound notebook rather than play outside at recess.

The thirst for stories grew in college where she majored in print and radio journalism sharing the lives of the incredible people who live in Eastern Kentucky through the city radio station and multiple area newspapers. She possesses a Bachelor's Degree from Morehead State University for Convergent Media.

She sharpens her writing skills while recounting the heroics of her Dungeons and Dragons characters over dinner and co-running The Central Cincinnati Fiction Writers Group.

Jordan S. Keller lives with her husband, their bearded dragon, a goblin disguised as a cat, a puppy with airplane ears, and fourteen koi fish inherited when they bought the house.

TONI GLICKMAN'S

BITCHES OF FIFTH AVENUE
CHAMPAGNE AT SEVEN!
BOOK ONE

**For more information
visit:** www.SpeakingVolumes.us

LISA SHERMAN'S

FORGET ME NOT
FORGET ME
BOOK ONE

**For more information
visit:** www.SpeakingVolumes.us

MARK E. SCOTT

A DAY IN THE LIFE
DRUNK LOG
BOOK 1

**For more information
visit:** www.SpeakingVolumes.us

Upcoming New Release

BRIAN FELGOISE / DAVID TABATSKY

FILTHY RICH LAWYERS
THE EDUCATION OF RYAN COLEMAN
BOOK ONE

"The lightning paced humor provides a serious message about corruption in class action litigation. This is a hilarious satire about a very real problem." —Matt Flynn, author, *Milwaukee Jihad*

For more information
visit: www.SpeakingVolumes.us